**Also available from Therese Beharrie
and Carina Press**

*One Day to Fall
One Last Chance*

**Also available from Therese Beharrie
and Harlequin**

*The Tycoon's Reluctant Cinderella
A Marriage Worth Saving
The Millionaire's Redemption
United by Their Royal Baby
Falling for His Convenient Queen
Tempted by the Billionaire Next Door
Her Festive Flirtation
Surprise Baby, Second Chance
Second Chance with Her Billionaire
From Heiress to Mom
Island Fling with the Tycoon
Her Twin Baby Secret
Marrying His Runaway Heiress*

A WEDDING ONE CHRISTMAS

—

Therese Beharrie

carina
press

carina press®

Recycling programs
for this product may
not exist in your area.

ISBN-13: 978-1-335-28482-2

A Wedding One Christmas

First published in 2018. This edition published in 2020.

Copyright © 2018 by Therese Beharrie

This edition published by arrangement with Harlequin Books S.A.

For questions and comments about the quality of this book, please contact us at CustomerService@Harlequin.com.

Carina Press
22 Adelaide St. West, 40th Floor
Toronto, Ontario M5H 4E3, Canada
www.CarinaPress.com

Printed in U.S.A.

A WEDDING ONE CHRISTMAS

Chapter One

If the universe wanted Angie Roux to get home for Christmas, it had a hell of a way of showing it.

In the four hours she'd spent driving that day, Angie had been caught in stop-and-go roadworks four times; had been stopped by a traffic officer twice; had to change a flat tire, and now this.

People.

A crowd of them, standing outside the brick chapel next to the café she'd stopped at. She'd never actually seen the chapel in use before, though she wasn't surprised she'd encountered it now, considering the universe's current treatment of her. She just hoped the 'if you talk to me, I'm going to punch you in the face' expression she'd perfected at a young age would deter—

'How did you get outside so quickly?' a tall woman asked, walking toward her.

Angie looked behind her, and then, when she saw no one else, looked back at the woman. For good measure—her 'talk to me at your own peril' expression rarely didn't work—she asked, 'Are you talking to me?'

'Of course I am.' The woman frowned. 'You should still be inside. They're signing the register.'

'Okay,' Angie replied slowly. 'What should I be doing inside?'

'Waiting for them,' the woman answered with an impatient sigh. 'Have you never attended a wedding before? Aren't you thirty-two? Thirty-five? This can't possibly be…' She trailed off when Angie took a step back. Then another.

'Where are you going?'

Angie didn't answer. Instead, she turned around and began to walk back to her car. Her strides were slow, as if that would somehow mitigate that she'd left someone midconversation. Even if said person was trying to insult her.

The insult hadn't landed though. Angie had never thought looking older was an insult. In fact, she considered it a compliment. She carried herself maturely, which came with a certain amount of authority. Authority that had helped her growing up as the oldest of three girls.

She was more insulted by herself and how slow she'd been on the uptake. The people outside of the chapel were celebrating a wedding. Which seemed pretty clear to her now, when it was too late. When she'd already walked into a *wedding*.

She shuddered, her steps quickening.

'You've done enough to me today,' she muttered to the universe. 'Please, not this.'

As if in answer or punishment, a car turned into the gravel car park. Her feet stopped at her dilemma: because she'd taken the quickest route to her rental car, she was walking in the middle of the car park. She'd have to move to avoid being run over. Except she had nowhere to go.

There were empty parking spaces on either side of her, but that would risk being trapped or having to manoeuvre around the car—no, *cars*, she saw, taking in the line that had begun to form behind that first car—which would likely involve talking to people. Going forward wasn't an option at the moment and back meant…

She shuddered again.

But then she was hooted at—multiple times—and that first car edged forward, forcing her back. Resisting the temptation to show the driver an impolite hand gesture, Angie gritted her teeth and turned around.

She tried to walk stealthily toward the crowd, so the woman who'd spoken to her earlier wouldn't see her. Angie kept an eye on the woman, but she paid no attention to Angie. Relief soothed some of the apprehension in Angie's chest. She might be able to make it to the café she'd come to without attracting any more—

'Hey.' A young woman with pink highlights stopped her. 'Are you trying to get back into the chapel?'

Why did everyone think she wanted to get in the damn chapel?

'No.'

'Oh,' the woman said disappointedly. Seconds later she brightened. 'You're arranging something cool for them for when they come out, aren't you? Please tell me it's a flash mob!'

'It's not a flash mob,' Angie responded immediately. Apparently managing the woman's expectations was more important than getting herself out of her current predicament. 'I am trying to arrange something for them, but I have to get past you to do that.'

'You're too late,' the woman said, panic in her eyes. 'They're here.' Her expression turned sympathetic. 'I'm sure they'll forgive you though. You can go through here.'

The woman stepped back, creating a path for Angie before nudging Angie forward. The man she bumped into glanced back with a frown, then his eyes lowered over Angie and he nodded, shifting so Angie could move forward. The couple in front of him did the same, as did the people in front of them, until finally, Angie found herself with an unobscured view of the wedding party as they made their way out of the chapel.

Seeing the bridesmaids clarified why Angie was in this situation. There wasn't—as Angie had begun to fear—a sign on her forehead identifying weddings as one of her least favourite activities, challenging people to change her mind. She was simply wearing an almost identical dress as the bridesmaids.

Hers was shorter, with a deeper neckline, but she could understand why no one had noticed those differences. Hell, she was wearing the dress and it had taken *her* a moment to.

It was unfortunate, and reinforced the voice in her head that told her she was too dressed up for a road trip. But the dress helped her feel confident, which was something she'd desperately needed to keep the unravelling at bay.

It was there even now, taunting her. Telling her she should have listened to the rational part of her that warned her against stopping at the café. Claiming that being mistaken as a bridesmaid at a wedding was punishment for not listening.

She took a breath to compose herself, to push the unravelling away, and told herself she'd expected this. She'd known the trip back to Cape Town would be hard. When she'd seen the green board with its white lettering indicating the turn-off to Caledon—when she'd put on her indicator and turned—she'd known it would be a challenge, too.

It had been three years since she'd been in Cape

Town, after all. Three years since she'd seen her mother, her sisters. Three years since her father—

She stopped the train of thought. Tried to focus on something else. Like the fact that it had been even longer than three years since she'd been to Caledon. The last time had been with her family. Her whole family; not the incomplete unit it had become.

Fortunately, she didn't have time to dwell on that when the bride and groom appeared. The guests began throwing rose petals at the newlyweds, and it reminded her of the picture that sat on her mother's bedside table. It was of her parents on their wedding day. They stood at the top of the steps outside the church, looking at each other lovingly, happily, petals raining over their heads. The last time Angie had seen them together, the love had still been there, but the happiness had been missing...

You're unravelling.

She swallowed and moved to the basket that had the rose petals in it, grabbing a handful and joining in on the excitement. Though it felt cringey, she clapped. When the photographer announced they'd be taking group photos, she tried to slip away...

And was foiled. Again.

'You should stand right in front, young lady,' an old man told her, shifting and blocking her way.

His entire head was white, sharply contrasting his dark brown skin, his face lightly lined with deeper creases around his eyes. He seemed like the type of person she might have liked had he not just stopped her from escaping.

She almost growled, but instead managed a polite, 'I'm not a part of this wedding.'

'Of course you are. And you're beautiful.'

'I'm sorry—*what*?'

'You're beautiful,' he repeated. 'You don't have to be afraid of being in front of the photographers.'

'Wow, thanks,' she deadpanned, adding his face to her rapidly growing list of people who didn't have any boundaries with strangers.

'Could you let me past?' she asked, keeping to her strategy of pretence. 'I'm going to go around the crowd so I can get to the front quicker.'

'Good idea,' he said approvingly, moving so she could walk past him.

She could feel his eyes on her, so she walked slowly around the edge of the crowd. When she passed enough people, she hid at the side of the chapel, where she fully intended on staying until she was out of this nightmare. It was pathetic, but she was willing to be pathetic for the sake of self-care.

As if to test that willingness, a couple began walking her way. She slunk deeper into the shadows, but they kept moving forward. When the woman pulled out a packet of cigarettes—seriously, they were going to smoke right next to a *chapel*?—Angie stepped back again.

She wasn't obscured, and the couple was almost near her, but there was nowhere to go. Her back was against the wall—or against the shrubs, as it were. She panicked for about a second, then decided she'd had enough of the damn wedding.

Swallowing her pride, she ducked through the shrubs.

It rattled. Or rustled. Or made whatever sound a shrub made when someone went through it. She groaned and almost pleaded with the powers that be to make sure no one saw her duck through a shrub to escape a wedding. But with her current luck, that would all but ensure someone would follow her through to ask why she wasn't in the photos.

Fortunately, the shrub hadn't been a large one, and she made it through relatively unscathed. Her hair needed some convincing to disentangle from the branches, but rather that than the dress. It had been expensive. And it was gorgeous. She'd bought it to soften her mother up when they eventually reunited. Instead, she'd worn it for a five-hour road trip.

Maybe she already was unravelling.

When the thought had her heart thumping against her chest, she swallowed and took a steadying breath. She could do this. She could make it to the café and wait the wedding out. She *could*.

She straightened and tried to formulate a plan. She was currently on the edge of a large field that was a hub of busyness. People milled around, carrying boxes or guiding cars into what seemed to be designated spots. Some of the cars were sedans, others trucks, and their spots seemed to depend on that distinction.

Her eyes lifted before she could confirm it, settling on the road she'd taken to enter the town, visible from where she stood. It was a reminder that she'd consciously made the decision to come to this place. Despite the memories it had of her life before she'd left South Africa—or perhaps, because of the memories—she'd decided to stop there.

Almost instantly the lid of the container she kept those memories in popped open and she remembered.

The family trips to the Eastern Cape. How she and her sisters, Sophia and Zoey, would nag until their father stopped barely an hour outside of Cape Town. How he'd always made it seem like some huge concession, stopping at the small town where he and Angie's mother had once lived. In reality, Daniel Roux had been happy to spend time at the casino that had become a major tourist attraction for Caledon. Angie and her sisters would play games in the arcade, before they'd all take the obligatory drive through town so her parents could reminisce. The detour would end in a meal at the café that was just a few metres away from where Angie currently was.

Her heart broke a little, and she closed her eyes, forcing air into her lungs. She hadn't thought about any of this in years. Had actively avoided it. And for the life of her, she couldn't figure out why she'd decided to come here now when she knew it would force her to face those memories.

Unless it didn't, she thought, opening her eyes again. She needed to distract herself. Or, at the very least, figure out how she could put herself back together again before she unravelled completely.

She walked along the edge of the field, staying close to the shrubs—since she was so comfortable with them now—in case she had to hide again. To avoid the wedding, or in case someone on the field noticed her and tried to get her to participate in the activities. She wasn't in the mood for that either.

A few metres later, she found a well-looked-after pathway. She supposed it was the usual way people got from the property that held the café to this field, though she had no idea why they'd want to. How many people needed to seek refuge from a wedding?

And on a related note—what were the chances that, if she took this pathway to the café, she'd need to seek refuge again?

Realising she didn't have much of a choice, she took the steps down to the pathway, consoling herself with the idea of hiding in the shrubs that lined it if she needed to. Which was so ridiculous she almost laughed. Knew her sister Zoey would, too, when she told—

She stopped the thought midway. She couldn't keep doing this. She'd already exceeded her quota of memories and nostalgia for the day. Sticking to that quota was pivotal to her mental health. She'd learnt that very early on in the life she'd built for herself after she'd left Cape Town.

She shook her head and walked into the open air again, immediately bumping into the old man she ran from earlier.

Seriously—what did I do to you? she asked the universe silently, before fixing a smile onto her face. 'Fancy seeing you here,' she said in a falsely bright voice.

'Where did you just come from?' he asked without preamble. 'Are you alone?'

'I just—' *Oh, what the hell?* 'No. My boyfriend's still back there.' She smoothed her dress down and offered him a chagrined smile. 'I'm sorry. Weddings are just so romantic, and with the group pictures being taken, we thought we'd take a moment to ourselves. Very quickly,' she assured him, ducking her head as if embarrassed. 'I'm sure we weren't missed.'

'I'm not sure that's true,' the man said with a frown. 'You're a bridesmaid. Part of the group.'

'Yes, well… The family pictures are being taken,' she said, mentally crossing her fingers as if somehow, that would keep her from tripping over the elaborate tale she was weaving. 'I'm sure you can understand.' *And leave me alone.*

There was a pause, then the man smiled. 'Well, if the family pictures are being taken, I'm sure you aren't missed.'

'Me, too. I should probably run back though. Before they realise I've gone.'

Before you start asking about why my boyfriend hasn't come out of the shrubs yet, too.

She nodded her goodbye and walked in the direction of the café, hoping he wouldn't notice she wasn't heading back to where they'd first met. But at this point, she didn't care. She was counting on not having to see him again. Except when she looked over her shoulder, he was still following her.

She couldn't say anything about it. Perhaps the wedding celebrations had moved. Perhaps the photos were being taken elsewhere. Or perhaps he was checking that she was heading back to do her duties. He must have thought her a terrible bridesmaid. She didn't blame him.

The café was only a few steps away, and she didn't dare check if he was still behind her. Instead, she stopped walking and dug around in her handbag for her lipstick. She held it up triumphantly when she found it, before making as if she were heading to the bathroom in the café.

Her eyes widened as she entered and took in all the people there. People who were dressed smartly. Who were milling around as if waiting for something. Who were—

Damn it, who were wedding guests.

She didn't peek out the door to check for the old man as she'd intended to before snagging a table for herself. She looked, but none seemed to be free, and she was starting to draw attention to herself by not moving from the doorway. The last thing she needed was attention, especially not from wedding guests.

Wielding her lipstick in front of her as if some kind of shield, she moved farther into the café, her eyes sweeping over the room until it rested on a booth in the corner. There was only one man sitting there, papers strewn all over the table.

Not a wedding guest then.

Before she was fully aware of it, she was walking toward him.

And then she was sliding into the booth opposite him.

'Please,' she said, her voice surprisingly hoarse. 'Please pretend like I'm here with you.'

The man looked up and Angie blinked. Then did it a couple more times in case her mind was playing tricks on her. Or perhaps the universe was.

What were the chances she'd slide into a booth opposite a man who looked like he'd jumped straight out of her fantasies?

Smooth brown skin stretched over the angular features of his face. The lines of his cheekbones merged effortlessly to create a defined jaw that was currently peppered with the exact right amount of facial hair. It highlighted the curve of some very fine lips, and somehow complemented his sharp nose.

She swallowed. Forced her attention back to her current task. Which, when she saw the expression on his face, might not be as easy as she hoped.

'How about a deal?' There was urgency in her voice. 'I pay for your meal, you pretend like I'm here with you?'

'Should I take offence that you think I need you to pay for my meal?'

He had one of those voices that demanded the listener's skin turn into gooseflesh.

She wasn't even surprised.

'No,' she replied quickly, and her gaze rested on his left hand.

No wedding ring.

'Unless I'm taking up someone else's place here?' she asked demurely. 'In which case, I'll search for help elsewhere.'

His mouth curved up at the side as he set down his pen. Her eyes followed, noting the shirt that was rolled up at the forearms moulded to a muscular body. If it weren't for the papers, she might not have known he wasn't with the wedding.

'I'm alone,' he said.

'Oh.' It made something flutter in her stomach. Unreasonably so. 'Well, then, my plea stands.' She sighed a little. 'I'm desperate.'

'Why?'

'I didn't notice the signs as I drove into this place. For the wedding?' she prompted when he narrowed his eyes. 'Unfortunately, I'm wearing a dress similar to the wedding party and people keep trying to drag me into the celebration. Or into photos. Someone asked me if I was planning a flash mob. A *flash mob*.' She closed her eyes with a shake of her head. 'It's a nightmare.'

Interest sparked in his eyes. 'I thought all women loved weddings?'

'Now isn't that an ignorant thing to say?' she drawled. 'I thought more of you.'

'Really?' He placed those defined forearms on the table. 'Why? You don't know me.'

'I guess I wanted to believe a man so focused on reading he didn't realise there was a wedding happening around him was intelligent.'

'You could be wrong.'

'I could be,' she agreed, peeking at what he was reading. 'But since that's an article on the gender pay gap in South Africa, I don't think I am.' She paused. 'You're reading an article on the gender pay gap in South Africa? Not really the sort of thing someone reads at a café in a small town, is it?'

'What do people read at a café in a small town?' he asked seriously.

'I don't know. Thrillers? Maybe research on how to get away with the perfect crime?'

'Because they're planning on going on a killing spree?'

She pulled her face. 'I realised it sounded suspicious as soon as I said it.'

'It's not exactly the kind of thing you should say to a stranger,' he agreed.

'In case it's true?'

'In case *you're* the one with the killing plans.'

A grin captured his mouth and suddenly it felt as if the air in her lungs wasn't getting to where it needed to be. She couldn't bring herself to look away though. She was too enthralled at how a man she'd already thought sexy could become sexier.

No man should have that kind of power. No man should look like he did.

There was a certainty to those thoughts that surprised her. That should have had her getting up, walking away. Far away from this man with his amazing face and his hot voice and his sexy smile. Far, far away from this man who didn't inspire her usual reaction to strangers; who made her feel *comfortable*.

Despite how those thoughts had her stomach rolling, she didn't walk away. She greedily took in the overwhelming perfection in front of her. When she forced her eyes back up to his—and she saw a glint there—heat curled up her neck.

'I'm not.' She cleared her throat when a hoarse voice said the words. 'A serial killer. Or a criminal of any kind.'

'Good to know.'

'And I know you probably didn't come here for a stranger to interrupt what is probably pivotal "me" time.'

His lips curved. 'I didn't, but it's not unwelcome.' He lifted a hand and ran it through the black strands of hair. The result was untidy; his hair and the pounding of her heart. 'I could do with a break from work.'

'This is work?' she asked, trying to ignore the unfamiliar responses of her body. 'You're reading up on the gender pay gap for work?'

'Don't sound so surprised.' He leaned back now, lazily throwing an arm on the top of the booth he sat in. 'I'm preparing for a class I'm giving.'

'You're a teacher?'

'Lecturer.'

'In?'

The grin returned. 'Women's studies.'

'Really?' Angie's lips curved. 'I take it your earlier comment about all women loving weddings is a part of your teaching approach then? Antagonising them so you can have a greater look into their psyche?'

'Something like that,' he answered, but his smile sobered. 'I didn't mean to offend you. I just like seeing people's responses to provocative statements. It's a bad habit.'

'How did I measure up?'

'Pretty well, actually. Usually I'd get some sort of insult back.'

'Someone calling you ignorant isn't an insult?' He raised an eyebrow. 'Oh, ha ha,' she said. But smiled. And got one in return.

It couldn't have been more than a few seconds that they held each other's gazes. It felt like minutes. Hours, even. Her heart beat a strange, unfamiliar rhythm in her chest and her thoughts danced to it.

They told her the last thing she needed was a romance with a stranger she met in a café. A café that held memories she'd managed to ignore because of him. Until that moment.

It still looked the same. The exposed brick walls, the brown cushioning of the booths, the wooden tables. The pictures on the walls were different now though. The abstract photos of shapes and colours had been replaced with photos of people diving into the river at the edge of the property; couples laughing in their wedding attire as they stepped out of the chapel; and people sharing meals right here in the café.

Automatically her gaze found the booth she and her family used to sit in every time they were there. There was nothing special about it. It looked like every other booth in there. Except that they'd insisted on sitting there every time. With her father's steady charm—she wasn't sure how that worked as a description for him, but it did—they somehow managed to get it every time.

Suddenly the excuses she'd given for stopping at the café fell away. She didn't need to give her body a break from driving. She didn't need to give her mind a break from thinking. She wanted…to feel her father's presence.

She clenched her jaw and reminded herself of the quota. A part of her responded by entertaining the idea of romance with this strange man.

But there wasn't a romance, not really. Attraction, maybe, but certainly not romance. And the attraction would go nowhere. It could go nowhere. She was already fighting emotions off as if she were protecting a child who would save all humanity in a post-apocalyptic movie. She had too much to deal with to entertain a romance *or* an attraction. So she forced herself to see it as what it was; a reprieve from a wedding she didn't want to be included in.

Steadier now that she'd reminded herself of why she was there—now that she'd put the memories back where they belonged—she ignored the awareness that prickled up and down her skin and looked away. The café still held guests of the wedding. Some of them occasionally glanced her way with a frown.

She turned back to the man. 'Does needing a break from work mean you wouldn't mind if I stayed here? Just until the guests are called back into the event venue?'

'Sure.' He paused. 'I won't ask you to pay for my meal either.'

'Oh, no, I don't mind.'

'In return—' he continued with a small smile '—I'd like to know what your name is.'

'Easy enough.' She offered a hand. 'Angie.'

'Ezra,' he replied, taking it. That strange beat started in her chest again. As soon as it was appropriate to break contact, she did.

'Should we get the waitress's attention?' Ezra asked, already looking for the woman. When he got her attention, he indicated that they needed her, and his eyes returned to Angie.

They were a bronze colour, more gold than rustic, and incredibly distinctive. She didn't know how she hadn't noticed them before.

Her gaze flitted back over the sharp lines of his jaw and the stubble that covered it. She saw the sweeping— now untidy—style of his dark hair, and the way the not-quite-blue, not-quite-purple shirt he wore sharply contrasted his dark features. And then there were those muscles visible under his shirt…

Oh, yes. *That* was how she hadn't noticed those gorgeous eyes before.

Focus, Ange, she commanded herself. But it was so damn tempting to keep staring at the man in front of her. He was possibly the most beautiful man she'd seen, and she hadn't shied away from noticing them in her lifetime.

Although the last three years might have been an exception. Things had changed—she had changed—when she'd left Cape Town. Before then. So perhaps this was just a reaction to the fact that she hadn't really noticed men in recent times.

Oh, they'd been there. Some had even tried to flirt with her. She hadn't had the emotional energy to do anything other than give them a look that conveyed her feelings about their offers. Which was somewhere in the region of 'if you're not someone I have to deal with, then no.'

Of course, the same could have been said for *any* person who'd approached her in a nonpivotal way over the last three years.

And yet...

Her eyes moved back over him; her skin prickled again. *And yet.*

Relief shot through her when the waitress arrived, and she ordered a large chai latte. It was an indulgence, but it always calmed her. She needed calm now, with the weight of returning to Cape Town on her shoulders.

'What made you stop at a tiny café and lodge in Caledon where there just happened to be a wedding?' he asked when the waitress left.

'I'm on my way—'

She nearly said 'home' before she realised Cape Town wasn't her home anymore. It hadn't been for years. And she couldn't exactly dive into all the reasons she'd stopped in Caledon when she was only just beginning to discover how deep they went. She settled for the abridged version.

'I'm on my way to visit my family. For Christmas. We used to stop here on our family trips, and—' she lifted her hands '—nostalgia. You?'

'More or less the same. Besides the part about stopping here for family trips.'

'Where are you coming from?'

'Grahamstown.'

Surprise fluttered through her. 'That's quite the trip. You're a lecturer there?'

He hesitated. 'I used to be. For the last two years.'

'And now?'

'Now…' he trailed off and she thought it was because he didn't know what to tell her.

Which was strange. She hadn't pegged him for the hesitant kind.

Because you know him so well after these last fifteen minutes?

'Now you're preparing lectures in a café in Caledon,' she offered, ignoring the snarky thought. His eyes shone with gratitude. 'Is that an upgrade or a downgrade?'

'Neither, really,' he said with a smile that kicked her heart into overtime. 'I've worked in worse and better environments.'

'The academic year has ended though, hasn't it? Why are you still preparing lectures? And for where, if you aren't working at the university in Grahamstown?'

'The curse of being in academia,' he replied, but the muscles around his mouth tightened. He wasn't telling the truth, she realised. She wasn't sure why that bothered her.

'I knew I escaped for a reason.'

His eyebrows rose. 'You used to be in academia?'

'I used to be a tutor.' It felt like a long time ago. Everything had changed since then. 'I had every intention of studying toward a PhD until I did my Honours and realised I had no desire to study further. After I graduated, I taught at a small school in Cape Town for a little bit.'

'Which one?'

'Would you know it if I told you?'

'Maybe.' He fell silent, as if considering his next words. 'I told you I'm visiting my family in Cape Town. I grew up there.'

'Small world.'

Why did that fact send her stomach tumbling?

'Where are you coming from?'

'Knysna.' Because she didn't want to answer any more questions about that, she answered his previous one. 'The school I taught at was in Kuils River. Free Haven.'

His eyes rested on hers. It felt as if he saw too much. 'Durbanville.'

'So we're both going back to the Northern Suburbs as well,' she said. Again, she felt that strange frisson in her belly.

But did it matter that they were headed in the same direction? She would never see him again after she left the café. As soon as she finished her drink, she'd do some stretches, give herself a pep talk, and leave to spend Christmas with her family.

It would all be perfectly fine.

'So you are leaving.' Her sister's voice was flat. *'Why does this not surprise me?'*

'It's for a job.'

'Sure.'

'Sophia.'

'It's fine, Angie. Leave. I'll be here for Mom and Zo. You just...leave.'

Ah, yes, the reason 'perfectly fine' felt like a big ol' pile of manure. The reason she felt as if the world was slowly burning around her. Why she suspected going home and facing her sisters and her mother would be like walking through the fire.

'Can I get you anything else, miss?' The waitress set down Angie's latte.

'Please,' Angie said, and curled her hands around the mug. 'What's the strongest alcohol you serve?'

Chapter Two

Ezra's lips curled into a smile. It was the strangest feeling. He hadn't had many reasons to smile over the past year. Honestly, he didn't feel like he had any now.

Sure, he was returning to his home in Cape Town. He was reuniting with his family. He was heading to a new lecturing post. But his mind wouldn't let him forget *why* his life had taken all those turns. Or that returning would remind him of it—of his failures—for the foreseeable future.

Of course smiling felt unfamiliar. Foreign. Much like the attractive woman sitting across from him.

He studied her as she spoke with the waitress. She had a mass of dark unruly curls around a face that was only a few shades lighter. Her eyes were dark brown, too, and animated whenever she spoke. High cheekbones and slightly curved lips rounded off her utterly unique, utterly compelling face.

He could understand why people kept trying to lure her into the wedding celebrations. She would upgrade the aesthetics of the event without even trying.

The dress certainly helped, too.

'I'm only having one glass,' Angie said when the waitress left. There was a slight tremor in her hands when she lifted the mug to drink her latte.

'One glass of the strongest alcohol they have?'

She gave him a half smile. 'Yes.'

'Do you plan on driving back to Cape Town this evening?'

She nodded. 'You're not?'

'No. I've booked a room at the lodge for a few days.'

'You're staying at the lodge tonight? The night of a *wedding*?'

'Yep.'

He winced, though it was more for show than anything else. He wasn't sure how to explain why he was there. Hell, he was still trying to figure it out himself. Or maybe what he was trying to figure out was why he'd come for the wedding, but was now working in the most obscure part of the café so he wouldn't see anyone he knew.

Facing your fears, huh? his inner voice mocked. He sighed.

'You're not a fan of weddings either?' She sipped from her drink, watching him. 'Why did you give me such a hard time when I tried to escape it then?'

'Maybe I wasn't prepared to say "hello, stranger, of course you can join me."' He paused slyly. 'Or maybe I didn't want to say it to a stranger who has leaves stuck in her hair.'

Her hand shot up, and she patted her curls in every spot but the ones where the leaves were. He bit his lip to keep from laughing.

'Are you lying to me?' she asked.

'No.'

She merely looked at him. He grinned.

'I promise I'm not.'

He leaned over and took a leaf out of her hair, offering it to her. It felt…intimate, but he quickly brushed the thought aside as he handed her the leaf . She sighed, and proceeded to stare at it as if it were the cause of all her problems.

'Should I ask?'

'Let's just say you weren't the first one I turned to in my efforts to dodge this wedding.'

He stared at her. 'Well,' he said after a moment. 'Now you have to tell me.'

'Not much to tell,' she said coolly, looking at her nails. 'After the third person tried to get me to join in on the wedding celebrations, I hid in a shrub.' Her eyes lifted and they were alight with amusement. 'See? Nothing juicy there.'

An unfamiliar feeling tugged in his chest as he felt his lips twitch. He sat back, wondering if he'd drunk too much coffee and was now feeling the effects of it. Because there was no way he was responding to *her*. He hadn't been interested in a woman since—

Since his breakup.

Definitely the coffee.

He reached for the bottle of water he'd forgotten about in the hours he'd been there.

'What is it with people and getting married over Christmas anyway?' she asked, sitting back in her seat, watching the people around her with a perplexed expression. 'Is it a South African thing? A global thing? I feel like a festive season hasn't gone by without someone I know—or run in to, apparently—getting married.'

He looked at the guests milling around. It triggered some of the memories he'd tried to shut away for the past year. Of a wedding he'd pictured that would never happen.

Of the conversations, the plans, that had been made before there'd been an engagement. Like when they'd attended his brother's wedding, and Liesel had said they'd need to keep their guests occupied when they took their wedding photos someday.

As if she had every intention of marrying him. As if there'd been a chance at a future for them. As if walking away hadn't been an option. But in reality—

He shook his head. Ignored the accusations that echoed there. Ignored how there was a whisper beneath the screams. How that whisper was asking him whether she'd fooled him or whether he'd been gullible when he'd believed her.

Why hadn't he ordered something stronger, too?

'Must have something to do with the atmosphere,' he heard himself say. It almost sounded normal.

'You don't really believe that, do you?'

'Not personally, no. I know a lot of people who do though.'

'Christmas is such a weird time of year.'

'You're not a fan?'

'Most of my Christmases entailed long church services and awkward family reunions.' She tilted her head. 'That's not exactly the kind of atmosphere I imagined at my wedding.'

'So you *do* like weddings.'

'No.' Her head reared back. 'What? No. Why?'

Amusement shimmered through him. Since he didn't think she'd appreciate it, he fought to keep his face straight. 'You said you imagined your wedding. That means—'

'It means I was speaking hypothetically,' she interrupted. 'I have absolutely no desire to put on a flouncy white dress and make vows until death do us part in front of friends and family.' Her eyes met his, and— reluctantly, he thought—her lips curved. 'I've never imagined white flower petals being strewn across the aisle as I walked down in my flouncy white dress. Or about making those vows beneath a beautiful oak tree with its leaves going orange in autumn and it being draped in white chiffon.'

'Obviously.'

'Obviously,' she agreed with a quirk of her brow, her smile widening. She shook her head. 'I *may* have thought about it. Only when I watch movies, really.'

'Really?'

'Really. Besides,' she said, lifting her shoulders, 'a lot of that imagining is moot. My mother would kill me if I got married outside.' At his questioning look, she explained. 'We're a Catholic family.'

'Ah.'

'Ah? That's it?'

'I don't think religion is the kind of topic you're supposed to talk about at a first—' he stopped himself before he could say 'date' and hastily tried to recover '—meeting.'

Her eyes sparkled with the unsaid, but she nodded. 'You're probably right. Better keep to safe things like the gender pay gap in South Africa.'

He laughed. Found the tension that had started in him seconds ago dissipate as he did. She had that effect on him, he realised, but didn't know what to do with the realisation.

'You've surprised me, you know,' she said softly, pushing her mug aside when the waitress put down a glass of brown liquid in front of her.

How so? he wanted to ask, but stopped himself. That was the type of question that produced dangerous answers. That started dangerous conversations. Conversations he did not want to have with her.

'How can I surprise you when you don't know me?'

'Because, as you've already learned, I'm incredibly judgemental.' She grinned, and a ball of warmth burst in his chest. Spread through his veins. 'But I can also admit when those judgements are wrong.' She lifted her shoulder. 'I was wrong about you, Ezra.'

The warmth in his veins heated at the sound of his name from her lips. He desperately tried to remind himself of the hurt he'd felt when his seven-year relationship had fallen apart. Of the pain of it, the anger, that lingered. That had him doubting so many of the things he'd thought he'd known about himself and his life.

That pain—that doubt—had coloured every interaction he'd had over the past year, and yet now, when he needed it the most, he couldn't remember it.

He met the eyes of the woman who'd sat down opposite him less than an hour ago. He couldn't pretend she wasn't gorgeous. Or that she didn't intrigue him with the fire of her personality. With the honesty of her words.

But he wasn't interested in being attracted by gorgeousness or being intrigued by fire and honesty. No, he only wanted to build up the courage to face his family after the colossal mistake he'd made. *Mistakes,* he thought, since moving away from his family to start a new life with his girlfriend was hardly his first error in judgement.

'You've surprised me, too,' he said, picking his words as if they were explosive devices. 'Mostly because of the contradictions.' When she lifted an eyebrow, he elaborated. 'You've imagined your own wedding, but you're so determined to avoid one you hid in a shrub. You don't want to speak with the guests of the wedding, but you willingly sat down here to speak with me.'

She didn't answer him for the longest time. 'I suppose you're just going to have to be content with those contradictions, aren't you?'

He angled his head. 'Probably about as content as you're going to have to be with the fact that your initial judgement of me might not be wrong.'

'What does *that* mean?'

Angie kept her eyes steady on his, ignoring the sparks that flickered the longer she held his gaze. She wanted to see the emotion in his eyes. Wanted to know if it would reveal anything to her.

She didn't think he knew how expressive his striking eyes were. And though she couldn't put her finger on what all the emotions there were, she could see one. Caution.

'It doesn't matter.' He offered her a lazy smile. 'You'll be out of here before you have to find out.'

She didn't want to think about why, but the words stung. She made sure she remained impassive though.

'Of course.' She gripped her hand around the glass. 'I'll be out of your hair as soon as I finish.'

'I didn't mean—'

'It's fine,' she cut him off with a hard-fought-for easy smile. 'I need to be leaving soon anyway. If I want to make it home before dark. I mean, to my parents' house.'

Why did she keep doing that? Calling Cape Town home? She hadn't thought of it that way since she'd left. But then, her 'parents' house' wasn't accurate either. Not since her father had—

She shook her head. How many times was she going to have to remind herself about this? She'd given herself some leeway because her emotions were up in the air about returning to the place she'd grown up in, but she couldn't keep doing this. She couldn't keep exceeding the quota.

She'd established it for a reason. After the night she'd fallen apart in her living room. She had been in the middle of a foreign country with nothing and no one familiar around her, and she'd told herself she couldn't keep thinking about it. Yes, she was back home now. And yes, she was returning to her family. But that didn't mean she wanted to fall apart again. That didn't mean she wanted to go back to feeling that rawness, that helplessness, that *pain*.

She squeezed her eyes closed and listened to the internal voice screaming *I told you so* in her ear. Even thinking about it made the unravelling begin again. But even if she hadn't really stopped at the café to gain some semblance of control over herself, she would try. If not for her peace of mind, then for her heart.

'You don't see your parents' house as home anymore?' Ezra asked.

She opened her eyes, keeping them on her glass as she brought it to her lips for a steadying sip. 'I just haven't been back in a long time.'

'What's long?'

'Almost three years.'

He nodded. 'That *is* a long time. Did you move away for a job?'

'Yes.'

It was the simplest answer. It also sounded a lot better than *I was running from my grief.* Or it sounded less incriminating anyway. Every time she thought it, she was overwhelmed with guilt, and Sophia's words would replay in her head.

It's fine, Angie. Leave. I'll be here for Mom and Zo. You just...leave.

She didn't feel like revealing that to Ezra. It was too personal. Too closely entwined with the things she was fighting to keep from thinking about. Besides, he clearly felt the same way about boundaries when it came to personal issues. His comment about how she'd be leaving soon had left its mark. They were two strangers who didn't owe each other any explanation about their lives.

'So did I,' Ezra said.

'You left Cape Town for Grahamstown—to take a job?'

'Ridiculous, isn't it?'

Her lips curved. 'It must have been quite the culture shock.'

'It was. Cape Town has millions of citizens. Grahamstown doesn't even make it to a hundred thousand. And, of course, a good portion of that number are students at the university.'

'I got accepted there,' she said. 'But I couldn't bear to leave my fa—' She stopped herself in time. 'The city I'd grown up in yet. Besides,' she continued, hoping he wouldn't noticed her blunder, 'I wasn't convinced by the idea of living in a town so small.'

'You left Cape Town eventually.' It wasn't a question.

'I said "yet."' Her mouth lifted to a half smile. 'And this was for a job.'

'What job?'

'Teaching. Korea.'

'Oh.'

'Oh?' Her eyebrows rose. 'Did I just hear a scoff in your tone?'

'No,' he answered, but his lips quirked up, sending a flutter through her stomach. 'I would never.'

'That's probably a good idea.'

'Except that it's so *easy,* isn't it?'

'How so, Mr. Judgey?'

He grinned. 'Everyone here does it. You don't even have to have a degree in English to teach English in Korea.'

'Ah, okay.' She sat back now. 'If it makes you feel any better, I do have a degree in English. I also did my Honours in English and then taught it for a semester at Free Haven. When I passed my degree—with distinction, I might add—I went to teach in Korea so that I could save money to pursue my dream of writing the great South African novel when I came back.'

There was a beat before she sighed. 'Oh, you were being provocative again.' She rolled her eyes.

He laughed. 'I told you it was a bad habit.' He paused. 'Does it help if I tell you your resume is impressive?'

'Maybe,' she answered, then sniffed. 'Actually, yes, it does.'

He grinned. 'Great. Would it also allow me to ask you what your novel's about?'

'No.' She sipped her whiskey. 'Because if you did, I'd have to tell you I lied about what kind of novel I want to write.'

His smile widened. 'You mean you don't want to write the great South African novel?'

'Nope. Though only because there are already so many great novels. I'd never be able to match that.'

'Because you're not willing to write about the struggles of our pasts?'

'Or about the present,' she added. 'Mostly because I'm more intrigued by relationships than anything else.'

'So you want to write…women's fiction?'

'Romance.' At his expression, she narrowed her eyes. 'I've freely admitted to my judgemental ways, but honestly, Ezra, I think compared to you, I'm tame.' She paused. 'I'm not entirely convinced this comes from being provocative either. At least not this issue. Your tone clearly indicates you have an issue with entertainment for women.'

'It did… I don't—'

Angie bit her lip when he broke off. If she smiled now, she wouldn't be able to keep teasing him.

'It was admiration. The tone. I was admiring you.'

'Admiring me,' she repeated slowly.

'Yeah. It takes incredible skill to write romance.'

'And you know this because…?' She tilted her head. 'Have you written a romance novel in the past? Or is this just you mansplaining something I—as a reader and writer of romance—know much more about?'

'No!' He ran a hand through his hair. 'Are you trying to make me into the bad guy here?'

'Of course not,' Angie replied. 'Though I don't think I've enjoyed myself more than over the last few minutes…' she trailed off, waiting for him to realise what she'd been doing.

She wasn't disappointed.

A smile crossed his face, large and genuine, making his eyes crinkle and taking away a tinge of sadness she hadn't noticed was there until it wasn't. She couldn't say it transformed his features—not when they were already perfect—but it did soften them, making him look more personable. And *that* made him a lot more appealing.

She sat back now, wondering how her pit stop had brightened what she'd thought would be a bleak day. It hadn't started out that way, but it had taken a sharp turn since then.

Now she wasn't thinking about what she'd find when she got home. She wasn't worrying about having to face the blank look her mother had given her when Angie had told her she'd be moving. She wasn't remembering Sophia's judgement, or Zoey's sadness.

She wasn't thinking about the damage leaving might have done to her relationship with her family. She wasn't worrying that that damage was irreparable. And most of all, she wasn't thinking about how disappointed her father would have been in her for leaving them when they needed her the most…

'I'm not so sure I like you,' Ezra said.

'Well, that's what you get for your bad habit.' She took another sip of her drink, hoping it would settle some of the unsteadiness inside of her. 'Which, for the record, is probably going to get you into a lot more trouble in the future than anything I've dished out.'

'I think I can handle it.'

'Yeah, you did a pretty convincing job just now.'

Ezra chuckled softly, his face light with amusement. In that moment she knew *he* was the reason her day had brightened. That bantering with him had made her feel better.

Something flipped in her chest, then her stomach, and she pushed to her feet.

'Restroom,' she said quickly, when confusion replaced the amusement on his face, and she hurried away before he had the chance to say anything else.

The small restroom was as rustic as the rest of the café, and unfortunately, she didn't have it to herself. Two of the three mirrors had women fixing their make-up, while the third was being used by a woman styling her hair. *Not unusual,* she thought, *but untimely.*

She would have loved to have a minute alone to think, to process, but because there were also three women ahead of her in the line for a cubicle, she knew she wouldn't get it.

She briefly considered whether Ezra would notice if she walked outside and took a moment there, but she dismissed it. He would probably think she was bailing on him. After how kind he'd been to her, she didn't want that.

There was also the fact that she'd probably be dragged back into the damn wedding again if she went outside. She sighed. Told herself she could hold it together until she got a moment to herself again. She walked out of the bathroom—

Straight into the old man from the wedding.

Chapter Three

'What are you doing here?' he asked her immediately.

Because of course he did. Why would he do the courteous thing and pretend like he hadn't seen her come out of the bathroom? Why would he respect the idea that really, it was none of his business what she was doing there?

Angie closed her eyes. Then, not for the first time that day, and not for the first time with this man, she fixed a smile onto her face. 'Bathroom.'

'I thought you'd already gone—' he lifted his arm to look at his wrist '—almost forty-five minutes ago?'

'You're keeping track?'

There was a beat during which he had the grace to look embarrassed. 'Just looking out for Jenny, dear.'

Jenny must have been the bride, she thought, and huffed out a breath. 'I appreciate that, sir, but everything is fine.' When he opened his mouth to reply, she said, 'I'm not a part of the wedding.'

Because she was tired. The farce was becoming more annoying the longer it went on.

'I saw you in the crowd outside of the church.'

'I got caught in it when I stopped to come to the café.'

'But… Your dress?'

Clearly the man wasn't going to let things go easily.

She glanced over at Ezra, but he was looking at his papers intently. Apparently, he wasn't going to be much help… Unless she could get his attention.

She put her foot behind her tentatively. When she didn't feel anything alarming, she shifted her weight back on it.

'A happy coincidence,' she told the man, before repeating the action. She smiled brightly and hoped that the glare of it—because sadly, she couldn't actually glare at this frustrating man—would blind him to the fact that she was moving. Slowly, yes, but she was making progress.

But so was he. When he took a step forward, his trusting gaze still on her, it seemed as if he didn't even know he was moving.

Damn it.

'A coincidence? That can't be it.'

'Except I assure you it is.'

Ezra heard the words before his mind told him the voice was familiar. His eyes settled on Angie at the same time he recognised it was her voice he'd heard. She was holding herself up stiffly and he braced, preparing to defend her, though he had no idea from what.

Then Ezra saw the older man speaking with her. The man had a kind though intense expression on his face, and Ezra waited.

'Darling, look.' The man paused. 'I know that this has been an emotional wedding. Jenny and Dave are happy, and perhaps that's reminded you that you'd like to be happy in that way, too.' He lifted Angie's left hand up and stared pointedly at the empty ring finger, before gently letting her hand fall. 'You've told me you have a boyfriend here. Do you want me to talk with him?

Maybe convince him to think about making things official between you two? Because I'll do it,' he said graciously. 'I'll do it so you don't abandon my Jenny on her wedding day.'

Something inside Ezra stilled, and he didn't quite hear Angie's flat reply. But the reprieve was brief before his mind started spinning, picking information out of what the older man had just told Angie to form a narrative that sent nausea swirling around his stomach.

The first was confirmation that this was Jenny and Dave's wedding.

He wasn't sure why he needed the confirmation. He'd brought his invitation with him, hadn't he? Hadn't he stared at it before making the phone call to book his room as soon as he realised he'd be moving back to Cape Town? Hadn't he crushed the invitation in his hand and thrown it into the bin? Hadn't he then taken it out again, minutes later, painstakingly smoothing it out?

Though the invitation hardly mattered. Apart from confirming that his former students were getting married there, it meant nothing to him. *Nor would it to them,* he thought. He hadn't told them he'd be attending. He hadn't known he'd be attending.

He probably would have spent more time stewing in that if it weren't for the second piece of information Angie's companion had revealed.

She had a boyfriend?

'I'm not abandoning anyone, sir,' Angie said with a forced patience he imagined she used with unruly students. 'I don't know Jenny or Dave, so—'

'You don't know them as a married couple,' the man interrupted helpfully. 'Things aren't the way they used to be, you know. Young women these days still spend time with their friends when they're married. Even when those friends are unmarried.'

'Oh, how lovely,' Angie said. She angled her body so he could now see her face.

It was twisted with annoyance—and, he imagined, exasperation at the man's backward thinking—and her eyes fluttered over to him. Her brows lifted. When he shook his head, a grin claiming his lips despite the uneasiness fluttering around in his body at the news of her relationship status, she narrowed her eyes.

He couldn't blame her; he'd made no move to save her. Even though it had reminded him of the messiness of his mind since his breakup, he'd enjoyed finally witnessing what she was talking about. He understood now why she'd been so desperate to escape being dragged into the wedding. And he *could* enjoy it because he had confirmation that Angie wasn't available.

Not that it mattered, a firm voice said in his head. He almost nodded before he realised that that would be a sure sign he'd lost his mind. Instead, he just told himself to listen to the damn voice.

He'd silenced it too many times in the past. It had started when he'd been a stupid teenager eager for freedom. It had continued when he'd moved hundreds of kilometres away from his home. From his family, his career, his life.

When he'd spent years in a relationship he now saw had been lukewarm at best; downright chilly at worst. When he'd bought a ring and proposed. When he'd waited with bated breath for an answer...

He'd silenced his gut instinct too many times before; he'd suffered for it as many times. So he'd listen to the voice cautioning him about the woman he'd only known for an hour. Even if she made him laugh when he couldn't quite remember the last time he had.

'You know what?' Angie said, her eyes back on the older man. 'I think you're right. I'm probably just making up these very detailed lies—' her tone was so heavy with sarcasm Ezra was surprised it didn't drag her down to the floor '—because I'd like my boyfriend to propose.'

The tone had changed quickly, into something syrupy that matched the small smile she was aiming at the man.

'I think… Maybe I was hoping coming out here and spending time alone together would push him into doing it. Especially with the wedding and it being Christmas and all of that.'

She shrugged. Somehow her smile turned into a hopeful one. A shy one. If he weren't so stunned at her words, he might have laughed.

'Oh, darling.' The man's voice went soft, and Ezra struggled to hear what came next. The next thing he knew, Angie's head was tilting his way and the man was turning toward Ezra, face beaming.

They exchanged a few more words and with a wink, the man went off. Angie returned to her seat, an innocent expression on her face.

'You missed your calling,' he said, his voice steady, though his heart didn't feel that way.

'What? Oh, that?' She waved a hand. 'It was just a little something I picked up in acting class.'

'You went to acting class?'

'No.' She smiled. 'But considering your reaction and his—' she tilted her head toward where she had the conversation with the man '—I should have.' She drank the last of her whiskey, then frowned. 'Are you okay? You look…pale.'

'I'm fine,' he managed, and wondered if he could wish his heart calm. Or whether he'd ever be faced with the prospect of marriage or a wedding again and not feel as if he were falling into the hole he'd dug for himself with Liesel.

He'd hoped coming to where his students were getting married would help him get over it. Evidently not.

'Maybe you're picking up on your own guilt at throwing me under the bus like that,' he said, forcing himself to act like a normal human being again.

'Oh, I don't feel bad about that,' she answered. 'You did leave me there to fend for myself.'

'But you did it so well.'

'I didn't say I didn't enjoy it,' she said with a wink. 'Why didn't you come to my rescue though? I thought we were together in this whole "weddings are the worst" thing.'

He struggled for the ease to tease her when her words had his heart racing again. 'It was entertaining.' He paused. 'And maybe I was waiting for your boyfriend to show up.'

'You heard that?' She winced. 'I've had the worst luck when it comes to that man. He caught me after I made my escape through the shrubs.' She rolled her eyes. 'I was on my way here and I walked right into him.'

'That still doesn't explain the boyfriend?'

'I was getting there,' she said wryly. 'I didn't have to come back through the shrubs because there was a proper pathway a few metres from where I went through them. I know,' she told him, though he'd said nothing. He tried not to smile. 'Anyway, I had to make up some reason why I was so clearly not at the photos that were being taken. Somehow I ended up pretending I'd been making out with my boyfriend. He seemed impressed at the time, so you're welcome.'

He took a moment to process. 'I'm not sure what I'm supposed to be thanking you for?'

'For making your reputation a lot edgier than what you likely would have earned on your own.'

'Hey, I'm edgy.'

'Sure you are.'

He couldn't help the smile now, though that feeling spinning inside of him hadn't settled yet. 'Fine. But if I'm not, neither are you.'

'Oh, please,' she said, throwing up a hand. 'I'm edgy. I'm so edgy, I *live* on the edge.' And immediately pulled her face. 'I am so sorry you had to hear that.'

He laughed. It made no sense—what she'd said and the fact that he was laughing at all—but he did. He laughed. Those full lips of hers curved and he felt an answering pull in himself.

'I just hope he believes me,' she said after a moment.

'What did you tell him?'

'That Jenny and Dave were taking their solo photos.' Her face twisted again. 'I don't even know these people and yet I'm calling them by their first names.'

'Because you're edgy.'

'Wiseass,' she said, but there was no heat in it. 'You better hope that man believes me, too, or he might be back to find out why I lied to him about—' She cut herself off, considering. 'Well, about everything.'

'Let's get out of here,' he said suddenly. 'Let's go for a walk and let him and the guests settle in at the reception. By the time we get back, they'll all be too occupied with celebrating the wedding to bother you. You can finally enjoy a meal in peace.'

'By the time we get back, I'll have to leave,' she replied.

A weight settled in his chest and his mind tried to convince him to stay in the café so they could speak comfortably. So he could find out all the things it suddenly seemed incredibly important to know about her.

But his body, his heart told him he couldn't. Not when the realisation that he wanted to know more about her made his lungs cry for fresh air, even if the summer's day didn't mean that air would be cool.

His momentary dip into the past and the last few minutes—oh, who was he kidding? The last *hour*—with Angie made him feel...trapped.

He needed to not feel trapped. By his memories of Liesel. By his strange feelings for Angie.

He didn't know which of those had contributed most to the pressure in his chest. It didn't change the fact that he couldn't stay inside anymore.

'We could still go for a walk.'

She tilted her head, making her curls fall over her forehead, then nodded. 'Okay.'

He packed up as she settled the bill. She'd refused his offer to pay for their drinks, telling him she owed him one. He hadn't been able to muster the energy to complain. While she paid, he determined that his memories were the main cause of his need to suddenly go outside.

It was exactly why he avoided thinking about Liesel—about weddings, about relationships, about dating—as far as possible. He always needed time to recuperate after. Not too much time, otherwise he'd end up analysing every stupid decision he'd made since leaving for Grahamstown.

Since before.

He grabbed his bag, annoyed with the direction of his thoughts. He waited for Angie at the door, and they walked out together.

'I'm going to put this in my car.' He gestured to his things, nodding to his car ahead of them. 'Not sure carrying around this much weight is going to make for a relaxing walk.'

'Could I put my handbag in there, too? My car is further down the way, through those people.' She grimaced, then shook her shoulders. 'My subconscious must have known I'd need a quick escape when I parked.'

She smiled and he felt…different. He couldn't put his finger on how or why. He only figured out it was because of her smile when she sobered and he realised he'd been staring at her. Then he realised that her smile made him feel lighter, less weighed-down by his memories. Suddenly he was determined to make her smile again.

'You aren't afraid this is all a ruse to kidnap you?' He popped open the boot of his car.

'Wow, this conversation turned morbid quickly.' She placed her handbag next to his bag. 'But yes, I have considered it. I've concluded it would be terrible for you if you were a kidnapper. I would talk your ear off. I'd keep talking because that's the way I deal with weird situations.'

Somehow his determination to make her smile had ended up with *him* smiling.

'You're talking a lot now. Do you think this is a weird situation?'

'Honestly? Yeah, I kind of do. I mean, I'm a complete stranger who asked you for help so I didn't have to deal with being mistaken as a bridesmaid. And I pretended you, also a complete stranger, were my boyfriend to an old man who probably means well. All to avoid a wedding,' she added softly, a frown wrinkling the skin between her eyebrows.

He knew that last part had been for her. He almost opened his mouth to ask what she'd discovered about herself.

'Then there's the fact that *you're* acting weird.'

He blinked. 'What?'

'Ever since that man did what he did inside—and I guess, since I did what I did inside—you've been weird.' She moved away now and made her way down the gravel path. He stared for a moment, then followed.

'I haven't been weird.'

She didn't look at him. 'Okay.'

'No, really,' he insisted. 'Look, I just don't deal well with…strangers,' he finished lamely. Saying 'weddings' would have opened a discussion he didn't really want to have. 'You can sympathise, right?'

'I can.' She paused. 'Though I can also say that you're dealing perfectly fine with me.' The side of her cheek lifted in a smile. 'For the most part, anyhow.'

His mouth mirrored hers and he almost wished he could shake it off. Because how did any of this make sense? This woman saw what he didn't want her to—called him out on it, too—and it didn't make him want to run far away. It didn't change that he wanted to talk with her, despite what she'd see.

And yet being unwilling to share his feelings had been part of why Liesel had left him. At least according to her. *After* she'd staggered back and refused his proposal.

'How could I have known you wanted to get married? You never tell me what you're thinking. What you're feeling.'

'I moved all the way to Grahamstown for you, Liesel. Away from my family. What did you think that meant?'

'You didn't move for me. Not really.'

His foot kicked at the gravel path, his entire body tense, and he forced himself to snap out of it.

'This is beautiful,' he commented.

It had been an attempt to distract himself, but as he looked around, he realised it was true. Large trees stood boldly on each side of the gravel path they were walking down, their leaves bright green save for the few with edges wilted from the heat. Christmas lights stretched over the path from the branches of the trees. They were mostly fairy lights and not those pictures of Father Christmas and his reindeers Ezra saw almost everywhere in Cape Town.

Pops of colour came from flower bushes that peeked out around the trees. At the end of the path a pier led out onto the river that surrounded the property. His eyes found the white material waving in the slight summer's breeze before his mind realised he was looking at Jenny. Something in his chest contracted.

'Yeah, it's beautiful,' Angie agreed, her eyes on Jenny, too.

'You say that as if you're surprised.'

'I am. It wasn't like this when we stopped here at Christmastime.'

'This? As in these trees?'

She laughed. It didn't sound genuine. 'No, the lights. It's Christmassy without being tacky.' She tilted her head. 'Maybe they added this for the wedding.' The edges of her mouth tugged down in admiration. 'If so, it kind of makes me want to go inside the venue and check the décor.'

'Airtight logic.'

'Thank you.' She looked at him, then nodded her head. 'Ah, you're making fun of me again.'

'You make it so easy,' he teased, stuffing his hands into his pockets. 'Seriously though, this seems elaborate to add for just one wedding. And expensive.'

'Maybe Jenny and Dave are millionaires who want elaborate and expensive.'

He laughed. 'Er, no.'

'And you say that with such certainty because you know them so well?'

His head whipped in her direction—then he saw her expression. She was teasing him. He swallowed, tried for an easy grin.

'No, I say that because Caledon doesn't scream elaborate and expensive.'

'Maybe not,' she told him, 'but it does have a certain charm.'

She stopped walking, turning so she faced the eastern set of cabins that encompassed half of the lodge's accommodation. She began to walk in that direction, only checking that he was beside her when she was already on the other side of the path.

'Are you coming?'

'Depends on what you're going to do there.'

'I want to show you something.'

'And you can't show it to me here?'

'No.' She let out a little huff. 'Come on, Ezra.' There was barely a pause before she continued. 'Are you worried I'm going to do something to you? I promise I won't. My handbag's in your car and I keep all my weapons in there.'

He shook his head even as the smile claimed his lips. Even as his feet began crossing the path. Even as he followed her.

'Okay, so this isn't strictly legal—'

'What?'

She laughed and took his hand easily, as if they'd known each other all their lives. 'I'm kidding. But we are leaving the lodge's property right now.' They passed the final cabin as she said the words, continuing up a path covered with leaves now, not gravel. 'And we're doing a short walk up this little hill.'

'If someone had told me I'd be following a stranger up a hill in a town I've never been to before, I swear I'd think I'd been kidnapped.'

'Are you sure you weren't reading a thriller earlier?' she asked with a cheeky look on her face. 'Were you hiding a paperback under those papers? This is a safe space. You can tell me.'

'You always have—'

He broke off when she stopped walking and turned to look at him with a dopey grin on her face. He stopped next to her, though he wasn't quite sure what the smile was for.

Then he did.

They were standing at the top of a hill that gave them an aerial view of Caledon. It was a town of contradictions. There were large patches of land that were browning on one side of the town, with lush greenery on the other side where a large dam could be seen. Small patches of rural-like homes were spluttered along gravel roads, with larger areas of urbanised homes along stretches of tar next to them around what he assumed were stores in a busy central area.

'Wow.'

'Yeah,' she agreed. 'It's beautiful to see it from up here. It kind of reminds me of a lot of South Africa. Some breathtakingly beautiful spots, then the reminders of the hardship in the country's past.' She cocked her head. 'But mostly the beautiful.'

'How did you know it was here?'

Her face…crumpled. It was the only description he could come up with. 'My parents used to bring us up here. Me and my sisters.' She hesitated. Squared her shoulders. 'They used to live here. My parents, I mean. It was important to them that we saw where they'd started their family.'

'They had their first child here?'

'No. Well,' she said immediately after, 'they found out they were pregnant with me here. But they had me in Cape Town. I think they just wanted us to know this was where their married life began. And technically, I suppose this is where their family started.'

'They sound happy.'

'They were.'

He noted the past tense. At the same time, he felt his hand stretching out and clasping hers. He saw her look down and for a beat, he thought she might pull away. She didn't. Instead, she threaded her fingers through his, squeezing his hand as if to say thank you.

They stood like that, staring out over the town.

It was almost an out-of-body experience for him. Because he didn't do things like this. He didn't hold strangers' hands; he didn't watch it happen as if he were a bystander to a friendship blossoming. *Friendship.* He swallowed, but didn't question it. It felt safer. Friendship was easier to deal with than…than whatever else was crashing against his chest, demanding he name it.

So he stood. Looked. Admired. He would have never thought a small town could elicit such feelings from him. But then, he had spent the past two years in a small town. Maybe living in Grahamstown had encouraged a deeper sense of appreciation in him for spaces where people actually knew one another.

'Do you see that grey building over there?' Angie asked, breaking the silence.

'The one with the red roof?'

'Yeah. It's a diner.'

Ezra turned at the emotion in her voice. On her face, he saw nostalgia. And a twinge of sadness. His grip on her hand tightened.

'That's where my mom told my dad she was pregnant.'

'Wow.'

She gave him the side-eye. 'There was an awful lot of emotion in that one word.'

He laughed. 'I just— Okay, I think it's a bit weird you can point out where your mother told your father she was expecting.'

'Why?' she asked, turning toward him, dropping his hand and folding her arms. He felt an inexplicable emptiness at the loss of contact. 'Don't your parents have places special to them? Or rather, don't they share those places with you?'

Ezra thought about his parents. About their easiness around each other. About the clear love they showed. He ignored the pang in his chest.

'Sure. But this is a little extreme.'

'Well, then,' she said after a moment. 'It's a good thing I didn't point out the house they told us I'd been conceived in.'

His head whipped around so quickly he belatedly worried he'd caused permanent damage. She widened her eyes—which were now bright with amusement— and he shook his head.

'Oh. You're messing with me.'

'You're not the only one who can be provocative.' She grinned. 'We better get back.'

'You're right. The twenty minutes this walk has taken has probably made all the guests forget about you.'

Her eyes widened again, though this time she looked stricken. 'Are you messing with me, or do you really think they're looking for me?' She gripped the arm of his shirt. 'Ezra.'

He laughed. In amusement, yes, but also to cover up the way his body was heating at her touch. 'I'm not sure. There isn't one way to do a wedding, so Jenny and Dave might not be back yet.'

'If they're not back yet, the guests won't be distracted enough to ignore me.' She groaned and moved her hand from his arm to her forehead. 'What am I going to do?'

'This isn't an existential crisis, Angie,' he said, amused. 'We can just avoid them.'

'*Yes.*' She brightened. He felt something inside him do the same. 'When I was, um, removing myself from the wedding celebrations earlier—'

'When you were hiding in the bushes, you mean?'

'I noticed,' she continued, ignoring him, 'that there seemed to be something going on on the property next to the lodge. We could go check that out?'

'Sure,' he replied too quickly, then offered her a smile he hoped wasn't too eager. 'You can tell me why you hate weddings so much while we walk there. Or why you pretend to.'

'I don't pretend to,' she said. They started walking. 'And I guess "hate" is a strong word. It's… They come with a lot of baggage for me. The ones I've attended have been unpleasant. Those were ones that were supposed to mean something to me. Friends. Family.'

The last word came out softly. She blew out a breath. 'They're probably not like that for everyone.'

'What happened?'

'Nothing specific.' Her face tightened. He wondered if it meant she was lying. 'They've just been awkward events, particularly in my family. My aunts saw them as opportunities to show each other up; my uncles as chances to get ridiculously drunk. My cousins used them to flaunt their achievements or money. They were never about the marriage. The union of two souls who love each other. Or whatever.'

She shrugged with a roll of her eyes, and he knew it was a way for her to shake off what she hadn't meant to reveal to him. She'd done it back at the top of the hill, too, with her parents. She would change the subject or make a joke. *Anything to avoid emotions,* he thought with a frown.

Interesting.

But he'd indulge her. For now.

'You sound like a romantic.'

'Well, I have to be, don't I, for the sake of my future career?'

'Ah, yes, the writing. I'd almost forgotten about that.'

'Here I thought I'd made such an impression,' she said dryly. She paused when they got to a particularly steep area of the hill.

'Let me.'

Ezra jumped down carefully and offered her a hand.

'I got up there by myself, you know.'

'I do,' he said, but kept his hand there.

She rolled her eyes again. 'Fine.'

Then she was gripping his hand and lowering a foot before placing her weight on it. She followed with her other foot. It had all been done very smoothly until that moment, when her foot skidded on the ground beneath her. His free arm immediately went around her waist, her body slamming against his with the momentum from her slip. But he had good grip where he was standing and the danger ended there.

Well, *that* danger.

With her body against his, he had the opportunity to feel the generous softness of her. His arm was circled around a waist that was full, though smaller than the breasts pressed against his chest. Breasts that he only had to look down to see more clearly.

Except that he couldn't. He was too caught in her eyes. In the surprise, the hesitance there. The interest, too, though the light of it seemed dulled. It was as if she felt it, but was refusing to acknowledge it. Which felt right, based on what he knew about her.

And yet his body was still tightening; something inside him still coiling.

The surprise of it had him letting go when she stepped back. And nodding when she offered him a shakily smile along with her thanks.

'Don't mention it,' he said.

'Okay.'

The silence that followed seemed heavy with what they weren't saying, and he blurted out, 'Why romance?'

She blinked. *Adjusting to the abrupt change in topic,* he thought.

'Probably the happily-ever-afters.' Her expression was pensive. 'That I can control it.'

'Oh. That's not what I was expecting.'

She laughed softly. 'Wouldn't you hand out happily-ever-afters if you could?'

'No, I meant being able to control it.'

'Life is unpredictable,' she replied after a pause. 'I

guess it's appealing to me. The idea that I can give people happy endings when that's not what happens in real life. Oh, no, wait,' she said, her eyes wide, 'that's not what I meant.'

'What—' He broke off when his mind replayed her words and picked up on the 'happy ending' comment. He chuckled. 'I'm sure some people are getting happy endings in real life.'

'Yeah, yeah,' she said, a pretty blush staining her cheeks. 'How about you? Why women's studies, I mean.' The blush deepened—as did his laughter.

'Just answer the question, damn it.'

He cleared his throat, though his lips were still curved. 'I was one of those weird kids who always thought really deeply about things that didn't require a thirteen-year-old's musings. It probably started with learning about women and their influence on the Apartheid fight when we were learning about it at school—"You strike a woman, you strike a rock" and all that—and then looking around and realising that despite that influence, I didn't see how they'd benefitted from it. Women, specifically. Not the entire country or a race in the country.'

They'd reached the gravel road again and Angie was leading them back toward the café. She wore an expression of concentration, though he didn't know whether that was because she was listening to him or because she was trying to see potential wedding guests before they saw her.

Either way, it was cute.

'There were other things, but long story short, they all got me interested in women's agency. Which, when I got to university, I realised I could study meaningfully.'

'Hmm,' she said. 'Seems like a thirteen-year-old's musings were exactly what the field needed.'

He cocked his head, his mouth curving. 'Guess so.'

'Well, since it only seems fair then, considering what I've shared with you, let's move on to question number two.' There was a brief pause. 'Why do you hate weddings?'

The words were out of his mouth before he could stop them.

'Because I thought I was going to get married and didn't even get as far as engaged.'

Chapter Four

'That's…possibly the worst thing I've ever heard.' Angie widened her eyes when he glanced over. 'Sorry.' She winced. 'Remember what I said about talking more in weird situations? It also comes with no filter.'

He gave her a look. 'Let's not pretend that isn't something you would have said in a normal situation.'

She blinked, then laughed. 'You're right. How well you've grown to know me,' she teased. His lips twitched, but didn't spread into a full smile. She sobered. 'I'm sorry, Ezra.'

And she was, even though she was glad for the clarity. The first—very selfish—piece of clarity was discovering he was single. Her brain offered the observation before she could force it to act with decorum. Her heart had responded in a similarly uncouth manner, relieved it didn't have any competition.

Once she got through that, she felt an ache in her chest at what he must have gone through. His hesitancy to open up suddenly became a lot clearer, too. And why he'd reacted so strangely to her telling that old man she was hoping he'd propose.

She groaned. 'Oh, Ezra, I'm so sorry.'

'Yes, you said that.'

'Yeah, but that was for—' She broke off, since she

wasn't about to say, 'for your non-fiancée.' That would have made her sound even more heartless. She cleared her throat. 'This is for what happened inside the café with me joking about the proposal. I'm an idiot.'

His mouth curved. 'You didn't know.'

'Yeah, well. I shouldn't have assumed.'

Because she had, she took a mental step back. Was grateful that she did when she realised she knew nothing about Ezra. He was…some man she'd met at a café. A man who made her heart jump in ways it hadn't for the longest time; or ever, if she was being honest with herself. A man who made her body feel things it hadn't ever. There was no point in denying that when she was still thinking about how their bodies had met at the bottom of the hill.

But she had to remember that he knew just as much about her as she did about him. She doubted she would have liked it if he'd made some cavalier comment about death. About family. Or if he'd asked more questions about *her* family and stirred up the memories she was desperately trying to ignore.

Though, as seemed to be the case that day, ignoring it still wasn't working.

She closed her eyes. Felt the grief, the pain wash over her as if she'd stood under a shower head and had it doused over her like water. Would it ever stop? The extreme reaction she could physically feel in her body. In her lungs. Her head. Her heart.

'I'm such an idiot,' she said again softly, though she wasn't sure if she was saying it to herself or to him.

'Angie. Angie.' She looked at him. Then blinked a few times when she realised she was acting like a freak. An illogical freak. 'You have nothing to apologise for. I overreacted with that man. It's not the end of the world.'

'You didn't overreact,' she said with a frown. 'You *reacted*. And in a politer manner than I would have, I guarantee you.'

He smiled. 'You're being nice. Generous, too, but I'll accept it.'

'I'm not being generous. I'm being...fair.' She paused. 'Why do you think it was an overreaction?'

'Because—' he lifted a hand, and there was a beat between then and when he continued '—because I asked to go for a walk because I felt suffocated at a pretend proposal. I wasn't even engaged. I have no reason to—'

'Respond appropriately to being faced with a situation that reminds you of something painful in your past?' She shook her head. 'I think you're being much too hard on yourself.'

I would know.

She sucked her bottom lip between her teeth, then deliberately let the air that had stuck in her lungs out. She had no desire to delve into how she was running away from her emotions. In fact, she *wasn't* running. She was...adhering to her quota.

She cleared her throat. Realised he'd stopped behind her. She stopped, too. Faced him.

'How do you do that?' he asked after a moment.

'What?'

'Make me feel better?'

Though warmth spread through her, she shrugged. 'Depends on who you ask. If you asked my younger sister, she'd say it's because I'm a smartass.'

There was a long pause as she realised what she'd said, and she swore silently. She'd been so desperate to brush off Ezra's comment—it had felt too intimate, too personal; too much like a symbol of their connection—that she'd stepped right into the danger zone by referring to Sophia. *Just* after she'd justified why she didn't want to, too.

'I'm sorry. I shouldn't have said that. It wasn't fair.'

'Sounds like you have a few issues yourself.'

She laughed. 'Slight understatement, if I'm honest.'

'Do you want to talk about it?'

She opened her mouth, then paused when she didn't know what she was going to say. Her instinct had been no. Why would she want to talk about leaving weeks after her father's funeral because she hadn't wanted to deal with her mother's feelings? Why would she want to tell him about the shame she carried about it? About the lies she told? The excuses?

It *had* been a lie, telling her family she'd planned to go to Korea before everything had gone south. When she'd said it had nothing to do with her father's illness when really, she'd applied for a teaching job the moment her father's health had taken a turn for the worse.

She'd made excuses about why she couldn't postpone it after her father had… After. She'd left her family because she hadn't been brave enough to stay. To deal with what she knew would come after.

No, she thought again. She didn't want to share that with him. But just as she was about to go with her instinct, she made the mistake of looking into his eyes. He wore the same expression he had when she told him about why she didn't like weddings. Pensive. Jarring. Because when he wore that expression, she felt as if he could see right through her.

Or no, not through her, but *into* her. Right to that place where she brushed her feelings under a carpet. And then, for good measure, weighed the carpet down with quotas. With excuses.

Now she knew Ezra wasn't only asking her if she

wanted to share because he was being polite. He was
doing it because he thought she needed to be prompted.
Because he thought—without truly knowing it, she
knew—that she needed a reason to set aside the excuses and pick up the carpet. To finally shed some light
on the pile of dirt that seemed an apt description for her
current emotional state.

He was doing it for *her*. Damn if she was able to resist it.

'My dad—' She took a deep breath. *Just rip off the
plaster.* 'He passed away before I left for Korea. Weeks
before.'

Passed away. Three years and she was still using
euphemisms because she couldn't say the actual word.

'My mom… She relied on him quite a lot, so it was
really an awful thing to do. Me leaving, I mean. Not
his—'

She shook her head. *Idiot.* It was like the guilt had
made her tongue clumsy. Which she deserved. She deserved a whole lot worse than stumbling over her words
for leaving her family when they needed her most.

'But you felt like you had to?' Ezra asked from beside her, and she realised she'd started walking again,
heading into the pathway that led to the field. She wasn't
sure when. Hadn't even checked to see if he was walking with her.

'Did you hear what I said? I left my mother behind
after she lost the man she loved more than anything
else in the world. When she was trying to figure out
who she was without him.' She cringed, hearing it out
loud. Saying it felt like she was condemning herself.
'It was selfish.'

'But you felt like you had to?' he said again, and
took her hand in his. The warmth of it slid through her

body, comforting her, just as it had when he'd done it at the top of that hill. Seemed like he had a knack for knowing when she needed it.

She had to clear her throat before she could speak again. 'Yeah, I did.'

Ezra nodded at her words, and silence followed them as they walked. Eventually she realised it was his turn. 'So, what happened with your girlfriend?'

'I proposed. She declined. Simple really.'

'Couldn't have been that simple if even the mention of a wedding bothers you.' She paused. 'How long were you two together?'

'Seven years.'

She almost dropped her jaw before she remembered she was trying to act more appropriately. 'When did you break up?'

'About nine months ago.'

'And you said you're going back to Cape Town to see your family for Christmas?'

'I'm moving back home permanently. But yes, to see my family, too.'

'Have you seen them since the breakup?'

'No.'

She winced. 'So this isn't exactly the homecoming you imagined.'

He pulled a face. 'It had to happen sometime.'

'But Christmas is a bit steep. People always try to make you feel bad about your life at Christmas.'

'You're not a fan of weddings *and* Christmas?'

Again, she kicked herself for revealing something she hadn't intended to. She was about to brush it off when she noticed they were at the foot of the step that led to the field. She could hear a faint drum of music coming from that direction now.

'What did you say was up here?' Ezra asked.

'I believed I used the very descriptive term of "something." The music wasn't here earlier.'

'Maybe it's a ritual of some kind. Some pagan sacrifice to the gods.'

'At Christmastime?' She wasn't convinced, but smirked when he cocked an eyebrow. 'I'm sorry, what I meant to say was that pagan sacrifices to the gods at Christmastime seems *extremely* legit.'

'Imagine how legit it's going to sound when we go check it out instead of talking about issues neither of us want to talk about.'

She stared at him for a beat. Then she began to climb the steps that led to the field. 'What are you waiting for, Ezra?' she asked over her shoulder. 'Let's go check it out.'

He was beginning to think Angie had a gift for him.

Or maybe it was that he had a gift for her. He'd seen the faint panic in her eyes when she'd told him about her parents—when she'd blamed herself for leaving—and he'd been determined to make the pain go away.

Because he was familiar with it, he told himself, now rejecting the idea of either of them having a gift for the other. He knew what it was like to regret a decision. More than most, even. So it was that they had something in common that was making him feel this way.

Not that that made any sense either. Ever since his final year in high school, he was careful about who he allowed into his life. It didn't matter if they were strangers, or friends of friends, or professional acquaintances; he'd learnt his lesson about bonding with people he shouldn't.

Spending time with Angie like this—at all, really—was…significant.

And he hadn't even got to the more disturbing parts of it.

Like how Angie had managed to get him to reconsider the end of his relationship with Liesel when he'd been beating himself up about it endlessly. How reconsidering it had him thinking that maybe all the aches, the memories, his reactions, were normal. Were fine.

Like how, when he looked at Angie, his body tensed in ways he didn't expect. Hadn't believed possible so soon after Liesel.

He didn't dwell on what it meant. On what it *could* mean. They'd be going their separate ways soon. There was no point.

That didn't stop the stir of anxiety in his chest.

Then they arrived at the base of the field and he didn't think about it anymore.

'This is—'

'Wow.'

They spoke at the same time, and when Ezra turned to Angie and she was already facing him, he thought her expression reflected his feelings exactly.

'I did not expect a little town outside of Cape Town to have this,' he said, turning his attention back to the field. The last thing he'd expected was to find Christmas floats there. Or to realise the faint drum of music they'd been lured by had been Christmas carols blasting through speakers all over the field.

As he took everything in, he noticed the floats had been divided. No matter how long he looked at it, he couldn't figure out whether they'd been divided according to logic or reason. Not when Father Christmas and the elves stood on a trailer next to the Three Wise Men, who in turn, stood next to a float dedicated solely to reindeers.

'Do you think it's for a parade?' he asked, his legs moving before he fully knew they were. Angie walked in step beside him.

'Um, I'm going to say yes because I feel really weird about not knowing this existed. Unless it happened after my parents moved?' She sounded as if she were talking more to herself than to him. 'Why wouldn't they tell us about this? Why wouldn't they bring us to this? It would have made their stories a lot cooler.'

'The story about your mom finding out she was pregnant wasn't cool enough for you?'

She made a face and he laughed.

'The other option is that maybe, they didn't want to expose us to all this paganism,' she said gravely, needing no time to bounce back. 'It would have damaged our Christian brains severely to watch a pagan ritual celebrating Christmas through floats and Christmas music.' She lifted a hand to her chest. 'The horror.'

He chuckled. 'Why is everything you say a quip?'

'It's my curse,' she said. When he looked over, she smiled at him.

Some version of himself stumbled at that smile. At the dimples he somehow hadn't noticed before. At how the smile crinkled the skin around her eyes. At how it quite literally took his breath away.

He wanted to lift a hand and pull at her curls. No, he wanted to slide his hand into them and tilt her head back, his mouth lowering to hers so he could—

'It's not a curse,' he said slowly, deliberately, almost as if he were telling himself that a version where he stumbled at this woman's smile—where he kissed her—

couldn't exist. Not when he was still reeling from the end of his seven-year relationship.

But what if you weren't *still reeling?*

'Ezra?' He blinked. Saw she was frowning. 'You didn't hear a word I said.'

'Sorry.' He resisted the urge to shake his shoulders. 'I haven't had much sleep these last few days. It's been hell driving so far.'

'I know.' There was a pause. 'Can I ask you what you didn't hear me say the first time again?'

He knew she did so purposefully, despite the easy smile on her face. Something must have told her he needed the distraction. He didn't acknowledge how that made him feel.

'Sure, go ahead.'

'You said it wasn't a curse. Earlier.' She lifted a hand, pulled at a curl. His fingers itched to do the same. 'What did you mean?'

'Exactly what I said,' he told her. Stopped walking. 'There's nothing wrong with being witty. In fact, it's one of the reasons I like you.'

Her lips curved, then her eyes shifted to behind him. When her gaze focused on his again, something on her face had his heart beating faster. It sped up even more when she gave him a sweet smile.

'I don't think you're going to like me very much after I do this.'

'What?'

She winked, moving past him. When he turned, Ezra groaned. Angie was heading toward a person holding a sign that said:

Elves needed for the Christmas parade. Speak to me if you'd like to brighten up a kid's day.

He didn't think this was going to brighten up *his* day.

Chapter Five

'Hi,' Angie said. 'I have a friend who'd like to become an elf. Do you still need them?'

'Yes, we do,' the woman holding the sign Angie had seen told her.

She was certain volunteering Ezra to be an elf was going to brighten her day. And hey, if it meant avoiding the awkward territory she and Ezra were heading toward with his talks of liking her, bonus.

'Could you speak to that guy over…'

The woman trailed off with a frown when she turned and saw the man she was referring to arguing with another woman. Angie didn't try to hide her own interest when the man stomped off, leaving the woman he'd been arguing with staring after him wordlessly.

'Nikki!' the woman who'd spoken with Angie yelled. 'Where's Simon going?'

Nikki turned to them. 'I'm…sorry, Dany. I don't think Simon is going to be able to do this. I don't think I can do this either.' Nikki gave a helpless shrug and walked off, leaving Dany and Angie staring after her now.

'So,' Angie said after a moment. 'I'm assuming Nikki and Simon are letting you down in some way.'

'I'll say.' Dany tossed the sign on the table behind

her. 'Four months. Four months my husband and I—along with our *former* friends, Nikki and Simon—have been planning this float for the Christmas parade. And just like that—' she snapped her fingers '—our plans have gone up in smoke.'

'Oh, I'm sure it's not that bad.'

'Angie,' Ezra said from behind her. 'I think this nice woman is trying to tell you she doesn't need us anymore.'

'You,' Angie corrected immediately, before turning her attention back to Dany. 'I'm sure two people can't spoil all the work you've done.'

Dany sighed and lowered onto a chair Angie hadn't noticed before. When Dany's hands began to rub her stomach—her decidedly swollen stomach—Angie realised she might need to work on her powers of perception.

'In any other year they probably wouldn't have. But this year—' She broke off. Sighed again. 'This year, my husband had a work function in Cape Town that he couldn't miss. I know this because I asked. Several times.' She rolled her eyes. 'Eventually, I agreed that it would be fine for him not to be here for the actual parade because part of the fun of it is making the float anyway. We all did that together.'

'Okay, so why can't it still work?'

'I'm supposed to drive the car in the parade because, you know.' She gestured to her stomach. 'Simon and Nikki were supposed to be Father Christmas and Mrs. Claus respectively. Our float with *just* elves won't work.' She blew out a breath. 'And by the way, I know that technically, Father Christmas isn't wed like Santa Claus is, but we didn't think anyone would care.'

Angie forced herself not to smile. 'I think you're right.'

'Except now I don't have either character. Oh, well. It probably wouldn't have worked anyway. We wouldn't have got volunteer elves. Who would have volunteered for that? Except you.' Dany winced. 'But that's because you're from out of town. Small place,' Dany said when Angie's eyebrows rose. 'You don't even know about the prize. A year's worth of donuts.'

'Is that, um, usual?' Angie asked, keeping both the amusement and confusion from her voice. 'The donuts, I mean.'

For the first time since Nikki and Simon stormed off, Dany smiled. 'Not in the sense you mean it, I don't think. Each year one of the local entrepreneurs sponsors the Christmas parade. It's tradition, and really, we don't do it because we want the prize. Although there *were* significantly fewer entries the year the printing store sponsored the parade.' Dany wrinkled her nose. 'Free ink cartridge refills for a year.'

Angie laughed. Heard Ezra laugh behind her, too. Then she was speaking, and hoping Ezra would hold on to his amusement for a while longer.

'You know, Dany, donuts sound really good.'

'They're *so* good.' Dany rolled her eyes in mock ecstasy. 'The bakery is the best in town. Which might not sound all that significant considering the size of the town, but I've eaten my share of donuts from Cape Town and I'm pretty sure it would hold its own there, too.'

'That's some recommendation.'

Angie turned to Ezra. There was a pause as he looked at her without saying anything. Soon he was shaking his head.

'Oh, no. No, no, no.'

'Oh, come on. It's Christmas.' She waited a beat. 'You'd look really hot as Father Christmas.'

'What?' Dany exclaimed at the same time Ezra said, 'No.'

'You'd do this?' Dany asked again, the excitement clear in her voice.

'No,' Ezra repeated.

'Ezra, do it for the children.'

'Screw the children,' Dany said. 'Do it for the donuts.'

Angie blinked, then she burst out laughing. When Ezra didn't laugh—she swore she saw his lips twitch though—Angie sobered, nodding solemnly. 'Do it for the donuts, Ezra.'

'I mean, you could do it for the children as well,' Dany said, grimacing when Angie turned back to her. 'There's only one Father Christmas allowed per parade per year for the sake of the children. Each year, one float gets a turn. This year was ours. The next time we'd have our chance again would be in over ten years' time. And we wouldn't even be able to participate normally for the next couple of years either since we're having the baby, and who knows when we'll have the time to do something like this again.'

Dany's eyes moved from Angie to Ezra. She looked down.

'Besides, it's Christmas. My last Christmas before some of my independence disappears because of the baby. I was looking forward to being able to say I did this, you know? But alone. Without my husband, I mean. So I could prove that I *could*. In some stupid way, I guess I was trying to prove to myself that I can do things without my husband. He got a new job recently that requires him to be out of town a lot, and I'm going to have to look after the baby myself a lot of the time.'

She heaved a sigh. 'If I could pull off something as important as this alone, I'd know I could be alone as a mom, too. So...' she trailed off, lifting her eyes slyly.

'Damn, Dany,' Angie said with a slight laugh, respect going through her. 'You sure know how to guilt someone into doing something.'

'Sorry. I inherited it from my mom. And since I'm going to be a mom...' She lifted a shoulder.

The words shifted something inside Angie's chest. She ignored it. 'Oh, it wasn't a criticism. I'm impressed. So, Ezra.' She turned back to him. 'What's it going to be?'

Ezra gave her a steady look. Finally, he sighed.

'Fine. But it's just as much for the donuts as it is for the kids.'

'I look like an idiot.'

'You look fine,' Angie replied dismissively. 'I, on the other hand, am wearing a dress from that period in history where women were prohibited from looking attractive.'

Ezra took in the frumpy red-and-white dress and grinned. 'Yeah, you're right. At least I actually look like Father Christmas.'

He hadn't enjoyed stuffing the pillow under his shirt, but he supposed that was part of the deal. Along with the white beard and hat. He just wished there was a summer version of Father Christmas's outfit. Maybe a short-sleeve shirt and some formal shorts.

If he were going to brainstorm a summer look for the man, Ezra would also have suggested perhaps trimming the beard to a short stubble. Attractive and modern. And making people who dressed up as him in thirty-degree Celsius weather less miserable about their life choices.

'Does the hair even make it more convincing?'

Ezra laughed as she fiddled with the wig, which looked exponentially larger since she'd only just managed to tame her curls.

'Do you want an honest answer, or do you want me to lie?' he asked. She grunted. 'Hey, you're the reason we're in this mess in the first place. You should let me enjoy this.'

She gave him a fake smile now and he laughed again. He couldn't remember the last time he felt so free. So light. It must have been some time during his relationship with Liesel, except that as he scraped through his memories to try to remember when that was, he couldn't find a single memory of when he'd felt this good.

Which begged the question: why had he packed up his life and moved away from his family if he couldn't even *remember* being happy with his girlfriend? Why had he proposed? And why had he been so surprised—so hurt—when she'd refused?

The thoughts were unwelcome when he felt so detached from the situation. But then, when had he ever really been detached from it? It followed him around like a curse he couldn't shake. He'd thought leaving Grahamstown would help, but it only seemed to have amplified it.

His eyes rested on Angie. Maybe it wasn't leaving that had amplified it…

'There are at least two upsides,' she said when Dany gave them the sign and they began to walk to the North Pole-themed float. There were no elves, unfortunately, but Dany seemed content with managing to secure another Father Christmas and Mrs. Claus.

'One, this could have been much worse. Dany could have chosen to have Mrs. Claus be sexy. While I'm all for sexual empowerment, I don't think dressing in a skimpy dress in front of thousands or however many people would have done us any favours.'

'Not sure that's true,' he commented, desperate to get the disturbingly enticing image she created out of his head.

'I mean in terms of characterisation,' she said dryly. 'I don't think Mrs. Claus would want people to gawk at her in the way a skimpy dress would have elicited.' She lifted a brow. 'In the way you're gawking.'

He grinned. 'Thanks for clarifying.' He waited a beat. 'Your dedication to portraying Mrs. Claus authentically is something I'm sure will be noted during award season.'

'Two,' she continued flatly, not acknowledging his comment, tossing her head back. He didn't think it had the effect she'd hoped for with that wig. 'I know none of these people, so I'm fairly certain this won't end up biting me in the butt.'

He grimaced.

'What?' He pulled his face again. 'Ezra,' she growled, 'if you don't tell me what that expression is about, I'm going to push you off the float and pretend it was an accident.'

He climbed up the stairs Dany had put up next to the trailer, and glanced back. 'Has this been your plan all along? Murder because I talked about kidnapping?'

'No,' she said sweetly. 'But if you don't tell me what you were pulling your face at, I won't be able to tell the judge I was remorseful if I *did* murder you.'

'I was only thinking that you shouldn't have said it,'

he relented. 'About knowing people here, I mean. It's the kind of thing that causes people you know to pop up.'

'I don't have magical powers.'

'It's called the law of attraction. I don't make up the rules,' he said with a shrug when she narrowed her eyes at him. She hissed out a breath.

'It would be just my luck, too, if someone I knew saw me here.'

'And didn't you say your parents lived here?' he asked.

She blinked up at him, then began to climb up the stairs slowly, as if his question had weighed down her limbs. He immediately regretted asking it. He also knew that if he asked whether she was okay like he wanted to, it wouldn't go down successfully.

She was like one of those plants that closed up if someone touched them. If he asked her about something she didn't want to talk about, she pulled back and he wouldn't even get the surprise revelations she shared with him. That…would have been a shame. A disappointment. A loss. So he didn't say anything. Held out a hand instead.

She blinked again, but gripped it, before lifting her leg and climbing over the low railing keeping everything from toppling over. It brought her closer to him, like they'd been at the hill, and his body immediately thanked him for it.

He was a head taller than her, but her expression made him feel as though they were of equal stature. Or perhaps that feeling came from somewhere deep inside him; somewhere more significant. Somewhere that knew he wasn't referring to her height, but her character. Strong. Steady. A perfect fit for him.

The thought had him stepping back. Releasir hand. Taking an unsteady breath.

'You okay?' she asked quietly when he turned away. He took a moment to process, and she must have known he needed it because she didn't repeat her question or say anything else. When he felt better, he turned back and answered.

'Sure.'

She nodded. Seconds later, Dany called from the car's window that they'd be joining the convoy soon. She'd barely said the words before the traffic officer gave his signal, and the car roared to life under them. It edged forward slowly, and Angie gripped his hand.

'Sorry,' she said when he looked over. 'I've never done anything like this before.'

'Nor have I.'

'Yeah, but you look steadier for some reason.'

'Trust me, I'm not.'

She turned to him. 'I'm not talking about your emotional well-being. We both know I'm more stable in that department.'

She winked and his mouth curved, though for the life of him, he knew he should have felt more offended. He also knew that he should have looked away, let go of her hand; he did neither.

They stood like that for the longest time. And when the spell ended—though a part of him worried it never would—he cleared his throat. 'I guess the only way we're going to get through this is if we stick together.' He squeezed her hand. 'Let's go win some donuts.'

Chapter Six

They did not win the donuts.

There hadn't been any clues of this result as they'd gone through the motions of the parade though. For the most part, it had been fun. It would have been *all* fun if Angie hadn't felt the memories chasing after her as the car slowly drove down Caledon's main street.

In some ways, this was unavoidable. She'd been to Caledon's main town a few times before. Always driving through; always for a handful of minutes. She thought now that perhaps her parents had merely been doing it for their own sakes rather than that of their children. Regardless, it meant Angie had something to compare what she was seeing to.

Nothing had changed.

Perhaps that's what sent the wave of longing through her. As they waved to the cheering crowds—as Ezra dug deep into the red bag he'd been given for the 'presents' of marshmallow chocolates for the kids, deftly throwing them into the crowd—it washed through Angie, forcing her to cling to whatever she could find to keep steady. It worried her that she immediately looked to Ezra. Which had been the reason she refused the impulse to take his hand, letting herself be dragged by the wave instead.

The parade had started just off the national road,

giving them a glimpse of the tail end of the casino and spa that acted as one of the main tourist draws for the town. Then they slowly went through the middle of the town, following a designated route that took them through roads Angie hadn't seen before. It didn't matter. The feel of the town was the same.

There was no one style of building here, which was part of the town's appeal. Old mixed with new in a quaint combination of past traditions and what would become future traditions. Red buildings stood next to cream buildings, which, in turn, stood next to historical buildings; churches and government buildings stood opposite liquor stores and furniture shops. The roads had been cordoned off for the parade, and people pressed against the barriers separating the road from the sidewalk, eager to get a view of the floats.

Not all of them though, Angie thought, handing out the cookies she'd been given as part of her Mrs. Claus character. Her eyes settled on one young girl standing at the top of a step far from the barrier. Her arms were folded, her mouth turned down, and she was leaning against the wall of a convenience store. Everything about her screamed that she didn't want to be there.

Angie's mouth curved up. She'd seen that stance before. In many of the teenagers she'd taught over the years, but also in her sister. Sophia would have hated this. She would have protested vehemently at being forced to attend, and because she would have been forced to attend, she would have made sure everyone knew how much she hated it.

Which, of course, would have made Zoey determined to get Sophia to smile. Their youngest sister would have teased and joked and threatened. Hell, there might even have been bouncing and some very bad gymnastics.

And if that didn't work, Zoey would have resorted to drastic measures: roping Angie in. Together, Angie and Zoey would have done the only thing they knew would make Sophia smile: The Terrible Dance.

Someone handed her the empty plate back, and Angie offered a smile as thanks. She was afraid of what it might have looked like though. She was in no state to offer a genuine smile.

'Are you okay?' Ezra asked, edging over to her as smoothly as he did everything else. And annoying the hell out of her in the process.

'Fine.'

'You don't seem fine.'

'You're an expert now that we've spent—what, ninety minutes together?'

He lifted his free hand in an easy surrender, but his gaze was shrewd. 'Just making sure my partner in Christmas is okay.'

Despite herself, her lips twitched.

Which, again, annoyed her, because how was this man so charming? He said he didn't do well with strangers, and yet he smoothly interacted with the crowds watching the parade. And she didn't want to start on how well he was dealing with her. How despite her moodiness, he took her hand and drew her gently to his side, pointing out the spectacles of the other floats now that his gift bag was empty. He did it seemingly knowing she needed to be distracted.

At the end of it, Angie was smiling, laughing, as if Ezra had banished the darkness of those memories for her. Perhaps it would have been easier to let him steady her right from the beginning, she thought. But then her stomach flipped and something in her chest constricted, and she ignored that, too. Which meant that she was ignoring almost all her thoughts, and even she could admit that was ridiculous.

'I'm sorry we didn't win the donuts,' Angie said after the winners had been announced and Dany stood waiting as Angie and Ezra got off the float.

'It was a long shot,' Dany said, waving a hand. 'I'm just glad I got to participate.' She gave them a genuine smile. 'Thank you so much for helping out. I know this probably wasn't what either of you wanted to spend your afternoon on.'

'I don't know,' Ezra said, glancing over at Angie with a small smile. 'I think it worked out okay.'

'It was certainly preferable over other celebrations today,' Angie added, which got her a wider smile from Ezra and a look of confusion from Dany.

'Anyway,' Dany said after a moment. 'Just because you didn't win the donuts, doesn't mean you shouldn't have some.'

She tilted her head toward a booth that had a Do It Donuts sign standing at the front, and then waddled over. Angie exchanged a look with Ezra—*Do it Donuts? Really?*—before following Dany.

'Give these people some donuts, Ben,' Dany said, ignoring the long line and walking to the front, slapping money on the counter.

Ben smiled—*a kind smile,* Angie thought, smiling back—and nodded. 'You got it, Dany. I'll give you chef's choice since you're not from around here.' He winked at them before folding a box and selecting donuts from beneath the glass casing.

'Small town,' Dany said when she stopped in front of them again. 'You have a certain look about you when you're not from around here.'

'Though shouldn't that mean we have to stand at the back of the queue?' Angie asked, amused.

'Nah, you're with me.' Dany grinned. 'Ben's an ex-boyfriend. Part of our breakup agreement was that he gives me donuts whenever I want them.'

'Sounds like a pretty good deal,' Ezra noted. Angie glanced over at him, but he was looking at Dany, no indication that the ex-talk was making him uncomfortable.

'Yeah, we both knew it wasn't going anywhere.' Dany lifted a shoulder. 'Sometimes you get bored in a small town and end up doing things you shouldn't. Things ended amicably, as you can see.' Ben gestured to her and she waddled back over, grabbing the box from him. 'And now you get donuts,' she said when she returned.

'We're grateful.'

'Me, too.' Dany smiled. Her gaze narrowed on one person and she sighed. 'There's Nikki. I better go talk with her. The sooner I do, the sooner I'll forgive her for letting me down. Thanks again.'

She hugged them both, and left with another sigh.

'You know,' Angie said minutes later, studying her half-eaten donut as they made their way back to the café, 'this might actually be the best donut I've tasted.'

'Definitely,' Ezra agreed, licking his fingers after finishing his own donut. She was distracted by it for a moment—what else could he do with that tongue?—before shaking her head.

'I bet you're glad I volunteered now.'

'I'm not planning my revenge anymore,' he allowed.

'That's something.' She laughed, and smiled at the young boy who shrieked with glee before running off to catch an elf.

'This feels almost festive, doesn't it?' she asked, finishing her donut. 'The parade, the aftermath.'

She gestured around at the busy street, wondering now at the fact that it had been successfully cordoned off. In Cape Town, it probably would have caused a number of traffic incidents. She was sure there would have been a significantly higher number of disgruntled citizens, too.

In contrast, the residents of Caledon seemed to have embraced it. Hundreds of people were roaming around them, enjoying the food stalls that had been set up or rushing toward the entertainment areas. There was a Christmas-tree decorating competition in front of them, and a cookie-decorating competition behind them. The air felt happy and calm. Angie breathed in deeply, as if doing so would help her hold that feeling inside her.

'It does feel festive,' Ezra said after a while. 'But the real question is whether it's festive enough to change your mind about the festive season?'

'What do you mean?'

'Do you still hate it?'

'I don't hate it.' She felt his gaze on her, but she refused to look over, afraid of what he might see.

'Fine,' he said. 'Only weddings then.'

'I thought we already established I don't hate weddings. I hate the baggage they come with. I've also told you about why that is.'

'Not everything though,' he commented, and she blew out a breath. How could he see through her when she wasn't even looking at him?

'How do you know that?'

'I don't know. Instinct.'

'Instinct,' she repeated. Shook her head. 'Well, since your *instinct* is on point, I suppose I'll tell you.' She paused. 'Weddings force me to face my family. Whatever you're sensing about my feelings about Christmas is probably because weddings at Christmas give me an *overdose* of family interactions, which I was thinking about earlier. That's not really something I relish anymore.'

'Who does?'

'I used to.' The aftertaste of the donut somehow went from sweet to bitter. 'There was a period of time where we were happy as a family.'

'What changed?'

'I… I don't know.' She kept her gaze on the ground. 'I want to say that something happened. So there's a clear delineation, you know? Then I can tell you about the pre-something period, and the post-something period. The truth is…more complicated.'

'You do know then,' he noted. 'It's complicated, but you know.' When she looked at him, he shrugged. 'They're not the same things.'

'No, they aren't.' She took a breath. 'I think I got to see the cracks when I was older. Or saw things for what they were.'

'Which was?'

She didn't answer for the longest time. 'I thought my parents were happy. They were, I guess. But when I got older I realised that happiness didn't come from a healthy place. My mother was so dependent on my father. My father liked that, and they had this… I don't know, I guess symbiotic relationship would describe it best. Where they're both benefitting on the surface, but in reality, they're hurting one another.'

'Or maybe just you?'

She looked over at him. 'No. No,' she said again with a slight shake of her head.

'Okay,' he said. 'What about your sisters?'

'What about them?'

'You don't like spending time with them?'

'No, that's not it. We…grew up. We went through those awful, awkward stages fairly close to one another because the age gaps between us are close.' Her stomach churned at what she was leaving out—at the years she'd spent taking care of them—but she forced herself to at least say this. 'My father got sick before things could get better. That…that in itself changed things. Then I—I left, and there were no more chances.'

'There'll be more chances,' he said softly.

She made a noncommittal sound, already afraid she'd revealed too much. Her insides were almost vibrating from the vulnerability, and she didn't like it. She glanced over when she heard an intake of breath—like he was going to ask her something big, or try to make her feel better—and she held her own breath.

But he only said, 'Families are hard.'

She let out the air slowly, watching his face as she did. She narrowed her eyes.

'You know, you say that, and yet there's something about the way you've said it—and your expression—that makes me think you don't believe it.'

He didn't look at her, but the side of his mouth curve. 'This is beginning to get creepy.'

'It is, isn't it?'

Now he did look at her. 'What do you think I'm talking about?'

'The fact that our *instincts* are telling us things about the other even though we've only known each other for a few hours?'

'Like I said—creepy.'

'I agree.' And she knew when they parted ways, she'd wonder about it. 'So stop avoiding the question and tell me why you're lying.'

'I'm not. Not in the way you're thinking.' His hands

tightened around the box of donuts. 'My family's pretty close-knit. It's great most of the time. Not so great when you've done something stupid and you don't want to be called out on it.'

'That's why you're dreading going home?'

'Yeah. Part of it, anyway. I'm not looking forward to having the post-breakup conversation.'

'But they know, right?'

'They know.'

They walked in silence for a few seconds, and then Ezra said, 'Your turn.'

'What?'

'There's more to this whole "I don't like Christmas and weddings" thing, isn't there?'

'I told you a lot of it already.'

'Angie.'

'What more could there be, Ezra?'

'Angie.'

He stopped then, forcing a young couple who'd been walking behind them to part. They got stern looks in return, but Angie didn't mind it as much since it gave her a moment to compose herself. When she turned to face him, the plea saw in those incredible eyes made the words slip from her lips almost as if they'd been oiled.

'My parents were married around Christmas. They celebrate—*celebrated*—' *so hard*, she thought, and forced herself to continue '—their anniversary around this time every year.' She swallowed down the bile. 'They renewed their vows months before my father—' She took a breath. Cleared her throat. 'Around this time, too.'

'Which is the real reason you hate being at this wedding,' he said softly, almost to himself. He shook his head. 'The memories must be hard.'

'Yeah.' Her feet began to move again, as if they wanted to run from the emotion weighing down on her chest. 'The memories are there, but they're not—' She broke off when she realised she didn't know how to finish that sentence. She pivoted. 'I haven't actually been home since…since we lost him. I haven't hadn't the chance to be reminded of it.'

'You didn't have to be home to be reminded of it,' he said next to her.

'Not sure that's true,' she replied. 'I've never been around my mother since then to figure out how she feels about spending her anniversary without my father. Or Christmas, for that matter.' *Or any other day,* she thought, but didn't say it. 'He… It happened at the beginning of the year. I left in February. And now I'm back. Three years later.'

'Which makes going back so much worse,' he said softly. 'You *have* to spend Christmas around your mom and be reminded of it. Of being without him.'

She swallowed when his words, his understanding fed the lump of emotion in her throat. She took a deep breath, kept it in for a few seconds, then let it out. She did that four or five times. Though it didn't cause the anxiety or hurt to disappear, it faded them enough for her to speak again.

'It makes absolutely no sense, but I'm mad at them for doing it. For getting married at Christmas. It's so stupid. It's…selfish.' She turned away from him, tucking her hands into her armpits though there was no chill in the breeze that flew over them. 'It feels like I have two reasons to dread Christmas now. A memory of their anniversary, and a memory of how…' She sucked in air, let it out slowly. 'The last Christmas I spent with them hadn't been great either. My father was sick, and he got sicker—'

She broke off. Shook her body to try to get out of it. She felt the pain of it. Of this this very clear evidence of why she'd gone away; of why she refused to think about it more than she had to. She felt the guilt in her bones.

'There's nothing wrong with dreading Christmas,' Ezra said.

They started down the gravel path where all of this has started earlier that afternoon, toward the café. Angie's eyes flitted over her rental, but she kept walking, noting as she did that there were barely any people around this time.

'There's especially nothing wrong with dreading Christmas when it has painful memories of someone you were close to,' Ezra added.

'It's funny,' she said after a while. 'When he was still here, I don't think I'd have described us as close. We were much too similar.'

Which has been part of the problem, she thought. Her heart thudded painfully, and she cleared her throat. He was getting hopelessly too much information from her. Besides, she needed the distraction.

'What ended your relationship?'

His eyebrows rose, and he stuffed a hand into his pocket while the other held the donut box against his hip. 'This is revenge, isn't it?'

'No.' But his eyebrows went even higher and she nodded with a small smile. 'Maybe a little.' She blew out a breath. 'I'm sorry. I'm not used to—'

'You don't have to apologise.' He offered her a smile that had her gut twisting and a voice in her head scolding her for being callous. 'I was pushing.'

She didn't reply. Wasn't sure what she should say.

How could she tell him it was less about him pushing and more about the fact that she still struggled to speak about her father? About the complicated mess of her feelings about what had happened? About her family? About the guilt that drove her? The responsibility now, too? And the fear—always the fear—that she'd take over from her father and be her mother's entire emotional support? That feeling responsible for her mother, her sisters meant that she was already doing it?

Her heart pounded in her ears, making the silence stretching between them so much worse. Making the ache in her heart, her lungs, her gut, her bones so much worse. And then she was wishing she could say something to break it. To go back to the ease they'd shared earlier.

But she was beginning to realise that things with *Ezra* were complicated, too. They could go from easy to difficult and back within minutes. She let the silence ride—breathing, letting her body slip back into its natural rhythm—and told herself to be comfortable with the knowledge that she and Ezra were complicated.

'To be perfectly honest with you,' Ezra said into the silence. She nearly smiled that her instinct had been correct. 'I'm not sure what ended my relationship. Maybe it was never meant to become what I thought it would.' He paused. 'Sometimes I think I imagined it all.'

'Seven years is a long time to imagine things,' she said after a moment. 'No offence, but I don't think you're that creative.'

He laughed quietly. 'You're talented.'

'Thank you. And yes, I *will* sign all the copies you'll buy of my book someday.' They shared a smile. 'It does suck though,' she continued, 'the whole end of your relationship. I'm sorry you had to go through that.'

He blinked. Frowned. Shook his head.

'What?' she asked.

'Nothing,' he answered. 'It's… You're right. It *does* suck.'

'Why are you saying it like that? Like you've only just realised it?'

'No, I always knew it. I haven't spent much time thinking about it like that though. It seemed…too simple, almost.' He stopped walking. 'But it does suck.'

She stopped, too, and turned to face him. 'Sometimes the best answer is the simplest one.'

And in that moment, as they stood looking at one another, something shifted. Angie's mind scrambled to figure out what. What had changed? How had it changed so quickly? But then the air snapped between them and she had no more opportunity to think. Not when her lungs had gone heavy, as if there was too much air in them. Or not enough.

She wanted to tell herself to breathe. To take a moment and *breathe*.

But she couldn't.

Because all her wants had suddenly been ensnared by the man standing in front of her. The man who looked at her as if she were the only person in the world. The man she'd shared more with in the last hours than she had with anyone else in the past three years.

Maybe even before that.

How had things gone from teasing, to sharing, to… to *this*? Was it that complicated thing again? And how could things be complicated after such a short period of time? Why did she feel like the fact that they were was significant somehow?

Heat shimmered through her belly. At her thoughts, at the way he was looking at her. At the way that look made her feel.

As if she were the only person he'd ever looked at. As if she were the only woman he ever wanted to look at.

As if she'd been swept into one of those romance novels she'd read growing up. Into the happy tension of them that she wanted to create as an adult. Where people didn't die or grow apart. Where there was only one ending and it was happy; for ever, or at the very least, for now.

Something inside her acknowledged that she wanted to feel that way. Happy. It didn't seem to matter if it was for ever when it was for now. Damn it, she wanted to feel—she wanted to believe—that they were the only two people in the world.

If she did, she could step forward, lay her lips on his without consequence. She could run her hands over the ripples of his muscles. Slide her fingers through his thick, dark hair. She could find out if he was as attentive physically as he'd been emotionally.

'Stop,' Ezra said suddenly, his voice hoarse.

'What?' Her tone echoed his.

'Looking at me like that. It, this, isn't a good idea.'

'No,' she agreed. 'So it makes absolutely no sense that I don't care about what kind of idea it is.'

She stepped toward him, leaving just enough space that he would have to close the distance between them. If they were going to do this, both of them had to participate. In the decision. In the desire.

The slight curve of his lips as he stepped forward told her he was more than willing. She let her eyes flutter closed—heard the rapid beating of her heart in her ears as she did—and waited for his lips to touch hers.

And was startled when instead, his voice sounded in her ear.

'We have an audience.'

Chapter Seven

Emotions warred inside him at his situation. The situation where he'd been about to kiss the most captivating woman he'd ever known, but had been interrupted by an elderly couple watching them. It was only slightly more disturbing that the man was watching them with undisguised approval; the woman clasping her hands in unbridled joy.

Or *bridal* joy, he thought, when he recognised the man from the café.

'Did you do it, son?' the man called when Angie moved away from him, stepping back quickly enough for him to brace to catch her. His eyes moved over her face, taking in the flush as she steadied herself. As she avoided looking at him.

'No,' Ezra replied with a sick feeling in his stomach, which deepened at the disappointment on the couple's face. 'The night's still early and I'd like it to be a surprise,' Ezra heard himself continue. He shrugged when Angie shot him a quick glance before looking back at the couple.

'Oh, Charles, we interrupted the surprise,' the woman exclaimed, slapping a hand lightly on the man's arm. 'And all because you wanted to neck in the woods while waiting for Jenny and Dave.'

'It's not my fault they decided to take photos—and

do only heaven knows what else—for two hours.' Then his face eased into a smile. 'Besides, I'd suggest it again if we actually got to do it this time.' Charles snaked a hand around the woman's waist and nuzzled her neck.

Ezra looked over at Angie. This time, she didn't look away, her eyes wide, alight with humour. It eased the tension between them; the tension inside him eased, too. It was strange, considering he couldn't his place a finger on what had caused it. Then his eyes moved back to Charles and the woman—*his wife,* Ezra thought, when he saw the ring gleam on her hand—and he felt a kick of jealousy in his chest.

It was so completely unexpected that he almost didn't hear what Charles said next, only tuning in again when Angie spoke. 'Oh, they won't miss us.'

'Of course they will. You should get back to the venue. They should be back any moment now.'

'Charles, look, I know what I said, but we're really not guests at the wedding.'

The desperation in Angie's voice told Ezra she was tired of the charade.

'But you're wearing—'

'The same colour and style of dress as the wedding party?' She looked down at the green dress that clung to the upper half of her body and swirled down loosely from her waist. 'I know. Like I said before, it's a co-incidence.'

'Charles, have you been accosting this poor woman and she isn't even a part of the wedding?' The accusatory tone Charles's wife used made even Ezra wince.

'I thought...' He paused, a frown furrowing his brow so that the white of his eyebrows stuck together. 'I suppose I've been terribly insistent, haven't I?' His tone was apologetic. 'I'm sorry, my dear.'

Angie smiled, though there was something beneath it that made Ezra's lungs feel as though they were constricting.

'What about the engagement?'

'That's real,' Ezra spoke almost without realising it. Charles brightened.

'Oh, good. It wasn't all for nothing. See, Becky?'

'Yes, darling,' Becky replied, tucking her arm into the crook of her husband's. 'We should probably get back. Jenny and Dave *are* on their way.'

'Yes,' Charles told her, patting her hand. 'You two are going to have a wonderful life together. I can just see it.'

Ezra offered the man an uneasy smile and watched as the couple walked away. He turned to Angie when they were gone, holding his breath at the look on her face.

'What was that about?'

'I couldn't disappoint them. They looked so…so… *excited* about the prospect of an engagement.'

'And that made you forget that you almost left me in the café earlier because even the word "engagement" spooked you?'

'I didn't—' He broke off. 'This was different.' And he was beginning to realise that it was.

'How?'

'I don't know,' he lied. Guilt nudged him, but he ignored it, unable to bring himself to tell Angie the truth. He was still trying to wrap his head around it himself. 'We should get back.'

'Actually, I should be leaving.'

Ezra had been shocked by the realisation of why it was important to him not to disappoint Charles and Becky. It was nothing compared to the way her words made him feel now.

'Is it because of this whole thing with Charles and Becky? If it is, I can—'

'It's not,' she interrupted. 'It's time for me to go. I have another hour before I get to Cape Town and it's almost peak traffic time.'

'But…' He trailed off, unable to offer her any reason to stay except…

Except *them*.

But there was no *them*. Which meant he couldn't tell her why he wanted her to stay. Hell, he was still trying to figure out what it meant that he wanted her to stay in the first place.

'Thank you,' she said softly. 'For saving me in there.'

'Not that you needed saving in the end.'

She laughed lightly. 'Yeah, that tends to happen with me a lot.'

He smiled, nodded. Felt a hopelessness in both gestures that churned his stomach.

'Good luck. With your family. You're nervous to see them again,' he continued, answering the question in the look she sent him.

'Yeah.' There was a pause. 'Very perceptive. Unsurprising, but perceptive. Thank you, Doctor. I assumed,' she said when he frowned. 'Lecturing positions are hard to come by. They don't just hand them out because the candidate is cute.'

She grinned, and his heart raced in his chest even as his mind told him he hadn't paid enough attention to her smile. To the kindness there; the proof that she had a big heart. Big enough that it had changed something inside him. He had no idea what. Had no idea why. But he wanted to figure both of those things out. He was terrified that if she left, he wouldn't be able to.

'Don't let her keep you from moving on,' she interrupted his thoughts, all traces of the smile he'd been admiring gone. 'You deserve to move on.'

'Even if I was the reason we broke up?'

'I'm not sure that's true,' she replied. 'If you were, you would have known why things ended. You seem like the type to,' she answered his unspoken question. 'Honestly, Ezra, I don't believe only one person is responsible for the end of a relationship. I think, once you have more time to think about it—once you've settled back into your new old life, or old new life—' she smiled, sobered '—you'll have realised your mistakes. And you'll learn from them.'

She lifted a hand to his cheek, smiled again. 'I have faith someone who managed to make me feel so much better about my own life is the kind who'll learn from their mistakes.'

Her hand dropped. 'Goodbye, Ezra. It was lovely meeting you.'

She walked away.

It was the dramatic walkaway Angie had always wanted to do. In her imagination, Angie had been walking away from a man who'd done her wrong. The path she'd walked on had been paved with pride and a sense of accomplishment. And she'd be walking to her future with her head high and her shoulders straightened.

There was none of that now.

No now, Angie was overwhelmed by the disappointment, the sadness, the regret. There was also a deep sense that she was making a mistake. Because the man she was walking away from hadn't done her wrong. Hell, he was the first thing that had felt right since she'd come home. Since she'd left. Since long before.

Her footsteps faltered on the gravel road; her breath

came too quickly. *Was* she making a mistake? Was she walking away from something important? Would she look back on this day and wonder what would have happened if she'd stayed? If she'd faced the drum of fear that had mentally provided a beat for her steps back to her car?

No, she told herself. There was no way she could do this. There was no way she could entertain this. Any of it. Yes, she'd spent a few hours in Ezra's company. Yes, she'd felt muscles she hadn't even known had been bunched inside her relax. Yes, she'd taken a walk with him, had been in a parade with him, had felt festive with him.

That didn't change that the time she'd spent with him had been in a world that would never exist for her. That could never exist for her. And she had to recognise that that was the very reason staying was so appealing.

Why wouldn't she want to stay in a world where she didn't have to worry about her family? About whether her mother was angry at her for leaving? About whether her sisters held grudges about what they'd been left with?

The closer she'd got to Cape Town, the louder those questions had got in her mind. Was her mother angry at her? Did her sister hold grudges? And along with the volume, the guilt had grown. She'd felt her family's disappointment consuming her; she'd felt her grief suffocating her. She'd stopped at a place that held positive memories of her family in hopes that the guilt, the disappointment, the grief would disappear.

Naïvely, she thought now, feeling those emotions pierce through the film of pretence she'd established with Ezra. But then, that wasn't quite right either. She'd been honest with him. More honest than she'd ever been with anyone before. More honest than she'd been with herself for the longest time.

She wasn't staying at the café to avoid her family anymore. Well, not only because she wanted to avoid the inevitable awkwardness of their reunion. No, her reasons had changed. Grown. Now it included whatever had been happening between her and Ezra.

But it couldn't. Not when the disappointment, the sadness, the regret—and now, confusion, too—were still there. She had to leave. She had to keep moving. She had to be brave. And then she got to her car, reached to her side to get the keys out of her handbag, and re-alised it wasn't there.

Panic thrummed in her blood before she remembered where it was. *Oh, great.* She'd put her handbag in Ezra's car before their walk. Why she hadn't re-alised it until that moment was beyond her. *Or not*, she thought, and cursed silently as her mind reminded her of its recent turmoil.

She closed her eyes, let herself stew in it for a moment, then headed back to Ezra's car to wait for him. She'd barely reached her destination when she saw him.

Her eyes greedily took him in, as if it had been years since she'd last seen him and not minutes. *Minutes, Angie.* Even with the chiding voice in her head, she couldn't stop looking. At the shirt over broad shoulders. At the easy way his blue jeans sat on his hips, stretched across legs that didn't belong on a lecturer, but an ath-lete. His hair looked like he ran his hands through it too many times; his face carved into features that made 'perfect' seem too inadequate a description.

Her lips curved as she thought of all the students who took his women's studies classes. Were they in-terested in the issues, or were they merely enthralled by their lecturer? She wouldn't blame them. She might have been tempted to change her major if Ezra had been her lecturer...

She offered him a small smile when he saw her, only then noticing he wasn't alone. He clearly had some effect on her. Especially since his companions were the reason they met in the first place.

'Angie. Why are you still here?'

'My handbag's in the boot of your car,' she said, smiling at the newlyweds. 'Congratulations.'

'Thank you,' the bride—Jenny—beamed at her. 'Are you with Dr. Johnson?'

'Doctor... Oh, Ezra.'

'Yes, *Ezra*,' Jenny said, nudging her new husband in the ribs. 'Are you two together?'

Ezra's eyes met Angie's; neither of them answered.

She pulled her gaze from his. Cleared her throat. 'Why does it seem like you all know each other?'

'Because we do,' Jenny answered with a grin. 'I was one of Dr. Johnson's PhD candidates.'

'And I was his TA,' Jenny's husband, Dave, spoke for the first time.

'Really?' She lifted an eyebrow at Ezra. He avoided her gaze, and was that a blush she saw spreading across his cheeks? Resisting the smile the image brought to her lips, she turned her attention back on the newlyweds. 'You know, a marriage born in women's studies is not quite as common as you'd think.'

'No.' Jenny laughed. 'But this one turned out okay in the end.' She turned and kissed her husband on the lips. It was a small, sweet gesture that had Angie longing for things she hadn't realised she wanted. She purposefully avoided looking at Ezra this time.

'So,' she said after a moment. 'My handbag. You can, er, have the donuts.'

He was still holding the box, and Angie thought she saw a ghost of a smile on his lips. 'Thanks. I'll get it for you,' Ezra said. He opened the boot of his car. 'Sorry about that.'

'It wasn't your fault,' she said politely. 'I didn't remember either.'

She waited for him to get her bag, and murmured a 'thank you' when he handed it to her. His fingers brushed against hers as he did, the feeling going right through her body. It rocked her, almost as much as the thought that she didn't want this to be the last she had of him. Of them. A brush of the hand she would think about for the rest of her life.

She put the bag over her shoulder and took a step back, hoping distance would help her escape the pull she felt toward him.

It didn't.

'Well, I hope you enjoy the rest of the wedding.'

'Join us,' Jenny said, her arm around Dave's waist.

'What? No, I couldn't.'

'As Dr. Johnson's date,' Dave continued from his wife. 'Maybe if you agree, he'll actually take us up on our offer this time.'

This time?

'Like I said,' Ezra said, 'you're both so kind, but I can't.' His eyes met Angie's before he continued. '*We* can't. We'd be taking up space you didn't account for.'

'Only because you didn't RSVP when we invited you,' Jenny scolded.

'It was a—' Ezra broke off, blew out a breath before giving them an easy smile. Angie saw through it. 'I appreciate the offer, but I'm not here to gatecrash your wedding. I'd forgotten it was even going to be here,' he said, running a hand through his hair.

Angie narrowed her eyes, but didn't say anything. Even though all of this was suspicious. Ezra didn't seem the type to forget things, especially of this magnitude. In the time she'd known him—which admittedly, had been quite short—everything he'd done had seemed deliberate. How was it that he happened to be at a wedding that a) he knew the bridal couple of, and b) he'd been invited to?

Something didn't add up. The longer she looked at him, and the longer he avoided looking at her, the stronger that suspicion became. Until finally her mind offered her a ridiculous answer to all her questions. Which in turn sparked an even more ridiculous idea in her head.

Ezra didn't want to attend this wedding because he was *afraid*.

This was simply conjecture, but Angie was pretty confident in her conclusion. Ezra must have known about this wedding. He must have come here and changed his mind about attending—though, apparently, he had never RSVP'd, so she wasn't quite sure of the details of that. But she was fairly certain he was here for a reason. He was just too afraid to face it.

Afraid of being confronted with the end of his own relationship. Afraid of facing how it made him feel about weddings. So, she would offer to stay with him. To stay and help him face his fears. Maybe, it would make him feel better about going home. About moving on. She wanted that for him, didn't she? She was doing this for him.

Why then did a voice in her head ask her if she was doing it for herself? It wasn't like she wanted to stay.

Okay, fine, she wanted to stay.

To help him, yes, but also to help herself. Delaying her reconciliation with her family would give her a chance to escape the cloud of disappointment. It had loomed over her even more ominously after she decided to go home. Besides, this was easier. She'd rather face his issues than her own.

It wasn't as if it were hurting anyone. Her family wasn't expecting her until the next day; another strategic move that had made her feel as if she had more control over the situation. When she'd decided to do it that way, she'd told herself it was to give her an evening to acclimatise to being back in Cape Town. Just like she'd given herself a month to acclimatise to being back in South Africa.

She ignored the reality of it. Of the fact that it wasn't even the disappointment that had her feeling so reluctant. It was the fact that she'd be returning to her family home and her father wouldn't be there. For the first time, she'd be going home and he wouldn't be there to greet her.

She sucked in a breath. Hoped it would steady the nerves in her stomach. But it had almost no effect. She opened her mouth to speak, to tell the people around her she needed to go and find some place where she could panic in peace. Except that when she looked at Ezra, when she saw the concern on his face, it calmed the fluttering in her stomach more than the air ever could have.

Go, now, her inner voice commanded her. *Run away from him before it's too late.*

'Please, Dr. Johnson,' Jenny pleaded. 'You're the reason Dave and I are together in the first place. We want you here, and you wouldn't be taking up space. Dave's aunt fell ill a few days ago, so she and her husband couldn't attend. We didn't have time to do anything about it.'

'I don't know.'

'If it's because you need a date,' Angie said softly. 'I think that can be arranged.'

His eyebrows rose. 'You're offering to be my date? To a wedding?'

'I think I am, Doctor.'

They held each other's gazes. Words passed between them in that look.

You don't have to do this.

I do. We both do.

She didn't know how long they stood like that before Ezra turned to Jenny and Dave.

'We're in.'

Jenny squealed and before Angie knew it, she was being pulled into an enthusiastic hug. 'Thank you,' Jenny whispered in Angie's ear. Angie frowned, before plastering a smile on her face when Jenny pulled back.

'I'm going to freshen up and then Dave and I will make our big entrance,' Jenny announced. 'An hour later than expected, but then, who could have anticipated how gorgeous this place would be? We had to take photos wherever we could.'

With one last beam at Angie and Ezra, Jenny walked away, Dave following dutifully behind her. Silence followed their departure. Angie resisted shifting her weight between her legs.

'Um,' she said with the silence became too much. 'Am I the only one who wanted to tell Jenny that anyone could have anticipated how beautiful a setting this is? Or that *she* should have anticipated how gorgeous this place would be?'

The corner of his mouth lifted. 'No.' Silence stretched

again. This time, he broke it. 'This messes up your plans. You're going to get stuck in traffic now, for sure.'

'I'll leave after rush hour winds down and miss it altogether.'

'You don't mind driving in the dark?' Ezra asked, but Angie heard the real question.

Why didn't you do that in the first place?

'I'm not a big fan of it after already driving four hours to get here. But resting will probably give me enough energy to make the drive. Besides,' she said casually, 'it's for a good cause.'

'And what cause is that?'

'Getting you over your fear of weddings.'

Chapter Eight

Ezra didn't answer immediately. 'I'm not afraid of weddings.'

'Sure you are,' she replied easily. 'Unless there's another reason you're here when you didn't RSVP to Jenny and Dave?'

'Yes. I had…'

He frowned, trying to think of a way to describe what he knew looked illogical. How could he explain what had gone through his mind when he'd got the invitation to Jenny and Dave's wedding? He'd still been in Grahamstown teaching, and the invite had been left on his desk by the faculty's secretary. He remembered looking at it and feeling a burst of happiness that his students had found love together.

Then he'd gone back to feeling sorry for himself.

Needless to say, he'd got the invitation a couple of weeks after his breakup. 'Feeling sorry for himself' had entailed crumpling up the paper, throwing it in the bin, then fishing it out again.

Try illogical *and* pathetic.

He'd stuck the invitation on his wall after that. It had been a sick reminder of how things could have turned out with Liesel. He hadn't RSVP'd, and yet, when he'd been making his plans to return to Cape Town, something had compelled him to pick up the phone and make arrangements to stay at the lodge on the day of the wedding.

He only regretted it when he arrived and saw people preparing for the celebration. He decided to hide in the café and work until he could make his escape back to his room for the night. And the moment he lost his mind would be but a blimp on the radar of his poor decisions.

It would have worked, too, if it hadn't been for Angie.

The irrationality of his decision was suddenly joined by an irrational anger.

'Anytime now,' Angie said, but her words were soft. Patient. And fanned the fire of his anger.

'I forgot about it,' Ezra said, edgy.

'Sure you did.'

'I'm not going to argue with you about this.'

'Because you know I'm right.' There was a pause. *'Because you're afraid of weddings.'*

'I am not—' He gritted his teeth. 'Look, let's just go inside and take our seats before Jenny and Dave come back.'

'You sound angry, Doctor,' she said instead of answering him.

'I am…frustrated by this conversation.'

'You're frustrated because I'm right.'

'I'm not afraid of weddings,' he snapped. His tolerance for the interrogation he was apparently under did, too.

Angie studied him. 'Okay,' she said, 'but you didn't forget about this wedding either.'

'What do you want from me, Angie?' he asked. 'Do you want me to tell you I came here on purpose? That I was compelled by who knows what to book a stay at the exact lodge Jenny and Dave were getting married at on the day they were getting married?'

'Yes.' Her eyes never wavered from his face. 'Were you?'

'You're infuriating.'

'I'm *right*. Why won't you admit that?'

'Because I don't want to talk about it. You of all people should respect that.'

Her head reared back, and for the first time since they started this conversation, she seemed ruffled. 'What does that mean?'

'It means you've run away from anything remotely emotional since you've been here.'

'That's not… I do not…'

'You do,' he said. 'When we spoke about your parents at the top of that hill? When you asked me about what broke up my relationship? When you lied to me and said you were okay during the parade?'

There were other instances he could name, but he'd made his point.

'I… I…' she stammered, looking genuinely stricken. The anger in his stomach melted into a pool of disgust. At himself.

'Angie,' he said, rubbing a hand over his face, 'I'm sorry. I shouldn't have—'

'No,' she interrupted, lifting a hand. 'Just… Give me a moment.'

She closed her eyes, took a breath, and opened them again. Doing so revealed a wealth of pain that had the disgust flowing into his veins, pounding along with his heart.

'I'm not saying you're wrong,' she said, choosing her words as if she were navigating a minefield. 'But—' she swallowed '—you're lashing out. And I'm not going to lay out my issues so that you can use them as a bridge to walk over yours.'

There was a long pause.

'I know this probably isn't the right time to bring this up,' he said, 'but that was a striking image.'

She stared at him, then she shook her head and bit her lip. 'You're an idiot.'

'With a PhD.'

'And the kind of humility rarely seen in your generation.'

His mouth curved, but he didn't smile. Didn't feel like he deserved to yet.

'You were also right.'

'I know.'

Now he did smile. 'I must have learnt my humility from you.'

Her gaze locked with his. 'You can't keep ignoring it.' She paused. 'I'm saying this to myself just as much as to you.'

His jaw clenched. 'I need to ignore it for today.'

'Except it doesn't want to be ignored, does it?' she asked. 'You freaked out when I pretended like you were my boyfriend who was about to propose. You came to a wedding of people you know and care about, and you refused to attend it. Doesn't that tell you you have an issue with weddings?'

'With engagements,' he corrected automatically.

The fight was still there, even though he'd already acknowledged he'd lost it. He wasn't even sure what he was fighting against anymore, but he'd known the moment Jenny and Dave had seen him—and his stomach had dropped to the pits of the earth—that he'd lost.

'Engagements,' Angie repeated. 'Why did you continue the farce of a proposal with Charles and Becky then?'

'Because they remind me of my grandmother and grandfather,' he said helplessly.

A part of him froze. He hadn't meant to tell her that. He'd just figured that particular fact out for himself. Like he always did, he wanted to set it aside. Think it through when he had time. Or avoid it until he was strong enough to face it. Which made the fact that he answered her *helplessly* a little scary.

'Okay. Why does that matter?'

'It doesn't.' When she stared at him, he sighed. 'I don't want to talk about it.'

'Fine. Your choice.'

There was a long, expectant silence, and it messed with his head. It was the only reason he could think of for blowing out all the air in his lungs and answering her.

'I didn't want to disappoint them.'

She studied him. 'Why do you think you would have disappointed them?'

Because they'd warned him about Liesel? First about his relationship with her, which his grandmother had claimed would go nowhere. Then about leaving with her, which his grandfather had called stupid. They were the best people he knew, and he'd already disappointed them before. Now he couldn't help but feel like an idiot for not listening to them. Especially since it had happened exactly as they said it would.

Especially since they'd been right… Before.

He didn't tell her that. And he couldn't figure out if his reluctance was because it was private, or because it made him look like an idiot. He'd already established he felt like one.

'You don't have to talk,' Angie said quietly. She was

watching him, he realised, and wondered what she saw on his face. 'I think you've faced it enough for now.'

He nodded, hoping she'd recognise it as a thank you. 'Do you want to go inside?'

'Yeah.'

They walked into the venue, an unexpected tension settling between them. Ezra was so caught by it that he almost didn't notice how the hall looked. When his eyes adjusted, his eyebrows rose.

The room was decorated in greens and reds, with tinsel used wherever possible, and looked more like an elaborate Christmas party than a wedding. Tiny Christmas trees sat at the centre of each table and a large one stood behind the main table, adorned with bright and sparkly ornaments. There was a bored-looking man dressed as Father Christmas near the gift table, and a sprite-looking woman beside him, accepting guests' gifts.

'I…' he started, but couldn't find the words to describe what he was seeing.

'Yeah, me, too,' Angie replied, eyes wide. 'You know how I said I wanted to see the inside of this venue to check if the wedding would be tacky?' He nodded, and she continued, 'I regret that.'

'You might want to keep your voice down,' he said when they got the evil eye from a couple walking past them. Angie grimaced.

'Thanks.' She looked around again. 'Is this what you were teaching your students back in Grahamstown?' she asked in a stage whisper now. 'How to be—' her whisper became genuine '—*tacky*?'

He grinned, noting that the tension between them had dissolved to a degree. 'No. Actually, I'm surprised. Jenny's tastes always seemed sophisticated.'

Angie made a face. 'Doesn't this change your mind then?' She frowned. 'Where are we supposed to sit?'

'I have no idea.'

'What's the strategy?'

'Wait until everyone takes a seat and check for two empty ones?'

Angie shrugged. 'That's probably our best bet.'

A few minutes later, the emcee announced that everyone should take their seats. Ezra's eyes flitted across the room, hoping to find the empty seats, and he almost groaned aloud when he saw where the only two empty ones were.

'Looks like we're going to have to keep the façade going for a bit longer,' he said, gesturing in the direction of their table. Angie looked over, sighed, but she nodded and they walked to their seats.

'I thought you two said you didn't know the bride and groom!' Becky exclaimed as they sat.

'Turns out Ezra did,' Angie said with a smile. 'And since Aunt—' she leaned back, her head lowering as she took in the names on the cards in front of them '—Jackie and Uncle Jim couldn't make it, Jenny and Dave invited us to stay.'

'What good luck for you, son,' Charles chimed in. 'You must be thrilled to have some more time to propose at the wedding.'

'Yeah. Exactly,' Ezra said lamely, forcing a smile.

He couldn't put his finger on what exactly it was about Charles and Becky that reminded him of his grandparents. It lay somewhere between how warm they were to complete strangers, and how affectionate they were with one another.

His grandparents had never shied away from affection. It had always been a point of extreme embarrassment and endearing sweetness. They didn't care that their kisses and caresses might have been strange for their children and grandchildren to see. No, their love and showing it however they felt necessary had always been their priority.

It sent a wave of longing through him, thinking of it now. As it had many, many times before. As it had when he'd seen Becky and Charles earlier. It didn't help that his parents had followed the example of his father's parents with their relationship, though they were less into public displays of affection. But they were happy. In love. Steady. And for as long as Ezra could remember, that was what he wanted. What he thought he had.

What you blinded yourself into believing you had.

He was such a fool.

He distracted himself from the unsettling thoughts by focusing on the reception, forcing himself to be present. Forcing himself to enjoy the celebration of a union of two people he genuinely liked; two people he knew would be happy together. Their family's and friends' speeches made him see another side of them—just as the questionable décor of the hall had—however this time, it stirred something inside his chest.

Dave's best man spoke of how much Dave had changed for the better since meeting Jenny. Jenny's mother spoke about how Dave was the only person she considered good enough for her daughter. The new husband and wife did their speeches together, thanking their service providers and their family for the support. When they spoke of each other, the stirring in Ezra's chest become a throb.

'I don't think I've ever found someone I like as much as Dave,' Jenny said. 'Which is a huge surprise to me considering how I felt when I met him. He was wearing a shirt at least two sizes too small for him.'

'I'd spilled coffee on my shirt,' Dave said as the crowd laughed. 'And my boss—' he gestured over to Ezra '—was kind enough to let me wear one of his, which clearly, I've never lived down. Thanks for that, by the way.'

A little mechanically, Ezra smiled, lifting the glass of water he was drinking in cheers.

'Regardless,' Jenny continued, 'I've forgiven him for that. Bonus is that I still like him, too.'

She smiled warmly up at Dave, who lowered his head and kissed his new wife. The crowd cheered, and Ezra told himself to do the same. Except he couldn't. It was as if the lump in his throat had spread to his hands, too. He couldn't lift them to do something as simple as cheer for the genuine love he saw in front of him.

Before he could admonish himself, a warm hand closed over his and he glanced at Angie. She was facing forward, her eyes on the couple, which he knew was more for his sake than because she was interested in what Jenny and Dave had to say. Which accomplished two things: one, it made him look a lot better since he wasn't the only one not clapping now; and two, it had gratitude joining the throb in his chest as he wondered at her.

She'd known him for all of a few hours and yet somehow, she steadied him. Despite the fact that she forced him to be honest—that she made him see things about himself he hadn't before—she steadied him. Even though she put a spotlight on all the issues he wanted to avoid, preventing him from keeping them in the dark, she steadied him.

He worried about what that meant. For him. For

them. Because the warmth from her hand had spread through his entire body. It even heated a part of his heart that Liesel had frozen. Except what would that get him? Angie would be leaving him soon. Hell, she'd already be gone if it hadn't been for the misunderstanding with her handbag.

No matter how grateful he was to her, for her, he needed to remember that. There was no use in unfreezing his heart if the remains of it stayed in a puddle in his chest. That's what would happen once she left. And if he kept entertaining the crazy idea of *them*, he'd slip on that puddle and break something he didn't think could be fixed again.

It was for the best that he didn't think about a *them*. If he realised there was only a him and a her. An Angie and an Ezra. Two completely separate beings. Almost kiss, intense chemistry, undeniable pull be damned.

Chapter Nine

Something had changed.

That's all Angie could think about when she looked at Ezra and saw the expression on his face. When she felt the angle of his body, away from hers. Her mind offered a reasonable explanation: he'd faced his fears. He'd seen that weddings weren't as bad as he made them out to be in his mind, after his own experience.

But maybe that wasn't it. Maybe she was projecting because that's what she wanted him to feel. She didn't want him to be suffering in the same way she was; with memories of his past, of his ex, of all the reasons he hadn't wanted to attend the wedding in the first place.

Her grip on his hand tightened before she could stop it. When he moved his hand away, her fingers curled into a fist. She dropped the fist to her lap, hating how symbolic that move seemed. He was pulling away from her. And she had no choice but to watch it because she was drowning in her own stuff.

The memories of her past. Of the last time she'd seen her parents happy together. It had been at their house shortly before he'd passed away. Her father had looked like a man with a brain tumour. Frail from the various treatments he'd been put through to make the tumour smaller so it could be surgically removed. Strong because of the recent prognosis that none of what they'd done in the two years since they'd diagnosed him had worked.

Because even in that moment, facing the end of his life, her father had been thinking of her mother. He'd been strong for the woman he'd married because that's what he'd signed up for. He'd done so willingly because he loved her.

Something that Angie apparently couldn't claim considering she'd run away when her mother had needed her to be strong.

The day her parents had celebrated their last anniversary together, they'd been happy. In love. Exactly like Dave and Jenny were now. So, Angie tried to give herself a break for feeling like her heart was being crushed by mortar and pestle. She forgave herself for grabbing Ezra's hand to comfort herself just as much as she wanted to comfort him. It was fine that something seemed to have changed. Not only for Ezra, but for them.

It was *fine*.

She almost sighed out loud when the waiters made their way to the tables with the starters. It was a sure sign that the speeches were over and the conversation could begin. Conversation meant distraction, and Angie desperately needed to be distracted from the fun way her mind was self-destructing.

'How do you and Becky know Jenny and Dave?' Angie asked Charles as a plate of mushroom risotto in the shape of a Christmas decoration was set in front of her.

'Jenny's grandmother is my sister.'

'So you're Great Uncle Charles?'

'I am, though she only calls me Uncle.' He gave her

a sweet smile. 'You could call me that, too, if you like. You would have to give me your name in return though.'

'Oh! I'm so sorry. I didn't realise...' She wiped her mouth with a napkin and offered Charles her hand. 'I'm Angie.'

'Charles,' he said, taking Angie's hand. It felt a lot feebler than he looked. 'It's lovely to meet you, Angie.'

'It's lovely to meet you, too, Uncle Charles,' she replied, and was pleasantly surprised to find it was true. Who would have thought the sexist old man—who she was convinced at one point had been stalking her— could be sweet, too? She was grateful she hadn't told him exactly how she felt about him now.

She picked up her fork again, then realised she was supposed to be a part of a couple. 'And this is Ezra.'

'Yes, we caught his name when you two sat down,' Becky said from where she sat next to Charles. 'I'm Rebecca, but you two can call me Becky. None of that "auntie" nonsense, please. I'm too young to be an aunt.' She winked at them, fluffing her completely grey hair.

'I wouldn't dream of it.'

Angie grinned, and risked a look at Ezra. His head was down, his hand bringing up bites of food to his mouth at steady intervals. She wanted to nudge him, to tell him he needed to act interested. She thought better of it when she remembered how far she'd already pushed him that day. She turned back to Charles.

'Are you from Caledon?'

'We are. Our whole family grew up here. I think that's why Jenny and Dave decided to have their wedding here. You must have wondered,' Charles told her.

'No, I wasn't...' Her voice faded when both Becky and Charles cocked their eyebrows. 'Okay, fine. Maybe

I thought about it. But only because I used to visit here with my parents.'

When Becky and Charles's faces brightened, Angie wondered why she'd brought it up.

'You visited the middle of nowhere with your parents?' Becky asked, a teasing glint in her eyes. 'Why?'

Angie glanced at Ezra again, hoping to send him a silent call for help, but he still wasn't paying attention to them. She swallowed thickly.

'My parents used to live here.' *Slowly*, she cautioned herself. 'Before I was born. We have family in East London. When we used to visit them, we'd almost always make a stop here. At the café, I mean. Then we'd get back on the road.'

There. That was a reasonable answer. It sounded steady, too.

'Oh, how lovely!' Becky exclaimed. 'What's your surname? Maybe Charles and I will recognise it.'

Oh, no.

'It's Roux?'

'Roux,' Charles repeated, those white brows furrowing together again. 'I think I remember a young couple by the name of Roux. They had a dog named Trixie.'

Her heart, which had started at a brisk walk when the conversation had begun was now flat-out sprinting. 'Yeah, those were—' she cleared her throat '—*are* my parents.'

'Daniel and Charlene?' Becky asked.

'Yes.'

'Oh, they were lovely.' Becky beamed. 'So in love, too. How are they?'

The world slowed around her, the only thing moving at its normal pace was her heart. Except that normal was relative. Now, normal sounded like tribal drums in the middle of a forest. It echoed through her chest as emotion danced up into her throat.

In some reasonable, rational part of her mind, Angie knew this was bound to happen. She'd been running from it the longest time. Just as she'd told Ezra, she'd have to face it at some point, particularly since it had been chasing after her for just as long.

In that same reasonable, rational part of her mind, she knew it was bound to catch up with her *that* day. The writing had been on the wall, quite literally in the form of a Welcome to Caledon sign. In some ways, she'd stopped the running when she'd stopped at the lodge, too. Which explained the quota that had been exceeded. It explained the memories, the guilt, the grief.

The grief.

One of the major reasons she'd run away had been because of it. She couldn't bear facing the way her usual life would change now that her father wasn't here. She hadn't wanted to visit her parents and see the empty chair where he used to sit. She hadn't wanted to go out to restaurants where they'd usually gone as a family and answer questions about where her father was.

How could she face telling someone her father had passed away? She had barely faced it herself. And now the universe expected her to break the news to sweet, lovely people like Charles and Becky? They would no doubt sympathise with her. They would offer her kind words. Words she didn't want. Words she didn't deserve.

If she needed any more proof she'd pissed off the universe, she had a clear sign of it now.

'They're doing very well, thank you,' she said before realising she'd spoken. She blinked. When panic threatened her entire being, she excused herself.

She ignored the confusion on the older couple's face

when she scraped back her chair and almost ran for the door. There were a few people outside, chatting and smoking. Angie forced a polite smile as she pushed passed them.

One more step. Just one more step.

She repeated the words as she put distance between herself and the venue. She was running again. This time, from the fact that she'd just lied about her father being alive so she could avoid having to deal with empathy.

Her stomach rolled. Telling herself to take one more step wasn't working anymore. She looked for the biggest tree and sank down behind it. Her one hand clutched at a throat that was closing; her other furiously brushing at tears she'd given no permission to fall.

But this was happening *because* she never gave herself permission to grieve. For as long as she could remember, she'd told herself to move on. To move forward. To run. When she had grieved, that one night in Korea, she'd broken down in the middle of her living room and sobbed so hard she thought she'd break into pieces, too. She'd felt so damn guilty for doing it, she'd told herself she would never give herself permission to do it again.

Except… Maybe now was the time to give herself that permission. It was time she stood still and let herself feel without trying to qualify it. Without trying to change it. To…to simply feel.

The first thing she felt was shame. Shame that she'd chosen to ignore the fact that her life had to change after her father. That she'd chosen to ignore that there *was* a life after her father. It had been easier to uproot herself, move to a different country, have a different job, and stay away for three years than it had been to face her grief.

Why wouldn't it be? Establishing new routines, new habits was easier than modifying old ones. In the process she'd forgotten that the old ones weren't things she could run from though. Not forever, anyway.

That realisation broke down the dam walls keeping out the extent of her shame. With the full force of it flooding her now, she sobbed. She covered her mouth with her hand to soften the sound, but the tears fell freely. Generously, and freely.

She cried because coming home gave her the reality check about losing her father that she'd been avoiding. She cried because she'd left her mother and sisters alone to deal with their grief. She cried because she knew she couldn't return and expect things to go back to how they'd been when she was younger and they'd been close. She cried because even though it was a decade later, she still wanted them to be close.

She cried because though she knew she'd hurt her mother, Charlene would be glad to see her. And would immediately find a way to make Angie responsible for her emotional well-being. She cried because she was afraid Sophia would hate her; because she didn't know what answer she'd give Zoey when her sister would ask her where she'd been.

She cried because she didn't even know whether she could say she was truly back. She didn't know which version of herself *was* back: the Angie who'd been spurred by guilt to come home and take responsibility for her family; or the Angie who hadn't been strong enough to give them what they'd needed from her when they'd needed her the most.

She cried because she was scared that despite her best efforts, she had broken herself. That breaking herself had turned her into her mother. She cried because she missed them, even when thinking of them turned her into a mess.

She cried because…

Because she missed *him*.

'Angie?'

The voice had her scrambling back against the tree. She wiped fiercely at the tears, but there was nothing she could do to obscure the fact that she'd been crying when Ezra found her. He crouched down until their eyes were level.

'Are you okay?'

'Fine. I needed a minute.'

'I didn't peg you as a liar,' Ezra said, lowering himself to the ground.

'I didn't peg you as someone who wouldn't have the decency to let a girl cry in peace,' she shot back. 'I guess we're even.'

He gave her a half smile. 'Careful, otherwise I might start to think you use sarcasm as a defence.'

'Aren't you a perceptive one?' she said dutifully, offering him a small smile when he cocked his head.

'I heard what happened inside there.'

Her eyes fluttered down. 'I didn't realise you were paying attention.'

'Which is fair. I've been acting like a jerk for the last hour.'

'I don't blame you,' she said quietly. 'It's hard to face your fears.'

'Like going home?' he asked and she nodded. 'It's fine that it's hard. No one expects you to sail through this without struggling.'

'You're wrong,' she replied, her voice catching. 'I know what I'm coming home to, Ezra. My mother… She can't deal with things by herself. At the slightest inkling of conflict, she shuts down. She looked to my father for as long as I can remember to direct her thoughts. How would they respond when we asked to have friends over? Or when we wanted to go out? Or when we were fighting with one another and needed a parent to intervene?'

'But she didn't only look to your father, did she?' Ezra asked.

Damn him, of course he'd seen that.

She took a shaky breath. 'No. Maybe it was because I was so much like my father that she let me lead her, too. If my dad wasn't around, she'd revert to me. For small things like whether we wanted to go to the movies or eat out somewhere. For bigger things like when one of my sisters had faced something at school and needed help through it. She'd either ask me what I thought, or she'd let me deal with it. Over the years it just…became my reality.'

She lifted a hand and brushed at the stray tears that were now coming down.

'It became kind of a bonding exercise for me and my dad. I'd take care of my sisters, and he'd take care of her. I'd make sure Sophia and Zo didn't get bullied at school, Dad went with mom to her Bible study to make sure no one messed with her.'

She almost smiled. Then she remembered what she was talking about and all amusement faded. She picked at her dress.

'That was part of the reason I ran. It terrified me to think that I'd have to deal with it alone. I wasn't sure I could be strong, and I knew she'd expect me to be. She'd need me to be.' She paused. 'It would kill her to see me struggling. To see me like this.'

His eyes swept over her face. 'What's been happening while you've been away?'

'I don't know. I've never had the courage to ask. My relationship with my sisters has been…strained since I left.' She snorted. 'Long before that.'

'I thought you said you looked after them?'

'I did, but they haven't needed me for the longest time, even before I left. Not that I let myself believe that. I used the idea that they still needed me as an excuse to not face the distance that's settled between us over the years.' She half smiled. 'Easier, right?' She rubbed a hand over her face. 'I'm a terrible person.'

'Because your sisters had to deal with something you've protected them from your entire life?' He took her hand. Rubbed his own over it. 'That doesn't seem like a fair evaluation.'

She hadn't thought about it that way. But it didn't matter. It wasn't only that she'd left Sophia and Zoey to deal with their mother. It was that she'd let her relationship with Sophia turn into little more than a utilitarian one. *Can you pick up Zo from school? Has Mom eaten? Who'll take Dad to radiation?* The closest thing they'd had to a real conversation had been when she'd told Sophia she was leaving.

And Zo… Well, Angie had let that relationship turn into one she imagined a ward and guardian would have. Angie would make sure Zoey had what she needed practically, and did the bare minimum when it came to Zoey's emotional needs.

After all, if she didn't have to take care of someone else's emotions, Angie wouldn't have to face her own.

She had told herself there'd be plenty of time to fix those relationships when they were all adults and out of the house. Then her dad had got sick… Then he was gone… And then she'd left them to deal—*ignore*—her grief on her own. She'd been selfish. She was their older sister, for crying out loud, and she'd been selfish.

She should have known better. She should have done better.

'You're still not being fair to yourself,' he commented, studying her.

Her face heated. 'You don't know everything.'

'Tell me.'

She barely needed a second to convince herself. Which would have surprised her, had it not been him. He'd caught her during an emotional breakdown in the woods. She was already vulnerable. Besides, his words seemed to have cast a spell on her lips.

'I… I've been back in South Africa for over a month,' she confessed. 'I rented a place in Knysna and stayed there without telling my family because I needed time to come to terms with being back.'

An unsteady breath released from her mouth, and she almost gasped trying to get air back into her lungs. Still, it was better than the tears.

'It started with me telling myself I needed a holiday. I hadn't taken one in the years I'd been teaching. I was…'

'Afraid?' he asked, when she didn't continue.

She nodded. 'Holidays meant stopping. Stopping meant thinking. I didn't want to think. I mean, look what's happening to me because I'm thinking. It's happened once before, so I know that's why.'

She laughed softly; it sounded suspiciously like a sob. A cry for help. A symbol of her current instability.

'I was right. This time has kept me thinking. Thinking and thinking and thinking even though I'd only designated an hour for myself to think about it each day.' It sounded ridiculous now that she said it out loud. 'When-

ever I thought about it, I could feel the weight of it—
of my decisions, of my grief, of everything—so heavy
on my shoulders and on my chest and…and I couldn't
bear going home until now. Day after day after day, I
couldn't bear it. I *still* can't bear it.' She lifted her eyes to
his. 'Tell me again how that doesn't make me terrible?'

There was a long pause, and Angie braced herself
for what she knew was coming. A confirmation. She
was a terrible person. She didn't deserve to be consoled.

'I stopped teaching at Grahamstown early in the second semester. I came to Cape Town once during that
time, for an interview for the new job. Then I went back
to Grahamstown. My family didn't know that I was in
Cape Town, or that I'd had an interview here.'

His eyes were a mixture of shame and defiance.
'They think I'm only coming home now because that's
when my teaching schedule let up. Does that make me
a terrible person, too?'

Chapter Ten

'Why didn't you tell them?' Angie asked, her voice husky, her eyes wide from the tears.

Was it wrong for him to think her beautiful now? Like this? Of course, she was beautiful without it. He didn't think he would ever get over how much. But now he had the honour of seeing her vulnerable. Of seeing the remnants of tears in her eyes; of seeing them red-rimmed and brimming with emotion.

Even though he hadn't intended on telling her everything, he found himself powerless against answering her question.

'I didn't want to see them,' he said simply, though the emotions were anything but. 'I didn't want to be reminded of…' he trailed off. Took a breath. 'My family is wonderful. For the most part, we have a good relationship.'

'But?'

'But they're incredible people. They're successful. They make great decisions.'

'And?' she prompted again. He nearly smiled.

Nearly.

'And… I don't fit.'

There. He said it. He told her his dirty little secret. He half expected the world to stop around him. Or, at the very least, for his companion to respond appropriately. For her eyes to widen; for the nod that confirmed she saw it.

Instead, he got a bland stare.

'You know that I don't know your family, right? You've literally just told me that they're great people, and while I believe you, I don't see how that makes you the odd one out.' When he didn't reply, she sighed. 'I'll say it more plainly. You're great, too, Ezra.'

Though his heart swelled, he shook his head. 'Did you miss the past where I said they make great decisions?'

'And, what? You don't?'

He gave a bark of laughter. 'I gave up my job, moved a thousand kilometres away from home and from my family for a woman who refused my proposal.'

'So you've made mistakes.'

'I've made poor decisions,' he corrected. 'They go back a lot further than this.' He let out a breath. 'They're different from mistakes.'

'Not sure I agree with that.' She tilted her head. 'Or why you think you have to punish yourself for being human?'

'It's not—' He broke off. Why didn't she understand? *Because she doesn't know everything.*

He gritted his teeth.

'Ezra, mistakes are a part of life,' she said softly. Kindly. Something twisted inside him. 'This won't be your last mistake either,' she continued. 'If you see them as lessons—and you should, being a lecturer and all—they won't paralyse you.'

'You don't… It's not…'

He couldn't bring himself to say it. Not even as she waited for it; quietly, patiently, as if he deserved it. As if he deserved her understanding.

How could he tell her that he *hadn't* learnt from his mistakes? He couldn't. He couldn't tell her that he'd made the same mistake twice. Or that he'd felt the same shame after. And there was no doubt in his mind that his family would feel the same disappointment they had after the first time, too.

'My parents didn't want me to marry Liesel,' he said slowly, wanting—needing—to give her something. He just couldn't bring himself to give her *that*. Not when it made him look like a fool. He didn't want to look foolish in front of her. 'My sister told me that after I called to let them know things were over between us.'

'Tad harsh,' Angie commented with a frown.

'No,' he denied. 'Jane was…trying to make me feel better, I think. I was convinced that Liesel was perfect for me. For our family.'

'For your family?' she repeated. 'That's not a conventional way of looking at relationships.'

'It isn't,' he agreed. 'But my family's important to me. It was important for me to have someone who got along with them, too.'

She stared at him. 'I'm getting that you have a… special relationship with your family.'

'But?' he asked with a slight smile, echoing her earlier prompt.

'But there are some serious cult vibes coming from this story.'

A beat of silence followed her words while his mind tried to wrap itself around what she was saying. Once it had, the amusement that resulted flickered through his body. It landed on his lips and he began to laugh.

'Cult vibes?'

Her lips twitched, but she nodded. 'I'm not even lying to you. I've never heard of someone wanting to be in a relationship for the sake of their family. Unless…' she trailed off, and he waited. 'Unless you're super rich and it was some kind of arranged relationship? For the sake of the family business?' Her eyes widened. 'To keep the bloodline—no, wait, gross —to keep the money-line pure?'

He laughed again. Harder this time, and felt the tension ease from his stomach. 'Are you thinking of writing an arranged marriage romance by any chance?'

Her cheeks pinkened. 'Maybe. I reserve the right to write whatever I want. Which, by the way, would be an excellent women's studies lecture. The power women exert through choosing what they want to read or write. But I digress.'

'Okay,' he said slowly. 'We'll come back to it.'

Though it made no sense, his fingers itched to write down the topic. Similarly, he felt a sudden urge to read through all the romance novels he could find so he could have this conversation with her.

She smirked. More tension dissolved out his body. How could it not? She was helping him breathe when his lungs sacrificed all its air for the sake of his mistakes. And she was making him smile while she did it. Making him remember his job that he loved and the passion he had for exploring the world. After he'd confessed his darkest secret to her.

It was enough to almost make him believe in miracles.

'My relationship with Liesel was a fantasy,' he told her honestly. 'My parents and grandparents, my brother and sister, were a part of that fantasy.'

'What was the fantasy?'

That I wouldn't be a disappointment anymore.

The words were so loud, so clear in his head it surprised him that he hadn't said it out loud. But it was the first time it had occurred to him. The first time he'd even considered it.

Of course, he knew that Liesel had seemed like the best fit for his life. She was the perfect girlfriend. Intelligent, social, funny. She handled his family with ease...

Why had it taken him so long to realise she was *handling* them? Or that handling wasn't what he'd wanted from a girlfriend? A wife?

It had taken her breaking his heart— *No,* he interrupted his own thoughts. She hadn't broken his heart. She'd shattered his illusion. Of her, of them. Of their potential life together. She'd broken the fantasy.

With the realisations pouring in, he couldn't figure out what to say to Angie. He'd first thought he hadn't wanted to go home because he hadn't wanted to remind his parents he was a disappointment. He worked damn hard to keep from reminding them of that fact. Liesel had been a part of that.

Returning home after a failed relationship, especially one that they'd apparently disapproved of, felt like an admission of sorts. A confession that he was, indeed, the same boy who'd decided skipping school and getting drunk with a girlfriend had been a good idea. Sure, the package was different. He was a man now. He had a PhD, an illustrious teaching job. He had some semblance of the stability he envied his parents and grandparents for. But the contents were the same.

Damn if that didn't suck.

'She, er—' He cleared his throat as again, he prepared to tell Angie a measure of the truth. '*She* was the fantasy. She was beautiful, smart. A doctor and the daughter of my parents' friends.'

'That's important? That she was a part of your social circle?'

'My family's circle,' he corrected.

'Oh, yes. Right. The cult.' She nodded, as if she actually believed his family was a cult. 'And that fantasy lasted for the full seven years?' she asked quietly. 'You had no idea it wouldn't work out for all that time?'

'I don't really know,' he said after a long pause. 'I didn't give myself a chance to think about it. Now...' He thought about it. 'I don't think I cared. At least not for the first four, maybe five, years. But then she wanted to open her own practice in Grahamstown. Wanted the quaint small-town experience, she told me.' He paused. 'I think I became a little more aware of the reality then.'

'You moved,' she said. 'Away from the cult—' she gave him a slight smile '—and away from where all those alluring qualities had been at their shiniest. What stopped you from seeing it then?'

'Man, you really like going deep, don't you?'

She lifted an eyebrow, and suddenly he heard his words and shook his head. Hoped it would shake away the blush he could feel creeping up his neck, too.

'You know what I mean.'

'Yes.' Seconds ticked by. 'Unfortunately.' She winked at him, and blood rushed to places that it shouldn't have considering what they were talking about. 'Sorry,' she said after a moment. 'I've distracted you. You were about to answer why you didn't see through the fantasy after you'd moved?'

'Right.' He sucked in a breath. Frowned. 'You don't actually know whether I was going to answer that.'

'Neither do you.' She grinned.

He laughed. 'Touché.' He waited for his blood to cool and the amusement to waver before he continued.

'I made excuses. Told myself it was the stress of moving. Of starting a new job, and for her, a new practice.' He paused. 'When things didn't change after we settled into a routine, I thought maybe she was hoping for a greater commitment from me. So I proposed.'

'And she said no.'

'And she said no.'

He could still picture her staggering back, lowering to the couch they'd bought together and shaking her head.

'What's wrong?'

'You. This. Why would you do this?'

'We've been together for seven years. What did you think would happen?'

'How could I have known you wanted to get married*?'*

He shook his own head now. Took a breath. Hoped the scene that played on repeat whenever it found a suitable moment would fade.

'The next day I came home from work and all of her things were gone.' The pain of it still twisted in his chest. 'I couldn't get a hold of her. Her phone was off. She hadn't been to her office. In fact, they told me she was on leave. When I called her parents, they said they hadn't heard from her either. A lie, likely.' He shrugged. 'That was that.'

'She just *left*?' The disbelief in Angie's tone soothed some of the pain.

'We said what we needed to the day before.' He'd realised that now, but it didn't change the truth of the words.

'Still selfish,' she said in disgust. 'She could have at least told you she was safe. You must have been worried.'

'Yeah.'

It no longer surprised him that she could see through

to more than what he told her. Worried him, yes, but there was no more surprise. Which told him he needed to prepare himself for when she saw how much of a disappointment he really was.

'I'm sorry, Ez.'

She squeezed the hand he'd almost forgotten held hers. He looked down, frowned. How he'd had all his realisations—how had he told her about one of his most embarrassing experiences—while holding her hand?

'Don't be sorry,' he told her, his eyes lifting to hers. 'This, *you,* have helped me to process it more than I've been able to in the past nine months.'

'Really?' she asked softly. 'Then why do I feel like there's more?'

He swallowed, though he'd known it would come. 'Look, I—'

'No,' she interrupted him. 'You don't have to tell me. We've done enough confessing for today.' She offered him a smile. 'Besides, you've helped me, too. I'm not still crying and shaking behind this tree.'

'Speaking of which…'

He used his free hand to hand her the handkerchief he retrieved from his pocket, and smiled when she grimaced and blew her nose. And then, though he agreed about the confessing, he asked, 'Has convincing me my mistakes are lessons made you see the same thing about yours?'

She opened her mouth, laughing lightly when he gave her a look.

'Oh, you're sneaky.'

'One of my many talents,' he replied with a smirk. He saw his hand lift to cup her cheek, and wondered how it had got there. Wondered whether he was controlling it. When his mind caught up with his body and his body told him *Yes, please,* he brushed a thumb at the trace of a tear she'd missed.

'I'm glad I met you,' he whispered.

'Me, too,' she whispered back, leaning into his hand, her eyes still on his.

He didn't know how long they sat like that before she set the handkerchief aside and shifted closer. Close enough that he could feel the warmth of her breath on his lips. His mind raced through all the reasons why he shouldn't kiss her. None of them stuck. He closed the space between them…

His heart stalled.

The moment his lips touched hers, his heart stalled. And then started again. And then raced so fast he worried he might be having a heart attack. Except he didn't think a heart attack would have every nerve of his body alight. Or make his blood feel like lava in his veins. It was an incredibly heady sensation, and he worried the novelty of it would have him coming back for more.

But it wasn't only that that had him wanting more. It was the way her mouth tasted of an incomparable sweetness. The tentative way she slid her tongue into his mouth, making the lava of his blood go even hotter, though he wasn't sure how that was possible. He wasn't sure how any of it was possible, really. They'd somehow skipped the light, tentative introductory kiss and gone straight to the kind that made him want to ditch the wedding and take her to his room.

The thought had him pulling back. He waited until he caught his breath.

'That wasn't…'

'Yeah,' she said, her chest heaving. There was a beat of silence before she spoke again. 'I'm really unhappy that that's the way our first kiss went.'

'What?'

'Oh, it has nothing to do with your skills. Which are very impressive, by the way.' She lifted a hand to her lips as though she were surprised by the fact. His pride took another knock.

'Are you trying to make me feel bad?'

She laughed. 'No, sorry. It's just that... I didn't think...' Her words faded, and then she looked at him. 'Honestly, Ezra, I think I convinced myself that there wasn't any spark between us. Clearly, I was wrong.'

His indignation eased. 'Why are you unhappy about our kiss?'

'Because it was too hot,' she said, and pressed a hand lightly against his chest. Taking it as a sign that she was tired of sitting, he stood, and helped her up. When she was standing, and had shaken her legs out, she continued. 'You weren't supposed to make me feel hot during our first kiss.'

'No?'

'No. The first kiss is supposed to be...sweet.'

'I thought that was quite sweet.'

She snorted. 'No, you didn't.'

He grinned. 'Why's sweet so important anyway?'

'Because,' she answered. Frowned.

He waited, but when she didn't continue, he asked, 'You don't know why you wanted it to be sweet?'

'No.' She laughed. 'All my first kisses have been sweet.'

'That isn't necessarily a good thing.'

'Why not?' She didn't give him the chance to reply. 'Sweet is romantic.'

He cocked his head. 'Are you willing to go on record with that?' He barely waited a second. 'You plan on consistently writing the first kisses your characters share as sweet?'

'Yes. No.' Her face twisted. 'Okay.' She paused. 'Look… Sweet is safe.'

'Safe,' he repeated.

'Yes, safe,' she replied in a faintly irritable tone. 'And safety means…' She hesitated 'Safety means independence.'

He studied her. 'Is it that important to you?' he asked. 'Independence?'

She gave him a stiff nod, though of course, he already knew the answer. Being independent must be vital if she was interpreting even the tone of the kisses she had as a possible threat to it. But he got it. She'd been responsible for so much growing up. Independence must have been a nonnegotiable in her life.

'It's not quite as fun though, is it?' he said, trying to lighten the mood.

'I don't know,' she replied after a while, her tone a complex blend of emotion and lightness. 'I've had plenty of fun in the past.'

'How about right now?' he heard himself asking. 'Would you like to have fun with me?'

'That was a pretty lame attempt at another kiss,' she said, the side of her mouth tilting up.

'Yeah,' he whispered, lifting a hand to her cheek. 'I guess you make me lame, Ange.'

That trace of her smile disappeared.

'You don't want me to touch you?' he asked, lifting his hand as his heart jumped into his throat.

'No, it's not that.' Her hand lifted to cover his as if to confirm it, gently bringing his hand back to her skin. 'You…you called me Ange.'

'You don't like it?'

'My dad used to call me Ange.'

'Oh, Angie, I'm s—'

'No, don't apologise,' she interrupted him. 'I didn't mind it.' She blinked. Smiled at him. Laughed. 'I didn't mind it at all.'

She kissed him again.

Chapter Eleven

Kissing Ezra again was probably not her best idea. But the moment she tasted his lips, she couldn't think of a single idea that was better.

This time, she slowed down what had been intense and eager before. Not because she wanted safe; after the last few minutes, she didn't think there was a 'safe' with Ezra. Hell, after the entire day, she *knew* there wasn't a safe with him. It should have had her running for the hills.

She was losing her ability to keep him at a distance. Which meant she'd soon lose control over what she told him and inevitably, over what she felt for him. She already had, to an extent. And that was dangerous. Controlling her feelings was how she lived. It made her okay with the responsibilities she shouldn't have had as a child. It allowed her to take care of herself. It gave her logic and independence. It kept her from turning into her mother.

It had also brought her guilt and shame. An inability to grieve. She used that as an excuse as she slowed things down with Ezra. Because she *needed* to feel. She had to balance out the damage not feeling had done. It had nothing to do with wanting to savour the moment.

It had nothing to do with the reckless excitement he stirred in her body. No, it was…for the sake of balance.

She took her time exploring his mouth, memorising tastes and revelling in the feel of his tongue sweeping against hers. It sent heat down low to the base of her stomach, and she pressed closer to him as though somehow, it would sate the fire.

It didn't. *Of course* it didn't. Instead, feeling his body react to hers stoked the flames. Her hands now had access to the body she admired earlier. Greedily, they ran over the planes of his chest, down the ripples of his abs.

'No lecturer should have these,' she said against his mouth.

He chuckled, sending vibrations through her body. 'I'm not your average lecturer.'

'Thank goodness for that,' she murmured, then stopped speaking when he pressed her against the tree behind her.

She could only think of the heat that flared everywhere he touched. Idly, she wondered if she'd see a trail of burns when it was over. His hands skimmed the sides of her breasts, and then back down, tightening slightly when they reached the curves of her waist.

She moaned, felt absolutely no shame in it.

She loved that he kissed her like she was his only purpose. Like *kissing her* was his only purpose. Though her body screamed for more—just as his did—he seemed content with the kissing. Just another sign of how considerate, how respectful he was, she realised. He didn't press because he wanted her to dictate where they would go with this.

As she realised it, she pulled back, and leaned her forehead against his.

'While I'm not against necking in the woods,' she

said breathily, repeating what they'd heard Becky tell Charles earlier, 'I think our friends at the wedding are going to wonder where we are.'

'Or they'll think we've escaped to neck in the woods.'

He nipped at her neck then, as if to emphasise his words, and she laughed even as heat exploded in her chest.

'While I'd love to keep doing this, we should probably head back.'

He sighed, but winked at her as he stepped away. She immediately missed the warmth of him; the smell of his cologne mixed with the scent of the trees around them.

She straightened her dress, picked up the handkerchief. She'd have to clean it or replace it; and how fortunate was it that thinking about that kept her from thinking about what had just happened between them? She brushed at the dirt that clung at the bottom of her skirt. When she reached up to her face, she realised her tears and the making out had probably not done it any favours.

'You should go ahead to the reception,' she told him, walking back to the pathway that had brought them there. 'I need to stop at the bathroom to assess the damage.'

'There's no damage.'

She laughed. 'I appreciate that, but I know there is. I don't blame you for not seeing it though. It's because of my super powers. When I kiss a man, he no longer sees any of my flaws.'

His mouth twitched, but he didn't smile. 'Why didn't you tell me that before you kissed me? Don't you think I should have been aware of what would happen to me after?'

'Oh, yes. You're right.' She stretched out a hand. 'My

name is Angie Roux. Kissing me makes you suscepti-
ble to my superpower of only seeing me as the perfect
woman I am.' Now he did smile, but she shook her head.
'Oh, no. No, don't smile. This is serious.'

He sobered immediately. 'Of course.'

'It is,' she affirmed. 'Some men have claimed it to
be a disease similar to gonorrhoea—'

She broke off when she heard his steps stop beside
her. When she turned around, the expression on his face
immediately had her laughing. Loud, and unruly, and
incredibly freeing.

As if she hadn't been sobbing her eyes out only moments before.

As if she hadn't been kissing her lips off only moments before.

'What?' she asked, when he kept staring at her. 'You
wanted to know.'

'I'm…processing.' He ran a hand through his hair.
'I've never had a woman tell me she might have given
me gonorrhoea before.'

'Well, we've already established you've been hanging out with the wrong women.'

She'd been teasing—knew he knew it, too—but his
face twisted into an expression she hadn't seen on him
before. Just like that, her stomach dropped. Turned.
She opened her mouth, but he smiled at her. A tight,
fake smile that turned the man she'd had her hands
over minutes before into the stranger she didn't think
he was anymore.

'I don't mind waiting for you.'

His voice was calm, steady. It sounded like a car
screeching to a halt at a stop street to her.

'You don't have to.'

'I know. I want to.'

'You don't have to pretend like—' She cut off. *Pull back, Angie.*

'What? What are you taking about?'

'Nothing,' she said immediately, forcing a smile to her lips. 'I'm sorry. I'm still a bit shaky about everything.' She cleared her throat. Because damn it, even if it *killed* her, she could be calm and steady, too. Prided herself on her ability to do just that, in fact. 'I really do think you should go ahead though. Make sure Becky and Charles haven't called the police on us.'

After the longest pause, Ezra nodded, and slowly made his way to the reception venue. She didn't wait for him to look back like she knew he would. Instead, she went straight to the bathroom in the café.

There was no one there this time, thank goodness. Which meant she had a moment—how long, she didn't know—to compose herself.

But her head was spinning with thoughts. Her heart was heavy with emotions. She didn't think about it. She rather chose to focus on touching up her make-up. She wore the bare minimum. She was lazy when it came to her looks, and frankly, her hair took most of her effort. So she washed her face, tidied up the smudged mascara, and took out her lipstick.

Her lips were slightly swollen, slightly red, and as she lifted the tube of colour, she saw her hand shaking. She pursed her lips when that simple thing made her want to cry, and took a deep, steadying breath. Then she straightened her shoulders and continued.

She would not let what had happened shake her. She wouldn't allow it to tighten her chest, or control the pace of her heart. She was better than that, damn it. She was a grown woman who could handle her problems. Who could handle that for the first time in her life, a man other than her father had seen her cry.

So what if her precious control was no longer protecting her? So what if she was feeling like she'd been afraid to all along?

It was just that she knew this would happen. She knew allowing herself to feel the grief for her father would do this. It was a slippery slope, opening up to feelings. Opening up to the grief had opened her up to more, too. And it would force her to feel more than the guilt that had brought her back home. It would force her to feel more than the responsibility that had kept her moving toward her family.

Like the disappointment that had come at having a mother who depended on her instead of the other way around. The anger that came along with that. The anger at her father for not doing anything about it, even when he saw how much it had affected her. How much it had affected her relationship with her sisters.

She had no doubt the responsibility she'd taken for them had contributed to the distance between them. She had to take care of them, which meant she couldn't be their friend. Or their sibling. And she hadn't wanted to think about that. She hadn't wanted to feel it. Thinking about it and feeling it would push her closer to breaking than anything else had before.

Except neither of those emotions was threatening to break her now. Oh, they were there, but they were swirling around beneath the surface, ready to pounce if she provoked them. No, *Ezra* was the biggest threat. And she hadn't anticipated it, so she had no idea how to protect herself against it.

How could she protect herself against a man who made her feel stronger? Who kissed as if he'd created the activity? How could she protect herself from what it felt like to have him pull away from her? That was what had happened outside. That was what that momentary pause he'd taken had meant.

She took a breath. Told herself she was fine. Fine because she was going to be leaving soon anyway. She would be walking away from Ezra. Walking away from the problems he presented...

And walking on to her other ones.

She cursed silently when the thought had her hand shaking so much her lipstick smudged. Two women came into the bathroom then, and Angie smiled at them before grabbing a tissue, wetting it, fixing the damage. When she was done, she looked at herself in the mirror.

And turned when she saw all the emotions she'd been running from as clearly as if they'd been carved into the lines of her face.

She was outside the reception hall in a few short steps, but before she entered, she reminded herself that she couldn't add to her problems. She couldn't be drawn into Ezra's problems. She'd already gone too far with the kiss. *No, long before that,* she thought. The moment they'd started sharing their lives with one another, things had gone too far.

Sharing meant connections. And Angie had actively avoided connections in the last three years. She'd played nice with her colleagues in Korea, but she'd never agreed to any social events. She'd chosen to go home and read or write instead. Reading had helped her forget; writing had helped her control. She wrote short stories with happy endings because all she wanted was a short path to happiness. Reality took much too long—if at all.

She spoke with her mother once a week; she sent

emails to her sisters twice a week. She might have called them, too, if speaking with her mother hadn't been so exhausting. Charlene would say more in her silences than her words, though Angie understood all of it. She was fluent in her mother's cues after all the years she'd spent studying them.

Zoey would reply to both emails in a cheery tone Angie somehow knew was false; Sophia would reply once, with a short paragraph detailing how their mother, Zoey, and she were doing—in that order. So Angie didn't even have connections with her family; there wouldn't be with Ezra either. Which was fortunate, since Angie didn't know long she'd be in Cape Town anyway.

She hadn't told anyone that part yet, but *she* knew. Knew she couldn't stay in a place that held so much pain for her. Her savings would tide her over while she did damage control with her family. But as soon as that was done—as soon as she knew more than just that she wanted to write a full romance novel—she would leave.

She couldn't be thinking about the man with a killer smile and even better kissing skills when she did.

And what happens to him if you go?

She frowned at the unwelcome thought and shook her head. But it wouldn't disappear, and she was forced to ask herself if she was disappointing him like his ex had. It made absolutely no sense that she was equating herself to his ex. It definitely wasn't the same thing, and yet she worried about it. Probably more than his ex had, too.

You're overestimating yourself.

Right. Yes. That was it. She was putting too much on two little kisses she'd shared with the man. When her fingers reached up to trace her lips, she dropped her hands to her sides, clenching her fists to keep them from misbehaving again. She couldn't be drawn back into the magic of those kisses. Because that's what they were: a spell that deluded her into thinking she had more power over Ezra than she did.

She wouldn't be hurting Ezra when she left because she wasn't that important to him. It was that simple.

Less simple was the fact that she couldn't say the same about her family.

'It's fine, Angie. Leave. I'll be here for Mom and Zo. You just…leave.'

Her heart raced as she tried to ignore Sophia's voice still echoing in her head; and then it tripped when she remembered she couldn't keep running anymore. She was hours away from seeing her family again. Which, with the emotion of Ezra's kiss still stumbling around in her chest, made her feel as if she'd been pinned under a rock.

'They want us to *what*?'

Ezra wasn't surprised by Angie's reaction. It pretty much reflected his own. Because when he heard that Jenny and Dave wanted them to join the Christmas parade again, he'd begun making up excuses as to why he wouldn't be able to go.

'It's a family tradition!' Becky said brightly, though her eyes flitted over Angie, and Ezra saw the concern there. Felt it himself. She looked…off. It didn't help that she was clearly avoiding looking at him.

'That a family wedding joins a Christmas parade?'

'That the family attends the Christmas parade,' Becky corrected him. 'We go each year.'

'But they've already finished with the floats,' Angie

said. 'I'm assuming,' she added hastily, when Charles and Becky both turned to look at her.

'Well, yes, they probably have. But that's not the only festivities. There are also contests. Of course, there's also the ad-lib nativity play—'

'Wait, what?'

He said it at the same time Angie looked at him with a delighted expression on her face.

'It's an ad-lib nativity play, Ezra,' Angie repeated with faux patience. 'Where the actors don't prepare their lines before performing the play.'

'Except they aren't actors, dear,' Becky interrupted. 'They're volunteers from the audience. Last year Jenny played Mary.'

Angie's eyes widened, and the glee in her smile had him shaking his head. 'Oh, no,' he said. 'No, no, no. You already got me to play Father Christmas today. There's no way I'm adding any of the characters from the nativity play to my résumé.'

'I have no idea what you're talking about,' Angie said innocently. 'I am quite eager to attend the parade now though. Shall we?'

He narrowed his eyes at her, though his lips twitched and it took all of his self-control not to smile. 'You first.'

'We'll go together,' Charles interrupted. Ezra blinked. He'd forgotten about Charles and Becky for a second. Hell, he'd forgotten about the entire wedding and its guests. During that short moment, it had been only him and Angie.

Which was a massive problem.

He waited as the rest of their table followed the crowd to the door, wondering how they were all okay with delaying their main meals for the sake of the parade. He paused at the thought. Maybe the main meals would be served *at* the parade.

It was a risky move, but as he looked around the venue one last time, he realised risky must have been the theme of Jenny and Dave's wedding. Perhaps not intentionally, he considering. But the tacky décor and feeding almost one hundred people at a parade—if his suspicions were correct—were definitely risky.

His suspicions *were* correct. But as he looked around at the field the parade had started at earlier, Jenny and Dave's plan didn't seem quite as risky. Tables were set out much like in the venue. Unlike there, they were decorated with white tablecloths and a single bowl of silver and white baubles surrounding a candle.

Food trucks enclosed the tables, making the area feel intimate, though a few metres beyond them stood a stage with people milling around it. Fairy lights hung between each of the trucks, reaffirming the impression of a boundary. It gave the entire space a festive feel.

'How did they do this so fast?' Angie asked at his side.

'I have no idea.' He gave it one last look before resting his gaze on her. 'I think we're going to have to re-valuate what we thought of this wedding.'

'No kidding,' she replied as she accepted a paper in the shape of a Christmas ball from one of the groomsmen. Moments later, they learnt the paper would give them access to any of the food trucks.

Ezra didn't miss the interest in the man's eyes as Angie thanked him with a smile. Nor did that man miss Ezra angling his body, or the message Ezra was giving him as Ezra blocked his view of Angie: *back off*. It made absolutely no sense. What right did he have to make any claim on Angie? And yet when the man gave him a slight nod and moved on, Ezra felt satisfaction replace the adrenaline that had been pulsing through him.

'Careful,' Angie said, her eyes lazily following the groomsman's back.

'Of what?'

'The weight of your ego.' Now her gaze met his. 'Or the size of your head. Either way, it might cause you to fall.'

She walked away before he could reply, and joined a line at a food truck serving pulled pork sandwiches. He stared after her. Knew that he was, but he was helpless to stop himself. And that was the problem, wasn't it? He was already falling. Too hard, too fast. And he knew that once he landed, he'd break something inside himself. Could already feel it cracking.

It had started long before she'd made that joke about him choosing the wrong women. Although that had succeeded in reminding him he had a history of making poor decisions when it came to women. That he'd gone from one extreme—wild, unpredictable—to the other: controlled and cold. Neither of them had been right. And he was convinced that he would learn from it this time.

Except that he thought he had, after Ana. He'd spent an entire term mucking about in school with her, failing every class—because who needed to go to class anyway?—and generally not caring. Since he'd chosen to do it in his final year at school, he'd tainted his perfect school record. It had been the reason his parents had sat him down and laid down the law. The law had stated that if he didn't pull up his socks, he'd be out of the house with no assistance from his family for living expenses or tuition when the school year was up.

It had shocked him into following the law, and he'd managed to still graduate with decent enough grades at the end of the year. After he'd broken up with Ana, of course. After that had come the disappointed talks. By then, he had no longer been a stupid teenager who hadn't cared. The talks had smarted, as they'd been intended to, and he'd vowed to never disappoint his parents and grandparents again. So he'd chosen the safe girlfriend. The perfect girlfriend.

And look where that had got him.

It was no surprise then that he didn't trust himself. Not when it came to women. *Especially* not when it came to Angie, who twisted his insides so tightly his instincts were lying in a puddle on the floor.

So there would be no more kisses. No more confessionals. They would just be two people enjoying a wedding together. A nice neutral event that by no means would remind him of romance or his twisted insides.

He groaned.

Chapter Twelve

It was strange to witness a wedding without tension.

Okay, there was *some* tension. A boy who looked to be about sixteen had tried to balance plates from four different trucks on his way back to his table and had dropped all of them. It had earned him a public and embarrassing scolding from his mother. Another boy about the same age had begun laughing at the scene; he had then walked into an older woman, spilling his soft drink down her front. He was less amused when she gave him a piece of her mind quite loudly. Also quite embarrassingly.

There were more instances of things like that, but Angie didn't see them as the kind of tension that would mar a wedding. It was the innocent kind, if something like that existed. Since she'd witnessed more malicious things at her own family weddings—petty cousins, gossipy aunts, drunk-and-flirtatious uncles—Angie could confirm that there was, indeed, an innocent tension. She quite liked it.

It distracted her from the sadness she felt at the memories of her parents' last wedding anniversary. She'd accepted that she wouldn't get away from them, which had in some strange way freed her from the turmoil of not wanting to feel the sadness the memories evoked.

It allowed her to eat her food contently, and she let herself be distracted by the events that created the innocent tension while she did.

Ezra seemed to understand that she didn't want to talk, only making the occasional comment which didn't require her response. It was a relief, since she wasn't a hundred per cent confident she'd know what to say to him.

'Did you enjoy your meal?'

The voice came from behind her. Angie angled her head so she could see who'd spoken to her. She smiled when she saw the bride, and barely had the chance to answer before Jenny had taken Ezra's empty seat beside her. He'd offered to get them drinks a couple of minutes before, and had been held up by Dave at the bar.

'Oh, it was delicious.' Angie gestured to the empty plates in front of her. 'Clearly, the buffet by means of food trucks was a smashing idea.'

'Thanks.' Jenny leaned back. 'It was worth the fight then?'

'Fight?'

'Yeah, to incorporate the parade into our wedding.' She rolled her eyes. 'If my mother had her way, we would have had our entire wedding in that tacky hall.' Now she shuddered. 'Thank goodness Becky took my side and convinced her the tradition of the Christmas parade and our annual family get together would make for an amazing wedding.' Jenny levelled a stare at her. 'You didn't seriously think I wanted my wedding to look like that hall, did you?'

'I, er… I don't know you.'

'Well, rest assured, I am not *that* in love with Christmas.'

Angie laughed, the unease of being put on the spot

when she had believed Jenny had wanted her wedding to look like that fading. She understood the poor woman's predicament. She remembered once for her confirmation, her mother had hired a hall to celebrate the event.

A hall. For a confirmation.

She hadn't complained to her mother because it was her mother. In all honesty, she couldn't bring herself to. It had been one of the few times Charlene had taken initiative with something. Angie had complained to her father though, who hadn't budged—*Have you seen how excited she is, Ange?*—and Angie had been persuaded—guilted—into letting her mother celebrate the event.

She imagined she'd be persuaded/guilted into a lot once she got home. Her mother would want Angie to do things and even if Angie didn't want to do them, she would have to. There would be no one to complain to now. Her life would be filled with conceding to things, just like she had with her confirmation. She was doomed to a life of feeling that same frustrated annoyance.

Except now it would be to an intenser degree; what her mother needed from her, what she felt as a result. Grief tended to amplify the negative in a person.

Like running away from your problems?

'Thank you, by the way,' Jenny interrupted her thoughts. Angie frowned over at her, and Jenny clarified. 'For that, I mean. For him.'

Angie followed Jenny's gaze and caught Ezra mid-laugh. It softened his features, made them more striking. Her ability to breathe felt as if it had stumbled and couldn't get up again. It took clearing her throat multiple times before she could reply.

'That isn't me.'

'You can't believe that.' Jenny turned her body so

that she faced Angie completely. 'Dr. Johnson took over the supervision of my PhD halfway through when my previous supervisor fell ill. We spent a lot of time together to try and make a mess into some semblance of an academic study. He's never looked this…calm, before.'

'He's calm because he's left a place where he doesn't know anyone and he's moving back home to a family whom he clearly loves.' She shook her head, as if somehow, it would take away from her defensive tone. 'It's not me.'

'If that's what you want to believe.'

An awkward silence settled over them for a moment. Luckily, Jenny didn't seem to be the type to let it linger. And then she said, 'I met his ex-girlfriend, you know,' and Angie found herself wishing for the silence.

'Hmm.'

'A couple of times.' Jenny clearly hadn't taken Angie's noncommittal answer as the sign Angie had hoped it would be. 'During none of them did Dr. Johnson actually look happy. Or calm. In fact, he looked like someone had tightened all the muscles in his body.' She paused. 'Which makes the whole calm thing now more significant.'

'Well, they probably broke up for a reason then.'

'Yes. And now you're his girlfriend.' Jenny brightened, before frowning. 'Which really makes you denying that you have a positive effect on him weird.'

'Because I'm not his girlfriend.' Angie wondered whether there were any rules against leaving a bride midconversation on her wedding day. But then she remembered it was rude to leave anyone midconversation—she sent a silent apology to the woman she'd done that to when she'd first been mistaken as part of the wedding—and nearly sighed. 'I met Ezra today.'

'What?' Jenny asked, and then gave a sparkling laugh. 'That explains a lot.' She sucked in a breath. 'I'm sorry, that must have sounded terribly patronising. And annoying. All of it.' She wrinkled her nose. 'I think my wedding day has turned off my empathy.'

Angie smiled. 'Today might be the one day you'll get away with it.'

'You're probably right.' Jenny's face softened. 'It means even more that you're here now. And that you've helped him be here.' She rested a hand on the one Angie had on the table, squeezing it before standing. 'And if you'll give me one more pass because I got married today?' Angie gave a curt nod. 'I do think you're good for him. I'm willing to bet he's good for you, too.'

Angie opened her mouth to reply, but they were interrupted by a man onstage trying to get everyone's attention. Which was good, too, since Angie had no idea what she would have said.

Her heart was beating so fast she couldn't quite catch what she was feeling; her mind laden with thoughts that made everything seem hazy. Which was the only reason she didn't immediately object when they called for volunteers to play Mary and Jenny said, 'Angie! Pick Angie!'

Watching karma do her thing was oddly satisfying.

No, Ezra corrected himself with a grin. There was nothing odd about. There was just a deep, simple enjoyment at the fact that Angie was being urged into playing Mary in the ad-lib production of the nativity story. Much like she'd *urged* him into playing Father Christmas. Much like she'd intended on him playing some other character in the play.

Karma was beautiful.

When Angie realised the crowd wasn't going to relent—he'd never appreciated the herd mentality more—her gaze met his. *Help*, it seemed to scream. But his smile only widened.

Her eyes narrowed.

He tilted his head.

Her jaw clenched.

He lifted a shoulder.

She let out a breath, then gave him a sweet smile. A warning alarm sounded in his head, but he ignored it. The opportunity was too good to pass by because of the possibility of retaliation. Besides, *he* hadn't done this. It had all been Jenny. Angie couldn't blame him for enjoying the show.

And yet the look she tossed him over her shoulder as she headed for the stage assured him she did.

He waited as Jenny moved through her guests, offering their names for characters as they were called. Ezra had angled himself behind a food truck so that she wouldn't see him. He only walked back to his table once all the roles had been filled. Then, with his beer in hand, he settled back to watch the show.

It was absolutely terrible. It was also genius.

None of the volunteers had been given costumes. Which meant that Angie was pretending to go into labour in her beautiful dress, surrounded by people making animal sounds in their Sunday best. There was one guy who clearly had no idea what was going on, which was almost certainly the result of alcohol. Whenever someone made an animal sound, he would follow.

He was playing Joseph.

The Three Wise Men had apparently followed Joseph into a bar, too, since they staggered across the stage and midway through the journey to see fake baby Jesus—thank heavens no one had had to volunteer for *that* role—they began to do the cancan. It was hilarious, but so incredibly inappropriate that everyone on stage and in the audience gaped before the giggles started.

And from there, things really went downhill. People began singing Christmas carols at inappropriate times or in lieu of their lines. One of the Wise Men had nearly fallen off the stage during an enthusiastic leg extension. He had to be helped up by a number of other characters. During the rescue mission, Joseph decided that it would be a good time to neigh loudly, sending a wave of surprise through everyone on—and offstage. Naturally, that led to a renewed rescue effort when the surprise caused the Wise Man to fall again.

Genius, Ezra thought again. He tilted his beer toward Angie in a cheers when she caught his gaze.

Oh, she was going to kill him.

It wasn't directly Ezra's fault that she was playing the Virgin Mary. However, she *was* attending the wedding because of him. He was the reason she was on Jenny's radar. Ergo, she could still blame him. And she intended to, particularly after she saw the smug expression on his unbearably handsome face.

She was distracted from planning her revenge when Joseph appeared at her side. She took a step back—he obviously wasn't a reliable acting partner—and his face turned wounded.

'Mary,' he said solemnly. 'Why don't you like me?'

She blinked. What the hell was she supposed to say

to that? And then she tilted her head, thought *what the hell* and sat on a pile of hay.

'Well, Joseph, you're never home.' She sighed dramatically. 'You spend most of your time in the tavern, you take me on a long journey in my ninth month of pregnancy, and you didn't even have the decency to book us a place to stay. How else am I supposed to feel about you?'

Joseph looked stricken. She wasn't sure if it was in character or whether the man hadn't anticipated this response to his tipsy question.

'But…you're my wife.'

'I'm also about to be a mother.' On cue, she panted, placing a hand on her back. She immediately stopped when she began talking again. 'And you're doing the cancan with three men you've only just met.'

'They've come to meet the baby.'

'You think that's okay? You're fine with three strange men coming all this way to see this baby?'

'One of them might be the biological father.'

Her eyes widened and she bit her lip. She knew she'd gone off script slightly, but she hadn't expected Joseph to pull out the receipts.

'No,' she said. 'The biological father is much more impressive than these men.'

'What do you mean?' One of the Wise Men stepped forward. 'We're all very impressive.'

The nerve.

'Didn't you just fall off the stage?'

Someone snorted loudly; someone else gave a *whoop*. She hid her smile.

'We're still impressive,' the Wise Man grumbled.

She sighed at the fragile ego. 'Of course you are. Though technically, you need to be impressive somewhere. You and your impressively wise friends only come visit when there's actually a baby *to* visit.'

'Oh. Right.' They shuffled off stage.

With a sigh, Angie gave birth, her drunk husband at her side.

She was fascinating to watch, he had to give her that.

Though Ezra gave it freely, since it really wasn't a concession. He loved looking at her. He loved hearing her sarcastic drawl, and how she didn't let anyone get away with being stupid, including him. She stood out whether she was the only sober person in a Christmas play or whether she was the only person in front of him in the woods.

She stood out.

It seemed too simple to attribute it to her beauty. Or to the fact that she seemed in control even when she clearly wasn't. In a play where everything was chaos, or in the woods, when she was crying. Perhaps it was a combination of it. Of her steadiness, her beauty.

Or perhaps it was because he was drawn to her. Inexplicably, stupidly. She demanded his attention; greedily, he gave it. Somehow he knew he'd always give it.

When applause erupted around him, he forced his thoughts away from their disturbing path and clapped along with the crowd. Then he pushed forward, ready to give Angie whatever she asked from him. And worried about the fact that she seemed to ask it without saying a single word.

'This might be the last wedding I ever attend,' Angie said after they'd been asked to return to the hall for dessert and the remaining formalities.

There were so many people making their way back

through the narrow pathway between the field and the lodge's property, an informal line had formed. She and Ezra were at the end of it; they'd hung back to give themselves some air. And distance. She'd spent much too much time entertaining strangers for the day. She needed to breathe with some familiarity.

Ezra's familiar?

She refused to indulge the concerning thought, instead focusing on the arch of the pathway. Lights had been strung around it since the last time they'd used it. She wondered if that had always been the plan, or if someone had forgotten their responsibility and had hastily tried to make up for it.

As they walked through the arch and down the steps, Angie saw that the ground had been covered with confetti. The shrubs that enclosed the path had been decorated with lights now, too. She probably wouldn't have become as close with them if they'd looked like this earlier, she thought, amusing herself.

Still, she lifted a hand and lightly brushed her fingers over them as they walked.

'The wedding hasn't been that bad,' Ezra said.

'Been converted, have you?'

He chuckled. For a while, they didn't say anything. Once they arrived at the reception hall, he spoke.

'I think the nativity play's the reason for my conversion.'

'Sure.'

'No, really. It was the highlight of my day.'

She angled her head. 'It was better than what your mouth did this—'

'Angie,' he said quickly when they saw Charlie and Becky heading toward them from the dessert station.

'A simple yes or no, Doctor.' She smiled sweetly.

'No. It wasn't better than that.'

Satisfied with the spark in his eyes—less so with the answering fire in her belly—she turned to smile at Becky and Charles when the couple reached them.

'You were lovely as Mary, dear,' Becky said, smiling at her. 'So witty. It really made this year's play the best in recent years.'

Angie opened her mouth, and quickly shut it again as Ezra chuckled beside her.

'Thank you, Becky.'

'Just telling the truth.'

Angie could see that she was, which was concerning. That play had been an absolute disaster. Maybe that was the point?

'You two get some dessert,' Becky said with a pat on Angie's arm. 'We'll see you when you're done.'

Nodding, they went over to the desserts. The table was decked out with a wide variety of deliciousness: cheesecakes, fridge tarts, jelly, custard, trifle, Malva pudding, ice cream, and some healthier options she ignored. She took a plate and cut herself portions of two different varieties of cheesecake, before adding one large portion of pineapple fridge tart to the plate.

Setting that down on the table, she took a bowl and dished herself a piece of Malva pudding before pouring some custard over it. When she was done, she picked up her plate and turned back to Ezra. He was staring at her.

'What?'

'That's…a lot,' he said after a moment.

'Yeah. It's dessert.' She shrugged.

'You ate a significant amount of food earlier. How do you have space for all that?'

She narrowed her eyes. 'Firstly, would you ask me that if I were a man? Uh uh,' she said when panic fluttered across his face. 'You have to check your bias if you want to be a good women's studies lecturer.' Her tone dripped with irony.

He sighed. 'Fine. I probably would have thought it, but I wouldn't have said it.'

'Hmm.' Her eyes narrowed even further before she shook it off. 'Secondly, everyone knows there's a separate stomach for dessert. No matter how much food I eat, there's always space for dessert.'

His eyes widened and he laughed. Just as it had when she'd seen him walk toward her after the play had ended, her stomach flipped. And then her heart got in on the action, thudding so hard she could have sworn it was sending Morse code to Ezra's.

Her reaction to him was becoming more and more ridiculous, but she was helpless to stop it. It had even shut out her nerves. She stilled, searching for them. They were still fluttering around the edges of her body. No doubt waiting for her to realise that she wouldn't always be so completely immersed in the present.

'Come on,' she said after a moment. 'I don't want to be one of those people standing at the dessert table when they start with the formalities again.'

Ezra smirked but he got his dessert—admittedly, less than hers—and they made their way back to their own table.

It was strange, but somehow eating dessert at a wedding, laughing with a man she had complicated feelings for and two quirky old people felt like it was exactly what she should be doing.

It could have been because she was avoiding thinking about going home, but her lungs felt a little looser. Angie chose to believe that for that moment, that was enough.

Shortly after she finished her dessert, the emcee announced that the newlyweds were ready to share their first dance. Angie turned with the rest of the guests to watch Jenny and Dave. Her lungs tightened again when the thought brought images of all the times her father had drawn her mother into an embrace when a song he'd liked had played.

She took a deep breath and told herself to deal with it.

It didn't work as well as she'd hoped. What else was new? She was glad when Jenny and Dave finished and the rest of her guests were invited to join them on the floor. She frowned when Ezra rose and, after bowing slightly, offered her his hand.

'Shall we?'

'I want to say no, but I feel like that might make you look bad.'

She amused him with that, but there was something else on his face that had the cells in her body on full alert.

'Humour me,' he said.

She swallowed and stood, because she was helpless not to. And then she was being drawn into his arms and into her own romance.

Heaven help her.

And it did seem to help her, to an extent. She didn't immediately lose herself in his intoxicating scent, even though it had her mouth watering. She didn't immediately tremble at the feel of his arms around her body, even though it was as seductive as it was comforting. She even managed to keep herself from asking him to take her back to his room. To seduce her until she forgot that they'd only just met and that having these thoughts was nonsensical.

Specifically that she, Angie Roux, was having these

thoughts was inconceivable. Yet there she was. She of the Controlled Emotions and Guarded Hearts was thinking about how the sway of their bodies together felt like the start of something. About how the contact of their bodies, their torsos touching, their arms around one another, their fingers threaded through the other's, felt more like foreplay than their earlier kisses had.

She didn't want to look at him. Into those gorgeous eyes that told her things before his words could. That saw things before she could say them. She didn't want to see the desire there. She didn't have to, considering she could feel it pressing against her belly, an answer throbbing through her body. More importantly, she didn't want him to see her own desire. Not because she was ashamed of it, but because of the desperation of it. Desperation that had fear joining with desire.

She drew a ragged breath when the next song had an upbeat tempo. Stepped away from Ezra on another breath. A grateful one, because she'd been able to step away from him. Because she'd been able to step away from him *and* maintain her dignity.

She moved toward the table, but Ezra caught her hand and initiated the back-and-forth step dance that was popular in South Africa. She followed without comment, though she nearly laughed in surprise when he twirled her around, before effortlessly leading her back into the main steps of the dance.

It was another thing she hadn't expected from him. As her mind told her to check her own bias—attractive men could dance—a *kwaito* song started and she nodded her head toward the table. What she and Ezra had just done was one thing, but *kwaito* dancing required a level of skill she didn't think he had.

'Where are you going?' he asked.

'Back to the table.'

He frowned. 'Why?'

Unsure of how to make 'because I don't want you to embarrass yourself' sound good, she said, 'I'm tired.'

'No, you're not,' he answered with a grin. 'You're underestimating my abilities. I'm offended.'

'Oh, no, I—' she started, and felt her words dry up when his legs started to move to the beat.

Check your bias, indeed.

Chapter Thirteen

If ever he was grateful for all the times he'd practised his dance moves as a child, it was now. Satisfaction filled him when Angie's jaw dropped; amusement joined when she shut her mouth again almost as quickly.

As he got lost in the music, he realised how long ago he'd done something like this. How long ago he felt like this. Happy. Free. Dancing brought him both, and yet he didn't do it nearly enough. When he had, he hadn't had a partner to join him.

Now, he pulled Angie in, tapping her hip with his hand, indicating that she should follow his lead. But she only narrowed her eyes, gave him a shake of her head, before launching into her own dance moves. He laughed when she wiggled her eyebrows at him, and they danced together, imitating each other's moves. It was the most fun he'd had in years. *Years.*

Before he knew it, they were in the middle of a circle. It was unsurprising, considering it was a South African party, though he wasn't sure how it had happened. Or how Dave and Jenny had joined them in the middle of the circle, with others sporadically walking in. When he realised they started something that no longer required them, he tried to catch Angie's gaze to tell her they could retreat.

Instead, he stilled as he watched her.

She was laughing, her curls flying around her face as she followed Jenny in an intricate dance move he was sure he'd never see repeated. Her expression was carefree, and he realised that in all the time they'd spent together, it hadn't been. Not so completely. Suddenly he understood how much what she was carrying around with her weighed on her.

With everything inside him, he wanted to help her carry it.

It took his breath away and he retreated to the edge of the circle, offering Angie a smile when she sent him a questioning look. He gestured toward the bar, then walked to it and gave his order. While he waited, he drank the water that had been put there as though he hadn't drunk anything in years.

When the barman set his whiskey in front of him, he downed it with one quick gulp.

As if it'll keep you from falling.

He shook his head, but the inner voice was right. He'd already known he was falling. Already knew it was a bad idea. He didn't know if she was another mistake, and he'd already established that falling for her would mean breaking once he landed.

Except now he thought it wasn't true. Because falling for her was like falling into quicksand. He was sinking slowly, without even realising it. Deeper and deeper, and soon it would be much too hard to get out. It was already closing in on him. The pressure around his lungs. The tightening at his throat.

As terrifying as it was, it also *wasn't*. A part of him believed he would never land with Angie. He would keep falling. She was…special. Though his instincts had let him down in the past, he didn't think they were now. Or rather, he could see he hadn't been listening to his instincts before.

He'd been a stupid teenager when he'd fallen for Ana. He'd done things and reasoned as only a stupid teenager could. But he'd punished himself for it. He'd punished his adult self for it because he wanted to fit in with his perfect family. With their perfect stability. So when his mind had identified Liesel as the perfect match, he'd willed his entire self to believe it.

But that hadn't been his instincts.

No, it seemed so damn clear to him now that he'd been running from those instincts more than he had anything else.

He'd found ways to drown it out after he'd believed it had led him astray. Had handily used his studies as a crutch, which in turn, had given him a new crutch— research. He read up on things, made notes, investigated, until logic was all he had. It pushed him into believing that gut feelings couldn't compete with logic. With reasoning.

If he'd had either with Ana, he wouldn't have allowed himself to be caught by her. He would have seen the propositions of the argument—that she had been unpredictable and he hadn't been, and thus, she'd appealed to him—and he would have seen the inevitable conclusion: that she wouldn't be good for him.

So he'd let logic and reasoning lead him from then on. He relished his research and had even found a job that depended on the skill he'd honed over the years. But he was beginning to think that reason and logic weren't everything. At least not in this case.

He angled his body, looking at the circle that had grown bigger in the few moments he'd been away. His eyes searched for the woman who'd turned his world upside down in one short day. She'd retreated to the edge of the circle now, too, but she was cheering on those in the middle as if she knew them personally. As if she were as much a part of the family as Becky or Charles.

There was something about her—the light, the energy—that sucked people in. It was hidden underneath acerbic wit and quick quips, but it shone through eventually. Which made the fact that she let him in to more than the light and energy all the more significant. She was falling for him, too.

He didn't know how hard. He had no idea what it meant for them. But he didn't care. It was enough that she was falling. That she was feeling.

It was enough.

He ordered her a drink and took it back to the dance floor as the music slowed.

'I thought you might like this,' he said, handing it to her.

'You were right. And a saviour,' she said, and downed the drink. She laughed as she laid the empty glass on the tray of a passing waiter. 'How very impolite of me.'

'Oh, I don't know,' he said, taking advantage of her distraction. He slid one arm around her waist and pulled her close. Her eyes widened, but her arm lifted around his neck, her free hand taking his as he began to move to the music. 'It looked fine to me.'

'I'll take it.' Her voice was low. Husky. 'Even though I know you're just charming me.'

He chuckled. 'I think I can spare some charm for the woman who convinced me to face my fears.'

'You do seem to have changed your mind about all this.'

'I've seen the light.' He wanted to pull her even closer. He wanted no space between them. But he wouldn't push her. 'It was never about the wedding.'

'Oh, I know.'

She leaned back, her other hand moving to his neck. It almost amused him, the stance that reminded him of his school days. He hadn't gone to his last school dance. He'd been too busy studying to make up for failing his first term. He wished he could go back to teenage Ezra and tell him he'd make up for it someday.

'We tend to project our feelings onto these events, don't we?'

'Because they make our memories sharper,' he said. 'My parents renewed their vows a few years ago. Thirty-five years of marriage.'

'Did it look like this?' she teased, though something on her face had wilted. It distracted him from the tension that had come from longing for what his parents had. From wondering if he was finding it.

'We did think about hiring Father Christmas, but he declined. Something about the North Pole being under construction.'

'The entire North Pole?' she asked in mock horror.

'The whole thing.' He grinned. 'Such a shame.'

'A pity you only discovered your talent for impersonating him now.'

'It is, isn't it?' He shook his head. 'My point was that that night was incredible. It made me believe that something like that existed.'

'Were you still with Liesel then?'

'Yeah.'

'And you saw yourself having it with her?'

He frowned. 'No. No, I didn't.'

'Okay,' she said slowly, after a moment. 'I'm a little confused.'

'Me, too.'

'Ah.'

They kept swaying in silence, and he was grateful

for a moment to collect his thoughts. He didn't need to think too hard. He knew he'd ignored signs that he and Liesel shouldn't have been together. Signs that would have told him proposing was the last thing he should have done.

So why had he allowed that memory to taint weddings for him when the last one he'd attended had been as beautiful as his parents'? And yes, he knew it wasn't the same thing, but it was still a celebration of love, wasn't it? It was still a proclamation of love. Of commitment.

'Man, I've been really stupid.'

She laughed softly. 'Happens to the best of us.'

'But I wouldn't have realised it if I didn't agree to attend this wedding. And if I had attended, I probably wouldn't have seen past the tacky décor.'

'Jenny's mom wanted it this way,' Angie said, her eyes not meeting his. 'Jenny wanted it to be tasteful, fun, enjoyable. Like outside.'

'Angie.'

'I know what you're going to say.'

'Let me say it anyway.' She met his gaze then. Her own was guarded, but she nodded. 'I wouldn't have seen past the tacky décor. I wouldn't have enjoyed the company—' as he said the words, he saw Becky and Charles slinking out of the hall. It solidified what he wanted to say to her '—I wouldn't have enjoyed any of it if it weren't for you.'

'Well.' It was all she said for a while, then she shook herself. Literally shook herself, shoulders and all. 'I'll be sure to send you an invoice.'

'Thank you,' he said sincerely.

Her mouth curved into an unconvincing smile. 'I'm glad I could help.'

'You did more than help.'

'Wonderful. Clearly my work here is done.'

He took a moment to keep himself from speaking out of panic. He knew she'd only stayed because she wanted to help him. If she thought her work was done, she'd leave. That was the last thing he wanted. He also knew that if he told her that, he'd basically be handing her the keys to her car.

'I suppose it depends on what you think your work here is.'

'You're here, aren't you?' Her face tightened. 'You're over your fear. You've had your realisations.'

'That was it?' He leaned back so he could see her face more clearly. 'You simply wanted to…help a stranger get his life back on track?'

'Call it a Christmas miracle.'

'Or fate.'

'Now you're just being greedy,' she said, her tone flat. He heard it as a plea for him to stop. He couldn't.

'You don't think the fact that you and I are both here today is fate?'

'I think that you're here because you wanted to face your fears yourself.'

'I didn't have the courage to until you encouraged me.'

'I didn't encourage you. You didn't even tell me you were here for Jenny and Dave. Not really.'

'But you knew, which is my point.'

'And my point is that it doesn't matter,' she exclaimed. 'You stopped her for this wedding, and I stopped here because it was a place I once shared with my family. My father.' She clenched her jaw, then continued. 'You spent today getting over your issues, and I spent the day stewing in mine. This wedding made you remember your parents' vow renewal and you were happy about it. I thought about my parents' last wedding anniversary and felt physically ill.'

'You think I was—' He broke off on a frustrated sigh. 'I understand,' he tried again slowly, 'that this wasn't easy for you.' She snorted, but he added the anger it evoked to the ever-growing pile of that emotion he was already ignoring to get through to her. 'It hasn't been easy for me either. I didn't just "get over" my issues. Remembering my parents' vow renewal has been more bittersweet than happy.'

He took a breath. 'But what are the chances both you and I—being who we are, having been through what we have—would stop here at this place? At the same time? Or that you'd join me at my table? That we'd be able to help each other?'

'Ezra,' she pleaded. 'We were—' She broke off. 'Don't. I want to keep enjoying myself. And pretending—'

'That whatever happens here doesn't matter?' he asked, grinding his teeth.

'Yes.' They'd stopped swaying now. 'Because it doesn't. How can it? When this dance is over, I'm going back to reality. So are you.' She released a shaky breath. 'We're both leaving this place and the magic that's happened here will fade, and our problems will still be there. So what's the point in believing it served a purpose when it's going to end anyway?'

She had a point. He knew she did; part of him felt the same way. But he also knew that if he let her walk away… If he let her leave… He knew he'd regret it for the rest of his life. So he clung to the hope.

'Magic deserves a chance, Ange. Even if it's for a few more hours.' Now was his turn to plead. 'Give it a chance.'

Chapter Fourteen

If she were in her right mind, she wouldn't even have considered Ezra's words. Unfortunately, at that moment she was distracted by the strength of his arms around her, by his body pressed to hers. And she was completely undone by his words, by the magic, and her mind flooded with reasons she should stay.

But she couldn't. She couldn't ignore her responsibilities. Not again. There'd been no spell over what she was going back to; her family was still broken. So was she. Which was the crux of it all, wasn't it? She'd been running away from breaking when she was already broken. From grief. From anger. From everything she'd run from.

This? Ezra? He was part of the make-believe world she'd been living in where she wasn't broken. In the real world, there was no magic that would change that she'd already turned into someone she could no longer recognise as herself.

She did see a lot of her mother though.

She drew a ragged breath and pulled away from him.

'Why couldn't you let it be, Ezra?' she asked, heartbroken.

Without another word, she left the dance floor, grabbed her handbag at the table, and headed outside.

She couldn't do this anymore. Couldn't bear it. So she'd leave. And try to forget about the magic she'd experienced a wedding one Christmas.

She manoeuvred through the same crowd of smokers as she had the first time she left the venue, though she'd already reached her car when she realised how dark it had got.

'Damn it,' she said out loud, and popped the boot to stuff her handbag in among all the other bags.

'You're not going to be able to leave right now,' came a voice from behind her. She clenched her jaw.

'Are you following me?'

'Yes,' Ezra replied tersely. 'It's evening. You're in a town that isn't your home. I'm making sure you're okay.' He paused. 'Jenny stopped me before I left the hall. She asked me whether you were leaving.'

'I should have said goodbye to her and Dave,' Angie muttered, mostly to herself.

'No, that's not it.' His tone was measured now. 'She said the roads are closed for the next two hours because of the parade. You won't be able to get to Cape Town until after then.'

She stared at him, as if somehow, doing so would change his answer. He lifted his shoulder in an annoyingly calm way, and she gritted her teeth, opening the boot of her car again. She reached for her handbag and took out the phone she hadn't checked in hours. There were no notifications of any kind, which made sense considering her lack of connections.

Even her family group chat was silent, though that wasn't anything new. They weren't a chatting kind of family. Besides, she'd told them she would be arriving the next day; there was no need to talk about anything else.

If she needed another reminder about why the universe was being so cruel to her though, she'd have found it in that. She'd thought she wanted a night to soak in being back in Cape Town. She'd thought she wanted to see the lights of the city, and Table Mountain, and feel what it would be like to be back home without the distraction of being with her family.

In reality, she was being a coward; she wanted more time before she had to face them. The universe was giving her what she wanted now though. She had another night away from them. It looked different—being stranded in a town outside Cape Town wasn't quite the same as choosing to be in a hotel inside Cape Town— but Angie got the point.

You wanted this? Well, here it is.

'What are you planning on doing with your phone?' Ezra asked, his expression unreadable, though his gaze had dipped to the phone in her hand. Only then did she realise she'd been staring at it with seemingly no purpose for she didn't how long.

'Checking whether Jenny's right.'

'How?'

'I don't know. There must be an official website for the Christmas parade. Or maybe somewhere on social media?'

She realised too late she phrased that last sentence as a question. But the doubt had crept in as she was speaking, mostly because she knew Caledon was small enough not to have to rely on the means used by larger cities. There might not be a website or social media.

Not that it mattered anyway.

'Problem?'

'Yeah,' she said with a frown. 'My network doesn't get any signal here, apparently.'

It didn't surprise her. She'd taken the cheapest plan she'd found since she didn't have any intention of staying in Cape Town long term. The plan happened to be with South Africa's newest network, which was, it seemed, still struggling to offer people in smaller towns reliable service.

'What are you going to do?' he asked almost lazily, and she narrowed her eyes.

'I'm going to have a chat with the lodge's receptionist about it.'

She started walking, heard his footsteps behind her, whirled around.

'You don't have to come with me.'

'I know.'

The look on his face told her he'd be accompanying her no matter what she said. She sighed. Didn't respond. What was the point?

She walked to the reception of the lodge, and after a short conversation with the receptionist, Angie learnt that Jenny had been right. She took a breath and tried to think through her options. If she left in two hours, she'd be driving in the thick of the night. It wasn't that she was afraid of it, but she hadn't travelled the winding mountain of Sir Lowry's Pass in years. The combination of the dark and driving a relatively dangerous road that was essentially unfamiliar didn't sound appealing.

She blew out a breath. 'Do you have any free rooms for this evening?'

'I'm sorry, ma'am,' the receptionist told her apologetically. 'Normally, it wouldn't have been a problem. But we're hosting a wedding, and with the annual Christmas parade, we're completely booked.'

Angie took a long, deep breath. 'There's a lodge down the road, isn't there?'

'Yes, ma'am. But—'

'But?'

'Well, ma'am… I wouldn't recommend staying there.' The expression on the brunette's face was tight, but she cleared her throat. 'Mostly because they'll likely be fully booked as well.'

But Angie knew that wasn't the reason. She'd driven past the place on her way to the café, and it hadn't changed in all the years since she'd last been in Caledon. It was still a little dark, a lot dingy, and the receptionist's face told her that in this case, it would be right to judge a book by its cover.

'Are you sure there isn't one room?' Angie asked, her throat thick. 'I just need a place to sleep. Nothing fancy.'

'I'll check again,' came the answer, though it was said in a tone that told Angie she shouldn't hold her breath.

How had things gone to hell so quickly? One moment she was in the arms of a man she knew she'd fantasise about long after she left—there was no point in pretending she could forget him anymore—and the next, she was stranded at a lodge that had no space for her.

'The irony of this moment is probably lost on you,' Ezra said softly.

'Enlighten me.'

'Well,' he replied, taking her surly tone in stride, 'there's no space for you at the lodge…'

'I'm aware.'

He gave her a look, his hands in his pockets. It put him in a stance that shouldn't have been sexy, yet somehow was, even with the faint anger radiating off him. Perhaps because of it.

'I still have— Oh. Oh,' she said again, when her mind finally cleared of the fog of Ezra's sexiness. 'I think it's safe to say Mary and Joseph's situation was a lot more serious than mine.'

'Similar though.' He paused. 'Almost as if there were some kind of outside force at work.'

He gave her a smile that was dangerous and unsympathetic, and annoyance bristled through her. At herself, too, because she found him sexy even when he was taunting her. Damn it. Damn *him*.

It was fitting then when the receptionist confirmed that there *was* no room for her. Angie thanked the woman and walked out of the reception area. She made it a few metres before her legs told her they were tired of keeping her up and she headed for the nearest bench.

Ezra sat down next to her. She nearly threw her hands up.

'You're right,' she said. 'Maybe it is fate that keeps doing this to me. Why else would I find you this annoying and still be attracted to you?'

He gave a bark of laughter. 'I could say the same thing about you.'

She snorted, though strangely, it made her feel better.

'If this was some kind of divine intervention, there should have at least been a stable that I could sleep in.' She paused. 'Do you think the stage is still set up from the nativity play?'

'I'm not sure that's your most comfortable option.'

'You're right. My car's probably better.'

'Yeah,' he agreed. 'But I think my bed would be best.'

'Excuse me?'

He smiled at the indignation. At the interest. He'd meant it provocatively. Hadn't been able to resist.

'You could share my room with me. We'll share the bed. No, not like that.'

Unless you want to.

'I think I'll take my chances with the car,' she replied dryly.

He chuckled. Couldn't blame her for the quip. But he wanted her to know it was a real option. 'You've spent most of your day in a car. I promise, I won't do anything inappropriate.'

She hissed out a breath. It felt as if something had punctured inside him and the air was hissing out there, too. Which of course, brought back the anger.

'I'm trying to help you, Angie.'

'Because you're the reason I'm in this situation in the first place,' she replied tightly. 'If I hadn't stayed—'

'I didn't ask you to.'

'Didn't you?' She turned to him. 'How was I supposed to leave when you were going through all this?'

'You don't know me, Angie. You're not responsible for me.'

'That's not true.' She straightened her shoulders. Lifted her chin though he swore her lips were trembling. 'The first part, at least.'

He nodded. Hated that he used it as a weapon when he knew it wasn't true.

They *did* know each other. They'd shared their fears, their vulnerabilities with one another. Most of them, anyway. It would forever be a mystery to him that he'd been able to open up about his failures. Because that's how he saw them. He hadn't spoken about them for most of his life because failure meant disappointment. He was tired of being disappointed.

He was tired of being a disappointment.

But then, there was something easy about opening up to a stranger. To someone who didn't come with the baggage or benefit of history. He'd been able to create a narrative that had put him in the best light. That ignored the darkness, the grey between the black and white.

If he'd had to describe it theoretically, that's how he would have done it. Except in practice it was decidedly different. Because sometimes the stranger was a woman who saw right through the bull. Who put the light on the darkness, on the flaws, and somehow made it seem less terrible.

Sometimes, the stranger was a woman who had darkness of her own. Who kept swatting away the light when her companion tried to help her. He didn't know what to do about it. He couldn't blame her when he'd resisted in some parts himself.

Or maybe he *did* know; he just didn't want to do it.

'You're right,' she said into the silence. 'You're not my responsibility. I stayed because…because I care.'

And didn't that strip the anger from him.

'I know.'

'And because I'm running from my real responsibilities.'

'Ange—'

'I always run when I'm afraid,' she continued as if he hadn't said anything. 'I'm running now, too. Because I care.'

It took him a moment to reply. The reply came in the form of a chuckle.

She was unimpressed. 'I'm sorry. I didn't realise that was funny.'

'It's not. It's just—' The chuckle died swiftly. 'It's just that I'm doing the exact same thing.'

'Running?'

'Yeah.'

'You could have fooled me.'

'What's that supposed to mean?'

'You invited me to spend the night in your bed.'

'I was teasing.'

'Were you?'

'Angie—'

'There's no part of you that wants to spend the night with me?'

How had he got himself into this? Oh, right. *Teasing.* His own fault then. 'I'll sleep in the car and you can take the room.

'That's not what I meant.' She sighed. 'You might think you're running, Ez, but you're not.'

'Of course I am.' He paused. 'Why am I trying to convince you of this?'

'Because you know I'm right, and you don't like admitting it. Just let me explain,' she said, when he opened his mouth to protest. 'You care about me, too.' It wasn't a question, but he gave a curt nod. 'And after what happened with your ex, you should be running from someone you care about. Especially when that someone's me.'

They hadn't been talking about the same thing, he realised. But then he thought that it didn't matter since what she'd said had taken over all the thoughts in his head anyway.

'Why you?'

She tilted her head. Angled her body toward him. 'Nothing can happen when we leave here, Ezra.'

'It could.' Taken aback by his answer, he frowned. But he…he kept *talking*. 'We're both going back home to Cape Town.'

'Ezra,' she said it quietly. Something akin to shame flushed his body. 'This makes no sense. You've come out of a seven-year relationship months ago. You proposed to her. How are you entertaining the possibility of something between us?'

'You think I don't know this doesn't make sense?' he asked tightly, the shame—the more, because damn it, there *was* more between them—spurring his words. 'Do you think I want to entertain an "us"? My track record with women is terrible. Which is what I was talking about, by the way, when I said I was running.' His breath pushed harshly between his lips. 'I've been consistent in my poor decisions when it comes to relationships. I *want* to run from you, Angie. I want to run so bad, but I can't. Every time I convince myself to—'

He shook his head then, hoping to regain his control. His dignity. Because he was acting like a fool and it was time he stopped. Before he could say anything more, she spoke.

'I'm leaving again. Cape Town,' she clarified. 'I'm going to get my family settled, clean up the mess I made there. Then I'm going to leave.'

'Where to?'

'I don't know.'

'Right.' He sat back. 'Of course.'

'Don't say it that way.'

He didn't reply.

'You don't know what it's going to be like, Ezra.'

'Neither do you. Not really.'

'I know my family.'

'Not after your father...' he trailed off when the words sounded harsh even to his own ears. 'Things have changed,' he said slowly. 'You don't know how because you left before you could find out.'

'Because I ran, you mean.' Her tone was flat.

'You're the best person to make that call, Ange. I'm only saying that maybe you should wait until you know what you'll be leaving behind this time.' And then, because he felt compelled to do so, he added, 'This has nothing to do with me. You'll never have to see me again if you don't want to.'

'Don't say that.' She faced forward again. Threaded her fingers together. 'You know it's not about that.' He didn't. 'And for the record, I'm not just running away from them. I'm running toward something, too. Toward a life I get to live for myself.'

'That's what your life in Korea was?' he asked. She nodded. 'That life wasn't in any way tainted by the memories of what you left behind? What you weren't facing?'

She didn't answer. Seconds later, a coarse laugh left her lips. 'You bastard.' She laughed again, except this time, she rested her head in her hands, and the sound ended on a sob.

He *was* a bastard.

'I'm sorry.'

'Don't be.' The words were stifled. She brought her head up and looked at him. Her eyes were dry. 'You're right.'

'Being right is overrated.'

'A social sciences lecturer would think that. No right and wrong, only shades of it.'

'No, that's not it. Being right just isn't worth you being hurt.'

She blinked, then reached out and took his hand. He shifted it so that their fingers tangled. They sat like that for a while, neither of them speaking.

'I'm sorry I broke it,' she said into the silence.

'What?'

'This.' She lifted their hands. Dropped it on his knee. 'Us.'

'How can you break something that wasn't whole in the first place?'

'Ooh.' She laughed. 'We're a mess.'

He smiled. 'Unfortunately.'

'So,' she said after a few seconds. 'Does this mean I don't get your bed tonight?'

Now he laughed, too. 'The offer still stands.'

'Thank goodness,' she answered sincerely. 'And I'm… I'm sorry about how I treated you earlier.' He squeezed her hand, she squeezed his, and then quickly cleared her throat. 'How about we take a walk down to the pier? Shake off some of the melancholy.'

'Sure.'

He stood, offered her his hand. Held his breath. He wasn't sure if that was because he didn't want to get a waft of her perfume—some powerful mixture of lilies and late spring—or because he didn't know if she'd take it.

But she did.

And damn if that didn't mess him up even more.

They walked down to the pier in silence. When they got there, they settled on one side of it, some distance from the edge, their feet dangling over the water. The pier was still warm though the sun had gone down ages ago. The trees on the embankment hung over the river as if designed to offer shade to those who preferred to cool off in its shadows rather than the water.

'I always thought my parents were strange for living here,' she said. 'In this small town almost in the middle of nowhere. But this—' she gestured around them with a hand '—makes me understand it. Today makes me understand it.' She paused. 'Helps me understand why Jenny and Dave wanted their wedding here, too.'

'I can't speak to your parents' motivations, but you know Jenny and Dave grew up here, right?'

She laughed. 'Yeah, but growing up somewhere doesn't mean you have to get married there.'

'So the autumn tree and petals didn't come from growing up in Kuils River? Your wedding fantasy,' he added when she frowned up at him. It made him feel foolish he remember the details of it.

'Oh, no. No, that came from a movie, like I said earlier.' Her lips curved. 'I couldn't have been older than seven. I don't remember much of the rest of the movie, only that I saw this woman walking down the aisle in exactly the way I described, and I just…' She lifted a hand, let it drop. 'I knew that that was what I wanted someday. It took getting a little older to realise fantasies don't come true because you want them to.'

'Sometimes they do.'

'Do they?' Her expression turned pensive. 'I haven't ever had a dream come true.'

'That doesn't mean it won't in the future.'

'Of course not,' she said dutifully. 'I'm obviously going to become a bestselling author before the age of thirty.'

'*That's* your dream?' he asked. 'A bit ambitious, I'll admit, but it could certainly come true.' There was a pause. 'Have you written anything that could be a bestseller though?'

She chuckled softly. 'Finding your motivational talk a little challenging now that you have the facts, Mr. Inspiration?'

'Inspiring people is not quite the same with facts,' he replied with a grin. 'Have you?'

'I've…written some stuff.'

'A book?'

'Short stories.'

'Which could be compiled into a book?'

'Which could be excellent kindling for a fire.'

'You're deflecting.'

'I prefer the term "running,"' she said cheekily, then sighed. 'I am.'

He didn't say anything when silence followed her words. He knew she'd talk when she was ready. The certainty of that knowledge should have bothered him. Instead, he patiently waited for her explanation, looking up at the night sky and quietly marvelling at its inky darkness. It was brightened by the stars and moon, which, in turn, brightened the water with their reflection.

'I've written one book.' She kicked her legs out. Drew them in again. Repeated the action. 'One full romance, from start to finish.'

'I take it it's not the one you'd like to become successful with.'

'It wouldn't be successful. It would be—' She broke off with another kick. 'The book is terrible,' she admitted. She turned to him, laughed. 'I haven't read it since I wrote it, but I have it on good authority.'

'Whose?'

'My dad's.' The smile lingering on her lips faded. 'I wrote it while he was sick. He found the pages I printed somehow before I got the chance to edit them. I got home from work that night and he was in my room and with this really serious expression he said, "Ange, girl—I think you need to do some work on your writing before you're published."'

Her expression was nostalgic. 'I was furious, of course. But he just waited while I told him he had no right to invade my privacy and how dare he read my book and—' she glanced over at him '—well, you get the picture. Anyway, he waited for me to finish and then he told me I needed work, yes, but I had promise. Which, for my dad, was a major compliment.'

'Not that you needed it.'

'What do you mean?'

'He told you your writing needed work before it was published. Which, if we look at it linguistically, implies that he believed someday, you would be published.'

She didn't reply for a while. Because of it, he could hear the rustle of the trees as a light breeze spun around them.

'I didn't ever think about it like that,' she said.

'Too busy looking at the negative, right?'

'Right,' she said with a small laugh. 'Kind of makes me regret not writing another book.'

'Why haven't you?'

'I… I couldn't.' The kicking started up again. 'It seemed like too big a task. Too big a commitment when I could only focus on smaller things.'

'Ah.'

'My shorter stories came with happily-ever-afters though.'

'I'm sure your father would have been proud.'

'Yeah,' she agreed after a moment. 'I've definitely got better.'

'Remember to send me a copy when your book's published.'

She smiled at him. 'I'll even put you in the acknowledgements.' She bumped her shoulder against his.

He had no doubts that she would put him in the acknowledgements. He also had no doubts she'd write another book. She'd put her life on pause the last three years, but he knew she'd pressed play by coming back home. And moving forward for Angie would mean pursuing her dreams. He knew it.

'What about you?' she asked suddenly. 'Did you have any wedding fantasies?' She closed her eyes almost as soon as she finished saying it. Opened them with an apologetic grimace. 'I'm sorry. I shouldn't have asked.'

'You don't have to filter yourself around me.' The truth of the words settled the tension. And he realised that if he didn't want her to filter herself, he needed to be okay with responding to it. 'I always wanted to get married on a lake. Like this, actually.' He paused. 'With Liesel... I thought we'd get married in Cape Town, at this gorgeous little quarry in Durbanville.'

'I know it. It's beautiful.'

'It is.' He took a shaky breath. 'I'd pictured all of it. Fighting with my parents to have the ceremony there because they'd want it in the family church. Coming to some kind of compromise because they loved me and I didn't want to disappoint them.'

He paused when the words sent an uncomfortable ripple through him. Not for the usual reasons this time. No, this time it was because he remember they loved him. It sounded silly—how could he forget it?—but he hadn't thought about it like that in the longest time. *They loved him.* That's where their concern was coming from. Concern he'd begun to see only as disappointment.

Huh.

'I'm sure it would have turned out perfectly. I'm sure it will, someday,' she added quickly. 'With the right woman.'

He almost laughed. Even when he told himself not to be, he was still surprised. But then, he already established things between them made no sense. So he gave up trying to hide his remaining insecurities.

He sighed. 'Exactly. The only problem is that I can't trust myself to judge whether a woman is right for me or not.'

Chapter Fifteen

It shouldn't have bothered her. Less than thirty minutes before, they'd had a painful discussion about why their feelings for one another couldn't matter. Less than ten minutes before, she'd told him about her writing dreams and how her grief for her father had forced them aside in the last years. Why then, did Ezra's admission feel like he stabbed her with something?

'Why not?' she forced herself to ask. Because she wasn't a fish out of water, flipping and flopping. She would be consistent in what she wanted from him. From them.

Because she wasn't a fish, damn it.

'Well, you already know about Liesel,' he started slowly. She forced air into her lungs when she realised she was holding her breath, waiting for him to continue. 'She wasn't my first wrong choice when it came to dating. There was…someone else. I met her the summer before my last year of high school.'

'Sounds like a suitable start to a tragic love story.'

His mouth curved. 'You're not wrong.' He took a breath. 'I was a pretty good kid until then. It helped that I had pretty stable older siblings. Great examples, but terrible standards to live up to. But I tried. Until my sister left her first year of university to follow some band across the country and I realised the bar to live up to had dropped significantly.'

She nodded sombrely, and then said, 'I know this is probably an inappropriate thing to say right now, but your sister sounds…strong-willed.'

He laughed. 'Bullheaded, you mean. She's kind of badass now. Anyway, back then, she was just acting out against our strict upbringing. Loving, but strict. She went a little bit overboard with her first taste of freedom at university. Realised it pretty soon when she came back six months later broke and completely jaded by the friends who'd convinced her to go with them. Turned out they'd manipulated her into spending the money she'd saved over the years—like I said, she was stable before then—and left her the moment it ran out.'

'When did that happen?'

'About a month in.' He grinned. 'I told you she was bullheaded. But we live and we learn.'

'What was your lesson?'

'Right.' He sobered. 'When I realised I had some space to mess up, I let myself do something I never had before: I went to a party.'

'You'd never gone to a party before then?'

'Not this kind. Thanks for the concern though,' he added, and she smiled. 'Anyway, this was the kind where adults weren't allowed at. And I kissed a girl no adult would have allowed seventeen-year-old me to kiss.'

'She was an alien?'

'She was older,' he said dryly. 'She'd been arrested for petty theft a couple of times'

'I'm almost impressed.'

'Don't be. It was stupid.'

Feeling the shift in him, she asked softly, 'What happened?'

'I became a nightmare. Ditched school to be with her. Did the bare minimum when I was there. Ignored my parents. Snuck out. Drank. Did pretty much everything you hear kids try to do as teenagers, but as one kid and all in the space of four months.'

'And then?'

'And then I failed the first term of my final year in high school and my parents told me if it continued, they'd kick me out at the end of the year.'

'That was enough to kick your ass into gear?'

'Yeah. Some part of me knew I was being an idiot. The relationship was terrible. I'm not sure why I stayed.' He winced. 'See what I mean?'

She did, and he was punishing himself for it. But she didn't say anything. Waited for him to finish his story instead.

'My parents worked their butts off for us. My mom got pregnant with my brother when she was a teenager and her parents disowned her. My father's parents took them in, but they didn't have much either. Every single day each of them worked to give us a life they didn't get. And I threw their efforts back into their faces.'

'You were a kid.'

'Yeah, but it made me work *my* butt off to keep them from ever looking at me that way again. With that… I don't know. A combination of disappointment and hurt.' He lifted a shoulder. 'It messed with me almost as much as the threat did.'

'So you stayed in line.'

'I did what I needed to do to pass. I messed up my grades so bad that I didn't get a bursary. Something else I regret.' He ran a hand over the back of his neck. 'But I did well in my first year at university.' There was a quick pause. 'And my second, and third, and post-grad…' He grinned. 'You get the picture.'

She rolled her eyes. 'Yeah, I do, *Doctor*.'

'I just wanted to make up for disappointing them. Making sure they didn't have to pay for another year of my studies seemed like a simple way.'

'And also, making sure you dated the right kind of women after that.'

His gaze flew to hers. He gave a slight shake of his head. It looked as if it were more to himself than to her.

'I only dated Liesel after that.'

'How old were you?'

'Twenty-four.'

She did the calculations. 'For seven years you didn't date anyone?'

'More or less.' He shrugged. 'I wanted to focus on my studies.'

'Did you have your PhD when you met Liesel?'

'I was two years away from graduating.'

'What changed?'

'I thought I'd met the right person.'

She considered it for a moment. 'Did your parents introduce you?'

His brows lifted. 'Yeah. How'd you know?'

'A gut feeling.' She paused. 'You said your parents didn't want you to marry her though?'

'Jane, my sister, told me they'd realised it somewhere during the course of our relationship.'

'Why didn't they say anything?'

'I don't know.'

They sat like that as the silence stretched. Somewhere away from the pier they heard the water splash.

'Maybe they thought you were happy,' she said slowly. 'Maybe they were willing to sacrifice what they thought because they thought *you* were happy. Because they loved you.'

The side of his mouth lifted. 'Sounds like them.'

'You already knew?'

'Not entirely. But before I told you that story I realised a lot of what I'd been doing was because I got stuck in the surface emotions and not the deeper ones. The concern and disappointment came because they loved me.'

There was a beat before she asked, 'You came up with that by yourself?'

He laughed. 'After *years*, yeah.'

'You've obviously earned your title, Doctor.'

He smiled lazily at her. Despite the sombre tone of their discussion, her belly flipped.

'I did study for seven years.' He leaned back now. 'So, is there anything you'd like to talk about since I'm an expert? Maybe your fear of commitment?'

She snorted. 'I do not have a fear of commitment.'

'What about your resistance to getting married?'

'It's not about fear of commitment.'

'You want to be in a committed relationship?'

'Well, yeah. Maybe.' She wasn't quite sure herself. 'I do like the *idea* of marriage.'

He straightened. 'Yeah?'

She laughed lightly. 'Yeah. I know, I'm a whole bunch of complicated.'

'Is the wedding stuff just because of your parents?'

'I said I like the idea of marriage, Ezra. I didn't cast a spell to make my soulmate suddenly appear so I could get married.'

His lips curved. 'But what does liking the idea mean? You don't want to get caught in the everyday of it?'

'No.' She took a deep breath, her lungs seemingly

knowing she was about to make the admission before her mind did. 'I don't want to turn into my mother.

The shame, the guilt, immediately followed her words. Because she deserved them, she let them flow through her body. Let them pulse in her veins. She let them remind her she was the worst daughter.

'Tell me,' he said softly when she closed her eyes, seeping herself in the feelings of it.

She opened her eyes to his concern; to his compassion. Somehow it undid the knot inside her. It shouldn't have, she knew. Because he was looking at her as if she hadn't admitted her darkest secret to him. His expression was exactly as it had been when he'd kissed her: as if she were the only woman in the world. As if she were deserving of this attention.

'She—' Angie swallowed when her throat went dry. Tried again. 'I told you about how much she depended on my father. And that he liked it. He liked that she needed him, I mean. I think it made him feel loved.' She paused. 'Maybe that's why he let me in to their weird dynamic. He wanted me to feel loved, too.'

She sucked in her lip. Let the air shudder through the side of her mouth.

'I protected my sisters from it for as long as I could, so I don't think they felt the burden of it.' She closed her eyes again. 'It didn't make me feel loved. It made me feel trapped. Making sure my sisters had everything they needed emotionally, and then protecting my mother from the fact that they needed it from *her* and that she couldn't give it to them.' She paused. 'I couldn't tell my father that though. Obviously, I couldn't tell my mother. So I just tried my best.' She opened her eyes. 'I think I did an okay job of protecting Sophia and Zoey.'

Until she'd left, when she'd seemingly handed the reins over to Sophia.

'It's fine, Angie. Leave. I'll be here for Mom and Zo. You just…leave.'

'It wasn't your responsibility though,' Ezra's voice interrupted the accusation replaying in her head. 'Not with your mother or with your sisters. Or your father,' he added. He gripped her hand when her head whipped so she could look at him. 'It's true, Angie. You were protecting him, too, by not telling him the truth.'

Tears pricked in her eyes. She nodded. 'I didn't realise.'

Breathe.

She opened her mouth. Sucked in air.

'I was going to tell you I didn't want to end up like my mother, in what would be the only example of marriage I've had. Being dependent on someone else. Not knowing who I was without that person. Being *broken* without them. That's why I ran. I was afraid I'd break after my father… That's why I don't want to connect with anyone either.' She paused when she ran out of breath. 'But earlier today I realised that I *did* break. After he passed away, I broke. Now here you are confirming that I'd broken long before he…'

She couldn't finish it.

'Angie,' he said softly.

'It's okay. It's okay,' she repeated, and squeezed his hand. 'It's part of what I've come home to face. Or what I will face,' she said dryly, pinching her nose, 'when I actually let myself go home.'

'Coming back to South Africa, back to Cape Town, already means you've come home. You *are* facing it.'

'Maybe. Or maybe I'm trying to figure out a way to work through how I feel about my father's mistakes now that he's not here.'

'You mean with you mother?'

'With me, too. And with my sisters. He wasn't a perfect man. He encouraged my mother's dependence. Expected me to carry some of the weight of that decision with both my mother and my sisters. He was honest to a fault, and annoyingly dry. I told you we were similar,' she said with a pained laughed, before exhaling shakily. 'He wasn't perfect, and it's so damn hard to say that.'

'It shouldn't be, if it's true.'

'Didn't your mother ever tell you we shouldn't speak ill of the dead?'

He laughed softly. 'She has, actually. But I think speaking honestly about the dead is more important. It does no one any good to pretend the dead were saints when they were only human.'

Her eyes widened; she didn't resist the smile that came along with it. 'I'm going to have to pay you for your services.'

'I'll give you the friends and family discount.'

'Is that what we are?' she asked. 'Friends?'

'I don't know.' He turned to her, resting his knee on the pier. 'It's complicated, isn't it?'

'Much like we are.'

He nodded. His hand lifted to cup her chin. 'I've never met anyone like you before.'

She wasn't sure she was breathing, which made the breathy tone of her reply impossible. 'Someone who runs from their fears?'

'You're not running anymore.' His hand slid to the back of her neck. 'I think you told me I need to learn from my mistakes because you need to learn from yours.'

She lifted her hand, intending to remove his hand from her neck. Instead, she gripped his wrist.

'I'm still a mess.'

'You're not a mess,' he said gently. 'We aren't either. We need work. We'll always need work. We're human.'

'How do you—how do you know how to make me feel better?'

'I have a gift,' he teased.

'Yeah, you do,' she replied seriously. 'For me.'

His body shifted then; his expression changed. Even though it was dark around them, and only the light of the full moon and the stars illuminated them, Angie saw the change. Felt it. In the sizzle in the air around them; in the tightening of her body.

Suddenly there were no past heartbreaks, no future uncertainty. There was no grief or families or problems. There was only them, now, and the demands of them in the now.

She was helpless not to give in.

So she leaned forward, lifted her hand to his cheek and tentatively touched her lips to his.

Chapter Sixteen

It went straight through her. The taste of him. The feel of his mouth pressed to hers. Her skin prickled. Her toes curled. Heat unfurled in her belly. She pulled back slightly.

'This is a bad idea,' she whispered, but didn't move any farther away.

'Probably.' The hand at her neck gently massaged her skin. She leaned into it, closing her eyes as she almost heard her muscles sigh with pleasure. 'Especially since we're sharing a room tonight. A bed.'

She laughed breathily, opening her eyes slowly. The effortless seduction in his eyes sent a thrill through her, the evidence of it gooseflesh on her body.

'If we get that far,' she replied quietly. 'I'm pretty content here.'

'Yeah?' His hand rested on her waist. Heat flared through her entire body. 'How lucky. I am, too.'

She smiled. Shifted closer to him. 'You know, I'd probably compliment your game right now if it weren't for the fact that *I* suggested we come down to the pier.' She looked around them. 'We're under the stars, under the moon on a summer's evening.'

'Alone.' As he said it, they heard a splash at the other end of the river. He smiled. 'Almost.'

'Still, not your idea.'

'And yet somehow, we still ended up with all this romance.' He cocked his head. 'Maybe my game is even better than you thought.'

She laughed. 'You're such a joke.'

'Hey, you were the one who started it.' His gaze dropped to her lips. His eyes were hungry when they met hers again. 'But I'd be happy to finish it.'

'Please do.'

His lips touched hers before she'd finished, and she was drawn into the magic again. It was as if the last hour hadn't happened. As if they hadn't run; as if they hadn't been vulnerable.

Or perhaps because of it.

Whatever it was—regular magic, Christmas magic—Angie relished the feel of it. Of the power of it. Because there was power in this moment. In the fact that she'd found this in the middle of nowhere. That she'd found it at a wedding. During the festive period. With a stranger.

There was power in the fire on her skin. In her body. Power in the smoke coming from the movement of their lips; the mating of their tongues. She deepened the kiss with the realisation of it, accepting the vibration of the moan Ezra gave in response. She almost smiled. Stopped herself only because she knew smiling would have meant breaking their contact.

That was the last thing she wanted.

And then his hands were moving. The feel of them over her body, and the taste of him—oh, the *taste* of him—had her answering his moan with one of her own. Passion shuddered through her body, and her hands fell to his shoulders, her fingers pressing into him so hard she was sure she'd leave marks.

Without warning and in one swift movement, he lifted her so she was sitting on his lap.

'This is incredibly inappropriate,' she said, pulling back to stare at her legs that were now stretched in front of her. Over him.

'So, kissing me—shall we say, enthusiastically?—in public is appropriate, but not sitting on my lap?'

'None of this is appropriate.'

'Fair enough.' His hands ran up and down her waist. 'No one's noticed though.'

'Someone might.'

'You're right.' His eyes glinted. 'We should participate in the activities the other people are doing to avoid suspicion.'

'Other people—'

She broke off when his one arm slid under her thighs, his other supporting her back. And then he was standing, and walking slowly toward the edge of the pier.

'Ezra,' she said softly. Sweetly. 'What are you doing?'

'What do you think I'm doing?'

'Something I think you're going to seriously regret if you destroy my dress.'

He paused. 'So take it off.'

'Fine. Set me down.'

'You're not going to run, are you?'

'Oh, hilarious.' She rolled her eyes. 'You were the one who gave me this option. Trust me.'

He nodded, then slowly set her down. Almost as soon as he had, she loosened the ties of the wrap-around dress she wore.

He was in front of her before she'd realised he'd moved, gripping the two sides of the dress she'd opened.

'What are you doing?' she asked, trying to keep her breath steady. It was hard to do with him so close.

'As much as I want you to continue, we've caught the attention of the others.'

Angie didn't bother looking over. 'Seems like you didn't think this plan of yours through.'

'There's always Plan B,' he said, and let go of her dress so he could pick her up again.

The air left her lungs at the move—how had she not realised what that muscular body could do?—and then again at the fact that he was studiously avoiding looking down at her. It took her a moment to realise it was because her dress was still open, falling lazily over her to offer glimpses of her body.

'I'm not sure your caveman tendencies would go down well with your students,' Angie commented, holding on to him tightly as he made his way down the incline of grass on the other side of the pier.

'Yeah, well, I'm starting a new job next year. I doubt any of my new students would find out.'

'Are you nervous about it?'

'The job isn't that different, regardless of where you go.'

Angie relaxed slightly when the ground became level. 'The environments are different though. You can be sure the students at Grahamstown and those in Cape Town won't be the same.'

'That might be true, but I've never had a problem.'

'I wonder why.'

'I'm an excellent teacher, Angie.'

She thought about how patient he'd been with her as she tried to verbalise her feelings about her family. And how kind he'd been when trying to show her where she'd gone wrong. Then there was his steady strength and easy confidence. The way he thought about what she said to him, engaging with it instead of merely listening.

Oh, yes—she had no doubt he was an excellent teacher. And she knew she would have had a crush on him because of it. His body was just a bonus.

Not that she'd tell him that.

'I'm sure you're a great teacher. But that isn't the reason you haven't had any problems.' She waited as he paused and looked back to the pier. He gave a satisfied nod and put her down. 'How attentive are your students?'

'Very,' he said, pulling the shirt from his pants and undoing the buttons.

Her mouth dried. Had she forgotten a swim would mean he'd have to undress, too? How could she have?

But then it didn't matter because his shirt was open, and she was treated to ripples and indents she'd never really seen on a man in person before. He set his shirt on the ground. Lifted an eyebrow.

'Oh, I was admiring your *lecturing* abilities,' she said, somehow managing to keep the lust out of her voice. When he chuckled, goosebumps shot out on her arms.

'You're saying my class is attentive because of how I look?' He shook his head. Began to pull off his pants. 'You're forgetting the content I teach. It's riveting stuff. People are genuinely interested in the issues affecting women, particularly in adverse political climates.'

'Of course they are,' she said sarcastically. 'That's why we've created an entire field of study focusing on those issues. Because everyone is interested in it. No,' she continued, narrowing her eyes. 'You're obviously in denial. Which would be fine until you see me in your class.' At his lifted brow, she smiled. 'I'm thinking of enrolling into university again just so I can take it. You know, because I'm genuinely interested.'

He gave her a sexy smile, though she couldn't tell if it was his normal smile or not. Maybe she was just projecting the fact that he was standing in front of her in only his briefs, leaving nothing to the imagination.

And her imagination wouldn't have been able to conjure up *that*.

'Having you in my class would be a nightmare,' he said, taking a step toward her. 'I prize being ethical. Most of what I'd like to teach you wouldn't be inside of a classroom.'

She nearly stumbled back, almost all the bravado she had earlier fading. Then she realised it was only because they weren't on an equal playing field. She bent down to untie her shoes.

'What would my first lesson be?' she asked, kicking her shoes aside. 'How to get a woman to strip down to her underwear on the day you meet her?'

'Probably,' he replied, his eyes going hot when she slipped off her dress and laid it over his shirt on the ground.

She wasn't wearing anything remotely seductive, yet her black cotton bra and panties seemed to be doing the trick nevertheless. Sometimes she loved the simplicity of sexual desire.

Though there was more with the two of them, she knew. Sexual desire had been intensified by the intimacy they'd shared. The emotional stripping, which had been as effective in creating this connection, this pull between them as the physical stripping had been.

If anyone had asked, she would have told them she'd been lured by the impressive body behind his clothes. If she was being honest with herself, the temptation was just as much because of his charm, his humour, his kindness, his heart—the list surpassed even that—as his abs.

'Well then,' she said slowly, forcing herself to focus on the seduction, 'what would my second lesson involve?'

She took a step back when he moved forward.

'Even less clothing.'

'Oh,' she said, her lips curving. 'When can I sign up?'

She deliberately lowered her voice.

'Right now.'

Just as he reached for her, Angie felt the edge of the grass at her heels. Giving him wicked grin, she twisted her body so that his arms reached for air. Then she pushed his shoulder, creating enough momentum for him to fly into the water.

Chapter Seventeen

He'd realised what she'd done too late to keep himself from falling.

But not too late to not take her with him.

He grabbed her arm, and had a brief moment of satisfaction at her widened eyes before the water engulfed them. His breath left his lungs—how was the water so *cold* on such a hot night?—but he put his arms around the figure in front of him, pulling Angie in so that they could surface together.

'Why'd…you…do that?' Angie spluttered once they did.

'You mean why did I pull you into the water with me after you pushed me in?'

She gave him a sly smile. 'You looked like you needed some cooling off.'

His lips curved, and he wondered what she'd say if he told her her plan had only worked for a few minutes. The desire was already back, stronger, more potent than before. He couldn't fight it. He didn't want to. Not when the memory of her stripping in front of him was as clear in his mind as she was currently in front of him.

His hands itched to touch the breasts that had spilled over the cups of her bra. To run up and down the smooth bronze skin of her belly. To feel the curves; the bumps and fullness of her hips.

The cold water did nothing to help him regain control over his body. He was grateful that he was fully submerged this time, so that she wouldn't have to see the effect she had on him.

How that made sense, he didn't know. He wasn't ashamed of what he felt for her. He sure as hell had never been embarrassed about his body before. Yet in some illogical part of his brain, he wanted to be...more respectful with her. In another, equally illogical part, he wanted to show her how much he respected her by making love with her.

He nearly rolled his eyes at himself. It was a good thing he already knew she turned him into a contradictory, illogical mess.

'This is so far from anything I've done in my life,' she said as she treaded water.

'Swimming?'

She gave him a look, though her eyes told him she was amused. 'No. This.' The amusement changed to something more sombre. 'With you. A man I only just met.'

His heart thudded. 'Is that your way of telling me you regret it?'

Her eyes were solemn when they met his. 'No. Which is probably the real reason I'm mentioning it at all. I don't regret it. Not one single moment.'

Warmth spread though him, though there was a slight panic there, too. Because he didn't regret it either. Not the fun they'd had; not the arguments. Not even the emotional confessions that had stripped him raw and laid him over the fire, turning the heat up until he couldn't help but face the reality of what he was running from.

She did that to him. And he wanted to be happy about it. He wanted to be thrilled. But he couldn't be. Not because he didn't trust his judgement. It was exactly because he *did* trust his judgement that was the problem.

He trusted Angie.

But this day together had been a fluke. A prank the universe or whatever force was in power had played on them. It would soon be over. They'd go back to the reality of their lives in less than twenty-four hours. Where there was brokenness. And people who loved them, but didn't understand them.

He wanted to go home, but it felt almost impossible to go home and face that. Or face it without her.

'Did I say something wrong?'

'No,' he replied immediately, forcing a smile onto his face. He couldn't show her that he was worried. If he did, they wouldn't even have this moment. He desperately needed this moment. 'I was thinking that it's… strange.'

'And you regret it?'

'What?' He swam a little closer so that there was no space between them. 'No. No, I don't. Not a second of it.'

She studied him. 'Not even when you found me crying behind a tree?'

'I'm a big fan of what happened behind that tree,' he teased.

She laughed. 'I'm sure.' Her eyes softened. 'What about when I volunteered for you to be Father Christmas?'

'Not quite as enjoyable.' His arms snaked around her waist. 'But memorable. As was your portrayal of the Virgin Mary.'

She smiled, and something completely unexpected

happened inside him. His heart filled. He could some-how feel it happening, though that was nonsensical. And yet it was happening. The cracks Ana had left; the holes Liesel had poked inside him. They filled, and he knew it was because of that smile.

That smile that was a perfect mixture of her strength, her empathy. That smile that warmed his soul even as it heated his body. It gave *him* strength even though it shouldn't have. Not if he wanted to go home and face his mistakes, face the disappointment, and not have it break him. Not if he wanted to go home and accept the disappointment as a part of his family's love.

He wasn't sure he could do all that without the strength Angie gave him. He wanted to, more than he ever wanted anything else before. He didn't want to depend on a woman to live his life fully, without fear. And wasn't that what he was doing now, giving Angie this power over him?

No, he thought almost immediately. He felt stron-ger because of her, yes, but she helped him to realise he could do it on his own. He'd realised the things that would help him to do it.

The real problem was that he wanted *her*. It was that plain, that simple. It had nothing to do with him going home. Or with what he'd face at home. It had every-thing to do with the falling. That after a day in her pres-ence, he knew he was falling, and could only imagine what another day—a week, a month, a year—would do.

He didn't want to have to imagine. He wanted to live it.

He didn't want to say goodbye.

His free hand lifted, almost of its own accord, and wiped the wet hair from her forehead. He replaced his fingers with his lips. It was surprisingly tender. To both him and her, he saw. This time, he very deliberately moved his mouth to hers. Found them already parted, waiting for him. *An invitation,* he thought, when she gave him a slight nod.

So he answered.

Her lips were soft, as was the sigh that left them before they were completely covered by his. The water sizzled around them, as if they'd put a hot pan into cold water. In some ways, he supposed they had.

What else could he have called the heat coming from the merging of their lips? What else could he have thought as his arm tightened at her waist, bringing her half-naked body against him, and feeling the fire of it ignite inside him?

All he knew was that it wasn't enough. She wasn't close enough. He couldn't feel enough. In answer, his hands slid over the curves he'd admired earlier, cupping her butt to bring her closer even as she hooked her legs around his waist.

He could have very well died in that moment; he would have died a happy man.

Or perhaps he *had* died. And if so, he'd gone to hell. Because it suddenly felt as if the night had turned into the hottest day. Or perhaps they'd merely been sucked into the core of the stars that shone down on them. Or perhaps he was just losing his mind.

His body.

His heart.

He didn't care. Not when losing felt this good. Not when being lost felt this good. Because that was what he was. Lost—so completely lost—in her kiss. In the sweetness of it, the passion. In the way her hands scorched his skin as they roamed over his body. In the fact that he could barely feel the cold water around them as they did.

Somehow his feet kept them afloat. Somehow it felt as if there were no other movements besides their bodies pressed together, her hips slowly rocking against his, his hands squeezing her butt, bringing her tighter against him, intensifying the pleasure shuddering through his body.

Though he wasn't sure how that was possible.

It didn't stop him from unclasping the back of her bra. She moaned into his mouth, sending vibrations through his entire body that somehow settled in his groin. He threw her bra onto the embankment, shifting his hands so that one held her more steadily while the other rose to cover her breast.

It felt as if the air around him had stilled. He pulled back, his eyes lowering to the full roundness of it in his hand. Tentatively, he squeezed. Heard the shudder from her lips as his hand kneaded. As his thumb brushed over the peak of her nipple.

He repeated the motion; groaned when her hips slowed to match the rhythm of it. He lifted his eyes, saw the heat in hers—the heady passion, the intimate surrender—and something inside him stopped. How, he wasn't sure, since everything inside him felt as if it were spinning, jumping, racing.

Except for that one part.

And in that part he felt a…reverence of some kind. For her. For what they were doing. For the fact that he was doing it with her. He hadn't kept falling, like he thought he would. Nor had he landed in quicksand. His feet were firmly on the ground. And he was walking toward her.

He'd always walk toward her.

His head lowered to her breast; his tongue gently swirling around the peak his thumb had abandoned. She gasped, her hands holding either side of his head. Ezra knew this moment would be imprinted in his brain forever. The rounded curve of her butt in his one hand; the soft mound of her breast in his other as he angled it for his mouth. The taste of her, the *feel* of her.

His head lifted and he nipped at her lips, wanting to add it to the memory. But then she gasped again, into his mouth, and he pulled back, following her eyes and seeing the movement that had distracted her.

He immediately let go of her, twisting his body so that he could shield her from view. He sagged with relief when he saw it was only some ducks making their way down the embankment into the water. The distraction pulled him from the haze of pleasure he'd been in, and he nearly winced when he turned back and saw the expression on Angie's face.

'Are you okay?'

'Of course.' Her voice shook. 'After all, you've just protected my womanhood from those birds who were clearly voyeurs.'

She offered him a wry smile; it hadn't changed the unsteadiness of her voice. Or that she was moving away from him. She stopped only when there was enough distance that neither of them could reach out and touch the other.

'Ange—'

'Could you…' Her voice went hoarse, and she cleared her throat. 'Could you please hand me my bra?'

Disappointment stole his breath, but he made his way to the embankment. He pulled himself up and turned around to give her privacy after he handed her the bra. It was foolish to be disappointed, he told himself. It wasn't like things could have gone any further than they had.

Want to bet?

He almost grunted at the thought, feeling like a complete ass as he did. What would he have done? Made love with her in a river? In a public place? Without knowing her for more than a day? Without having protection on him?

The answers made him ill, and he kept his back turned to Angie for longer than he needed to. Kept himself from offering her help, too, when he heard a sound that indicated she was pulling herself out of the river. She wouldn't have accepted his help. He wasn't sure how he knew, but he did.

Which was part of the reason he found himself in this…predicament. He knew Angie better than most people in his life. She knew him, too. She turned him into someone he didn't recognise. Someone who wanted to make love in a river—the lack of hygiene, for heaven's sake!—with someone he'd only met that day.

He shook his head, hoping the memories and the reverence that accompanied them would disappear as he did. Once he was sure he had a control over his emotions, he turned back to Angie. She'd replaced her bra, but not her clothing. Her arms lifted, but then she snapped them back at her sides and straightened her shoulders. She wanted to cover herself, but had stopped, he realised. If not for the colour that flared on her cheeks, he wouldn't have known she was uncomfortable.

Damn if that didn't make him respect her even more.

'I can't put my dress on while I'm wet, so I'm going to—' she cleared her throat again '—I'm just going to wait here until I'm not. You can go ahead.'

'Okay.'

He stayed where he was, his eyes on her face. He wouldn't look at her body. Not when he knew she wanted to cover herself. But he couldn't resist looking at her face.

'Ezra, I said you can go.'

'I know.'

'Why aren't you leaving then?' Her voice was sharp.

'I'm not going to leave you alone in the dark.'

'It'll be f—'

'—in a place we both don't know—'

'—honestly, I'll be fi—'

'—half naked.'

He almost winced at the sharpness in his own voice, but with each sentence, she'd angered him. He realised he was probably projecting his emotions; he couldn't bring himself to care.

'Nothing will happen to me,' she said finally, flatly, into the silence that had stretched between them.

'No,' he agreed. 'I won't let it.'

'Oh, for heaven's sake.'

'I'm not leaving you alone here.' His tone was harsh. He forced himself to soften it when he continued. 'Look, I know part of the reason you're sending me away is because you want space. I'll give you some. I'll go and sit on the other side of the pier if that's what you want. But please, don't ask me to leave you here.'

She didn't reply, and he sighed.

'Do you want to go up now then?' he asked. 'We can get you a change of clothing from your car.'

'I'm basically naked.'

As if he didn't know it.

'You can wear my shirt.' He handed her the shirt and

pulled on his pants before looking at her again. 'What's your decision?'

'We can go up. I'll wear the shirt.' She paused. 'Thank you.'

He nodded. Turned away again as she put on the shirt. It seemed like a futile gesture. Hadn't he had her breast in his mouth minutes ago? But she seemed to want privacy. He'd give it to her. Even though it was futile. The picture of her body was forever seared in his brain.

On the upside, it gave him a chance to ignore his emotions.

Except that they wouldn't sit back and obey his determination not to pay attention to them. No, as he and Angie made their way back to the lodge, his feelings sprung up and down in his head. They waved their arms around, demanding he pay them heed.

Of course, when he did, he realised how terrible he felt about the entire situation. About beginning the flirtation that had led them into that water. About leaning into the pleasure of it when he wasn't sure she wanted it.

That's what he felt now. Because of her reaction now. It was so far from the woman who'd moaned and writhed in his arms. Who'd eagerly kissed him and encouraged their seduction. Which made him wonder if that woman had existed at all.

Had he pretended she existed for the sake of his own pleasure? Had he pushed her into doing something that hadn't made her feel comfortable? Something she wasn't ready for?

A deep, crushing feeling overwhelmed him. Emotion thickened in his throat. He wanted to apologise, but apologising would be an admission that he'd acted like a complete asshole. And the fact that he was resisting the admission of *being* a complete asshole told him that Angie deserved an apology.

'Ezra?' Angie's soft voice interrupted his thoughts.

'What?'

'I asked if it was okay if I took a shower in your room.'

'Of course,' he replied. Then frowned. 'It's your room for tonight, too. You don't have to ask me.'

'Except that I do.' She pulled at the edge of the shirt with her free hand. 'I don't think it's such a good idea to stay with you tonight.'

Ezra groaned, shaking his head. 'I'm so sorry, Angie. This is—I'm so sorry.'

'For what?'

'I didn't mean to push you back there. I didn't mean for you—' He broke off, and then took a deep breath. He couldn't be a coward. Not with this. 'I'm sorry for making you feel unsafe.'

Chapter Eighteen

'What are you talking about?'

'What we did back there...'

He trailed off, his face twisted in anguish. It had her fingers itching to smooth the lines away. To kiss the furrow between his eyebrows. It had nothing on what happened to her heart when his eyes met hers.

'I'm sorry if you felt like I forced you.'

'Forced...' It took her a few minutes to process before the pieces clicked. 'No, Ezra. No,' she said again, shaking her head so vehemently she saw water flying on either side of her body. 'You didn't force me into anything.'

She pressed the heel of her hand over her eye socket, then shook her head again, though it was much gentler this time.

'I'm sorry I made you think that. I... It's not... This wasn't about me feeling unsafe. I don't feel unsafe around you.' She took a step closer but stopped herself before she could embrace him like she wanted to. That's what had got her into trouble in the first place. 'I probably feel safer than I ever have around you.' She swallowed when the words sent a thick lump of emotion into her throat. 'What happened back there... What almost happened... I wanted it, too.'

'You don't have to say that.'

'I'm not just saying it. I mean it. I was a willing participant. You did nothing wrong.'

She couldn't resist lifting a hand to cup his cheek. They stood like that for a moment, and then she heard laughter in the distance and she remembered where she was. What she was wearing. She looked down at his shirt that was now wet at her chest, displaying her black underwear.

'Obviously, we have to talk. But not here. Like this.' She gestured down to herself. When she looked back at him, he was watching her with careful eyes. It killed her. 'Unless you're still under the impression that you forced me into something, in which case I will stand here like this for as long as it takes for me to convince you otherwise.'

'We can go up.'

'Ezra.'

'It's fine, honestly.'

She stared at him. 'Is this how annoying I was back there? When I didn't want you to stay with me?'

His lips twitched. 'Possibly.'

'Probably.' She paused. Tried again. 'I understand that my reaction was…confusing back there. It wasn't because of you. Or it was, but not, you know, because I felt coerced in any way. I didn't. Absolutely not. And if I had, there would have been less of, you know.' She made a vague hip-circle gesture, avoiding his eyes when it made her blush.

He didn't reply to her words. When she turned back to him, he quirked a brow. 'I'm not sure I know what you were referring to.'

'Of course you know,' she snapped, more out of embarrassment than anger. But he grinned at her, and she wasn't so sure it wasn't anger. 'You're not as amusing as you think you are,' she told him.

'That's a certainty.'

He smiled at her. She didn't find it as seductive as she had his other smiles. She didn't think it was because it was any different. She thought it was because *she* was different. That they were. Because of it, she thought his smile was a little reserved and a lot more careful. It broke her heart that this was the result of her hesitance earlier.

The realisation of it sat in her throat, and she nodded when he told her they could go back to the lodge. Followed him as he led the way. It wasn't too far away, and she doubted people were paying attention to her anyway. It was that point in the party where people were either too drunk to notice anything they weren't directly confronted with, or too busy dancing to the music in the hall.

It didn't keep the relief away when they arrived at his cabin though. Nor did it keep her from clearing her throat. The emotion still sat there, unfortunately, but her voice was steady enough to ask Ezra if he could fetch her suitcase in the car.

'Any specific one?'

'Yeah, the small one on the back seat.'

He threw on a T-shirt that had been on his bed and took the keys she offered him. When he left the room, she took it in. It was very much a wooden cabin on the inside, large and spacious, clearly decorated with the winter months in mind. But still, there was an air-conditioning unit above the fireplace, a gorgeous canopy bed in the middle of the room, and a two-seater couch below the window with Ezra's bag on it.

Before she could do anything else, she heard the

click of the door as Ezra brought in her own bag. She murmured her thanks and took the suitcase with her into the bathroom. Mechanically, she locked the door, threw off the shirt and her underwear, and stepped into the shower.

She made it under the stream of water just as a sob escaped. She squeezed her eyes shut. It had come out of nowhere, the sound, the urge, and she'd be damned if she gave it free rein. But of course, pure will could only help her keep at bay for so long. She braced her hands against the shower wall, pursed her lips, but couldn't keep the tears from streaming down her cheeks.

Of course her mind wouldn't allow her to cry in peace. Nor would it allow her to delude herself into thinking that the crying had come from nowhere. She knew the urge had started the moment she and Ezra had been interrupted by that paddling of ducks.

When she realised how deeply she was falling for him.

When she realised she didn't want to say goodbye to him.

When she realised she had no choice.

She couldn't fall in love now. She didn't have her life in order. Hell, she'd realised only that day that the version of herself she'd been running from had already existed. She'd been shaped by her father's life. Now, she was shaped by the fact that he was no longer there. Wasn't that a form of dependence? Having her father dictate, even if it was indirectly, the way she lived?

Realising that was heart-wrenching. It had just as much of an impact on her emotions as the grief did. It was such a clear sign that she'd been broken even before the grief, too. Which made these feelings she had for Ezra even worse.

How could she trust them? How could she trust that they weren't those broken pieces inside her, looking for another person to depend on now that her father wasn't there anymore? What if those pieces were like magnets, searching for—and recognising, with Ezra—another magnet to be attracted to?

None of these fears even touched what she'd be going home to with her family. How could she explain that she'd been developing feelings for someone when they didn't even know she was in the country? She wasn't sure she'd be able to let go of the guilt of that simple fact, let alone the fact that she'd left at all.

She'd been right when she'd thought right at the beginning, right when she'd met Ezra, that there was no space for romance in her life. Where would she fit it in? While she was trying to be responsible for her family again? While she was trying to help them in any way she could to make up for leaving them?

Or would she wait until she had to tell them she was leaving again?

That last question had emotion rising in her body, threatening to drown her. The grief lapping at her heels, egging on the guilt and shame that had been her constant companions, even when she'd refused to acknowledge them.

She couldn't add romantic feelings into that. She couldn't take something so beautiful, so special and add it into the mess her life had become.

Because it was special. It was beautiful. It made her want to throw herself into Ezra's arms. She wanted to sink into the specialness, the beauty of it. Of him. She wasn't talking about his body, though her mind offered the memory of it to torture her. To add to the burden. She knew it because it didn't offer her only the memory of the image of his body—the rifts of it that looked as if someone had deliberately and loving carved each of them—but the feel of it.

Against hers. Pressed until there was no space between them. Until she could feel the ridges under the softness of her own body.

How he used it to pleasure her. The way his hands kneaded and squeezed the fullness of her. How he angled his body to shield her when he thought someone had caught them. The way his mouth showed her what those damn rats had felt when the Pied Piper had played his tune…

Torture, she thought again, and something akin to a whimper passed through her lips.

She straightened then, the sound reminding her too much of someone who was helpless. She might have been a mess, and a little broken, but she was *not* helpless. She was strong. She could do this. She could walk away from him. From them.

The thought sent pain washing through her even as the memories rained down on her. The way they'd spoken at his table. How he'd offered to help her. The honest conversations. Their foray into the Christmas parade. The wedding. The nativity play. His laughter after. Their dancing. His smile. His kiss.

Him, him, him.

And that was the terrifying part. Her feelings for him didn't leave any room for uncertainty. They demanded more. They deserved more. And if she paid any attention to her feelings, that more would cause her to stay in Cape Town. To live her life there.

Wasn't that exactly what Ezra had done with Liesel? Hadn't he moved his entire life to a different place to be with her? Look how that had turned out for him.

Coward.

No, she denied. She wasn't a coward. She simply knew that considering—*considering*—doing this because of her feelings for him was disturbing. It leaned a little too far in the direction of her mother, threatening Angie's tenuous grasp on her independence.

So maybe she was being a coward.

She ignored that thought and took a few deep breaths before making quick work of the rest of the shower. When she was done, she put on yoga pants and a loose T-shirt. She pulled her wet curls into a pineapple on top of her head, telling herself she'd deal with it later.

If she'd been in her right mind, she would have made more effort with her appearance. But she wasn't. Even if she had been, she was too tired for the effort. She consoled herself with the thought that she shouldn't be focusing on making herself attractive. She and Ezra didn't need any more incentive to pick up where they left off in that river.

Except that when she walked out, she realised it didn't matter what she wore. Because there was something between her and Ezra that would always be an incentive. A connection, a pull, some kind of Christmas magic that would always leave that hunger, that need on Ezra's face. That would cause that hunger, that need, to reflect in her own body. As would the emotion. As would the determination to be unaffected by it all.

What a hopeless pursuit. They would never be unaffected; they'd never even be able to pretend that they were. Which was why she opened her mouth to say something, but he'd already walked into the bathroom with a pile of his own clothing before she was able to formulate the words.

She sat on the bed. Moved to the couch when that felt

too intimate. A voice inside her asked why she didn't leave. Why she didn't climb into her car and drive away. But before she'd even fully processed the thought—or the logistics of it, considering her route home was still blocked—she realised she had no desire to hurt him.

She couldn't leave while he was showering. That would be the easy option. Which would eventually end up being the worse option. Because she'd done it before, hadn't she? She'd left before when she'd thought it would be easier. It had taken coming back now to re-alise how much harder she'd made it for herself.

She might not have been as completely independent, as completely unbroken, as she thought she was, but Ezra was right. She did learn from her mistakes.

At least she would learn from this one.

She curled her legs underneath her body, chewing on her nails as she waited for him to finish in the bathroom.

A few minutes later, he emerged in a cloud of steam. She stupidly thought it reminded her of a movie. He was the action star, and she was the woman helpless against falling for him. There was no way she'd be a damsel in distress. Even in her current state of mind, she'd kick ass.

He wore a T-shirt and tracksuit pants, and still, he managed to look as good as he had in his shirt and jeans. Possibly more now since the casual look contrasted so strikingly with his face. She would always think it was the kind of face that belonged to men in ad campaigns. The casual look he wore now made that fact—and how handsome he was—even clearer.

Her heart throbbed, a mixture of anticipation and disappointment. Despite all of the reasons why she shouldn't, she still wanted him. And knowing that she couldn't have him was as torturous as her attraction to him was.

His eyes flickered over her before he reached for the remote to turn the aircon on. Then he settled on the bed, directly opposite her. There was a long moment of silence before she managed to say, 'I'm sorry.'

'What are you apologising for?'

'What happened outside.'

'You don't have to.'

'I do.' She paused. 'I made you think that I didn't want you.' She lifted her eyes to his. 'You know that isn't it, right?'

'I'm not sure that I do,' he said after a moment. 'Things were pretty weird.'

'Yeah,' she agreed lamely. Because the description was apt. Things had become weird quickly, and she was the reason for it. 'I stopped us back there because if I didn't after we were interrupted, I… I don't think I would have.'

'That's a problem?'

'We both know it is.' She sucked in a breath. Hoped he'd understand that they couldn't entertain whatever was happening between them when they were going home to face their issues. 'We're making things awfully complicated for ourselves. For when the spell ends.'

'Why does it have to end?'

'Ezra—'

'I'm serious,' he interrupted. 'Why does it have to end? We're going back to the same place.'

'Because—' *you might end up being another crutch for me* '—I'm not staying in that place. I can't. I've told you that.'

'I thought you'd change your mind.'

'You thought…'

She trailed off when it made her head spin. Had she given him the impression she was staying? Did she somehow reveal her desire to depend on him?

Or was he just thinking what she'd thought? That she *could* stay. For him. With him.

But when she'd thought it, she'd instantly dismissed it. As she studied him, she realised that he didn't see why he should have, too.

'So,' she said after a moment, 'you thought I'd change my mind about staying. Who would I be staying for?'

There was a beat before he said, 'Us.'

A pang went through her chest as she thought about how much she wanted there to be an 'us,' but she nodded.

'Right. You didn't see anything wrong with that logic?' He didn't answer her question. She pushed more. 'You don't think staying for the sake of us when we've only known each other for a day is premature?'

'Things aren't normal between us.' His voice was tight. 'We both know it. We're living it right now.'

'Fine. Say I agree with you.' She paused. 'I do agree with you.' She could give him that. She could give them both that. 'You don't see any similarities between this conversation and the one you had with Liesel at some point in your relationship?'

His eyes widened, and in them she saw him processing her words. Realising the truth of them. Wanting to deny it but being unable to.

She hated that she'd done it to him, but she had to. He'd romanticised the idea of them to the point that it had obscured the truth. There was no future for them. He wasn't ready to be in a relationship. Neither was she.

And okay, yes, she'd done it because she'd seen similarities, too. Between how desperate they were to turn this into something and how desperately in love her parents had been. It wasn't strictly the same, but she knew how it went. How desperation turned into dependence. How dependence would complete her transformation into her mother.

Into relying on someone other than herself.

She'd already slipped into it without realising it. Having Ezra around would only make her desire to get out of it harder.

So she'd been blunt. It felt as if she'd stabbed him with a blunt knife; now she was watching the blood drip down his chest onto the floor.

'I'm sorry,' she said when all she could see was the blood. 'I know you don't want to think about it again. But I wanted to make you see that—'

'You don't have to apologise for being honest with me,' he interrupted. A beat later, he said, 'You don't have to apologise for being right.'

'Don't I?'

'No.' He lifted his eyes to hers. 'I did have that conversation with Liesel. In it, she told me I had a choice. Either go with her, or stay behind without her.' He paused. 'She was pretty clear about what without her entailed.'

'I... I didn't realise.'

'How could you have?'

'Still, I shouldn't have—'

'Angie,' he interrupted, and the courage she'd had for a brief moment—the courage that would have allowed her to tell him that what she'd said hadn't been entirely for his sake—vanished. 'Stop. Right until now, I hadn't thought about Liesel's words as an ultimatum. Which was probably why I didn't see the similarities between that and this.' He cocked his head. 'Well, that, and the fact that you and she have very little in common.'

'Thank you.'

His eyes widened and he laughed. 'How do you know I meant that as a compliment?'

'Because you haven't kicked me out of the room yet?' she asked wryly.

'True.' He leaned forward, rested his forearms on his thighs, then he shook his head. 'I did mean it in a positive way. You and she… You're different. I'm a different person when I'm with you.'

'In a good way?'

'Yes.'

His hand twitched, and she thought he might have wanted to take her hand. She tried not to feel hurt by the fact that he didn't. She'd put this distance between them after all. She'd reinforced it with all her logical observations. She had no right to be hurt by her emotional observations.

'I also wasn't giving you any kind of ultimatum,' Ezra continued. 'I was exploring a possibility. A viable one.'

'It's not though.' She released the air in her lungs. Sucked in some more. 'I can't stay here.'

'You can, Ange,' he said gently. 'You don't want to.' He continued before she could respond. 'Which is fine.'

'Is it?' she asked tightly. 'Because it feels like you don't believe it.'

'No, I think *you* don't believe it.' When she only looked at him, he sighed. 'I'm not going to pretend like I don't want you to stay. And I'm going to tell you that your family probably wants you to, too, but not because I want it to sway you. I just want you to—' He broke off on an exhale. 'Just be conscious of what you're choosing. Be, I don't know, active in the choice. You're in control of what you want to do. No one is keeping you from doing it, whatever it is.'

She felt it resonate within her, those words. Heard her own intake of air at the realisation. At the fact that she'd been choosing to live her life in such a mess almost without her knowing it.

She'd chosen to look after her sisters and support her mother. She'd chosen to become dependent on her father. First, during his life; now, because of his legacy. Being subservient to what she believed her family wanted from her was a choice. It was hard to accept that she didn't have to choose that life. She just…had.

It unsettled her. Made her restless. Because of it, she stood. Or maybe she stood because she wanted to choose something that made her life feel like her own again. She offered Ezra her hand.

'How about we go outside one last time before bed?'

He stared at her, but stood and took her hand. Questions spun in his head; they didn't matter. Angie could have told him she wanted to make love outside in the trees and he would have gone with her.

Not that that was as outlandish as he'd meant for it to be.

His body tightened merely at the thought of it. He nearly lost his breath when she opened the cabin door and his mind entertained that possibility again. It didn't take long for him to realise he was being an idiot, letting a body part other than his brain think for him. Slowly, the blood returned to his head.

When it did, he realised she'd taken the key of the cabin, locked the door behind them and was leading him to the back of the cabin.

'So you *are* planning on murdering me, after all. Ah, well, we had a good run.'

She snorted. 'Still on that, are you?' There was a pause. 'Why would I take you outside to murder you, Ez? I had the perfect opportunity in the lodge.'

'Less clean up?'

'Fair point. I'm pretty sure people have seen me take you to the back of this cabin though. I wouldn't have to clean up at all in that case.' She stopped. 'I'd leave your murdered body as is and accept my punishment.'

He narrowed his eyes. 'You're scary.'

'I know.' She smiled sweetly. 'Fortunately, I have no plans to murder you. I just wanted to be outside away from the party goers.'

'You mean you wanted privacy to kill me.'

'You realise that if anyone's listening to this conversation, it would incriminate me for a crime I didn't commit?'

'I do realise that.'

Her eyes turned to slits. 'You better not turn up dead in the morning, Doctor.'

He smiled. 'I'll try my best. So, if you didn't bring me out here for murder, what then?'

'I told you. I wanted to be outside.'

'We could have gone somewhere else. Somewhere better than…this.'

The main path they'd taken had split off into narrower pathways made of small brown rocks that led directly to the cabins' front doors. The narrow pathways, in turn, enclosed a large open patch of grass. Trees stood between the cabins, towering over parts of the pathway, though they didn't reach the grass where he and Angie were currently standing. Because of it, they had a clear view of the stars twinkling above them.

He supposed it wasn't the worst place to be. Plus, it was relatively quiet. Either the guests had already gone to sleep or they were still partying. Music sounded far in the distance, so he thought the latter. Still, he would have preferred something better for their last night together.

Angie was speaking before the pang of that thought could reach his heart.

'You're right. There probably is a better place.'

She stepped forward and he held his breath when she didn't stop until she was right in front of him. He slowly let it out when she put her hands around his waist, which no doubt made him look like an idiot. But he couldn't *not* breathe with her so close. Especially not when he wanted to inhale what the lemon body wash they'd used in the cabin had done to her scent.

He wasn't disappointed, though his mind quickly ignored how intoxicating she smelled and instead, focused on the fact that she was staring up at him expectantly.

He blinked. 'Did I miss something?'

'No. I mean, I was wondering whether you were going to put your arms around me, too. Granted, it *is* a bit presumptuous of me to hold you like this, but I didn't think you'd mind.'

'I don't,' he blurted out, and she smiled. He was acting like a fool; he didn't care. He put his arms around her, drawing her in closer.

'See, this is why I wanted to come here.'

'Why?'

'Can't you hear it?' she asked softly and began to sway with him. As she did, he listened to the faint music of the song that was playing. It was fast, not suited to what they were doing at all.

'I know,' she said when he opened his mouth. 'I was

hoping they'd slow it down to something more romantic—it *is* a wedding—but I guess we're out of luck.'

'Doesn't matter.'

'No.' Her eyes softened. 'It doesn't, does it?'

She lay her head on his chest, and they kept moving like that, despite the fact that they could barely hear the music. Perhaps that was a good thing, he thought with a smile, resting his head on top of hers. Now, at least, they could pretend the music was appropriate for their dancing.

What did it matter anyway? How could anything besides this matter? That they were standing here, together, in each other's arms. That they were present in this moment. That they didn't have to think about the what-ifs of tomorrow. That they didn't have to think about anything other than right now.

He tried to memorise it. The feel of her, the smell of her. He tried to memorise the song that was playing, and where they were standing. As the song ended, he realised that they were both barefoot. The grass was damp from the evening air, and they both looked as if they'd just stumbled out of bed.

'This is ridiculous,' he said, drawing back from her. 'You brought me out here without shoes.'

She blinked, looked down at her own feet, at his, and grinned. 'So I did. I barely noticed.' There was a pause. 'You must not have either, or you would have said something sooner.'

'Guilty.' A new song began to play. For some reason, it sounded louder. He frowned. 'You can hear that, too, right?'

She wrinkled her nose. 'I think it means we're at the portion of the evening where people need to turn up the music to keep the party going.'

After a brief moment, the beat began to play. It was a popular summer song that could be heard on almost every radio station, with a beat that begged to be danced to.

'Do you know how to salsa?'

She frowned. 'No. But I'm pretty sure you don't either.'

'Then you underestimate me. Again.' He shook his head. 'I'm disappointed.'

He went through the basic steps slowly, giving her a moment to join in. She didn't. She just stared at him. Realising she was surprised—really, when was she going to learn?—he bit back a grin and moved faster, including a hip movement he knew was better suited to the *kwaito* he'd been doing earlier.

Her eyes widened, and for a moment, he thought she'd stopped breathing. And then she laughed. Loudly, and he felt…refreshed. As if he'd spent the entire day doing physical labour and had just had a shower and settled down with an ice-cold beer.

Which made him want to continue the ludicrousness of what he was doing, and he did. She doubled over with laughter, her head tilted up to watch him, tears running down her face.

'Stop,' she said after what felt like forever. 'Please, stop. I can't keep laughing like this.' She straightened, wiped at the tears. 'Where did you learn how to do that?'

He took a couple of deep breaths before he answered.

'My sister needed a partner for some of her dance classes. She did it for fun and asked me to go with her.'

'You went to dance classes for *that*?'

The thought inspired a fresh bout of giggles. He waited for her to stop with a faint smile. When she was done, he said, 'Not quite that, but clearly you weren't interested in what I did learn in dance class.'

'I'm sorry, it was surprising.' She cleared her throat. 'Okay, okay, teach me, Master. I'm ready to learn.'

'Are you sure?' he asked dryly.

She lifted her hands in mock surrender, nodding at him. Resisting the smile, he began to show her the steps, and for what was left of the song, that's what they did. They didn't have very long, but they didn't need it— she was a fast learner. She fell into the rhythm of the dance quickly, moving her hips, her shoulders, too. By the time the song had ended, she'd got the gist of it.

'Do you think it would be weird to ask them to play it again?'

'Probably, considering how we look. And the fact that we're not there.' He grinned. 'But we already know we can dance however we like even if the beat isn't suitable,' he said when her face fell. 'Come on.'

As they danced, as they laughed, Ezra told himself to memorise this, too. Because when she went home the next day—his heart burned thinking of it—he wanted to think of them like this. Happy, free. And hopeful, he thought, dipping her, and relishing the laugh she gave for his efforts.

The smile that split across his face was the version of himself he wanted to remember, too. Not someone with a broken heart. Or someone fearful of moving forward again because of that broken heart.

He didn't want to be defined by his past mistakes. By his fear of disappointing his parents. Not anymore. It was time to move on. And maybe that had been the point of this day. This beautiful, magical rollercoaster of a day where he'd faced his broken heart and survived. Where his stupid gamble to come to his students' wedding despite his initial cowardice had paid off. Where he'd got to enjoy Christmas in its entirety. Where he'd felt part of a community as he did.

There was also the Christmas miracle in front of him. The woman he could have sworn he knew for more than one day. The woman who had quite frankly changed his life.

He stilled at the thought of it, and she stopped, too, out of breath.

'What? What is it?'

'Nothing,' he lied, heart aching. 'I'm just... I'm really glad I met you, Angie.'

'I'm glad I met you.'

There was a long pause where he thought they were both thinking about the next day.

'Do you know what I realised?' she said, frowning.

'What?'

'That since we've come here to this little spot, I haven't once thought about what I was going back to.'

'I guess I was doing my job properly then,' he said.

'No,' she replied, a bit dazed. He didn't think she was responding to him. 'No, Ezra, I don't think you realise...' Her eyes, wide with surprise, met his. 'I spent most of the past three years avoiding thinking about my family. About my mother, my sisters. About my dad.' She paused. 'Most of the time I was so aware that I was trying not to think about them. It took literal strength not to think about them. So this moment? And earlier, in the river? These moments are...' Her eyes fluttered up to his. 'They're miracles.'

He didn't reply immediately, recognising that it had taken a lot from her to say it. It had probably taken a lot from her to realise it, too.

'Would you,' he started slowly when the silence extended, and he thought she might need help climbing out of the depths of her thoughts, 'classify them as *Christmas* miracles?'

She rolled her eyes, but her lips curved. 'Fine. Yes. Christmas miracles. Because of you.' She pinned him with her gaze, speaking in a shaky voice. 'This is special, isn't it?'

He nodded. But instead of replying, he reached out a hand. 'How about we get some sleep?'

After a moment, she nodded and took his hand, gripping it so tightly he thought he must have lost circulation. He didn't mind it. Not when he understood it; when he was trying to hold on to it, to them, too.

When they reached the cabin, he took the keys from her hand and opened the door. And when they were safely inside, he lowered his head and kissed her.

She made some kind of sound—a sigh, a moan, he wasn't sure. Except he felt it go through him. Felt the emotion of it fill him. Because there was emotion, he thought, his hands running up and down her body, relishing the softness of her. Memorising the curves of her. There was emotion because this was a goodbye.

He didn't know how he knew it. Didn't know whether she felt it, too. It didn't matter.

He let himself fall into it. Let her know that she'd done something to him. Their mouths took, their hands feasted, but that was all there was. That was all there could be.

Somehow he knew that if they went further than this, he wouldn't survive it. Knew that she knew it, too, when she made no move to take things further. When they finally came up for air—when their eyes met, and with trembling lips, they smiled at one another—Ezra knew he'd remember it, *her*, forever.

In one quick movement, he leaned forward and scooped her into his arms, carrying her to the bed.

'This isn't our wedding night, you know,' she said in a shaky voice.

'Yeah,' he agreed quietly. He lowered her to the bed, then joined her on his side, fine with only their hands touching as they threaded their fingers together. 'But this is probably the only night you and I will ever spend together. This is how I want to remember it. With you, on this bed, holding hands.'

'Could you…could you hold me instead?'

His heart stuttered and he nodded, opening his arms to her and wrapping them around her when she shifted against him. He pressed a kiss into her hair, and reached for the switch that controlled the light from the bed. They stayed like that until Ezra heard her breathing deepen, steady. After still, he stayed, and let himself grieve.

It came in the form of a dull panic that crept under his insistence that he'd be fine when she left. A panic that taunted him for falling so deeply. For falling at all.

And yet the feelings he had for Angie were deeper than anything he'd felt for Liesel. Or for Ana. He could see those feelings for what they were now: his mind convincing his heart of something. But now his heart was trying to convince his mind of this, and the feeling was so distinct that he had no choice but to acknowledge it.

The acknowledgement pained him. Stayed with him until finally he closed his eyes in exhaustion.

Chapter Nineteen

It was better this way, Angie told herself as she rounded the steep mountain road of Sir Lowry's Pass. She slipped out of bed that morning, needing to get some fresh air. Ezra hadn't stirred beside her—nor was he awake after she took care of business in the bathroom—and she'd taken a lazy walk by herself.

When she passed her hired car, she had an idea: she could…leave. She hadn't been proud of the idea, but she couldn't stop thinking about it. Even though it would be no different to leaving him when he'd been showering the night before. Even though it would be no different to what she'd done to her mother and sisters.

Somehow though, it felt different. As if being aware of what she was doing made it different. As if choosing it made it different. But it was also because of their night, which had ended on such a heartbreakingly romantic note. She felt as though it gave her permission to run. So when she got back to the cabin and Ezra was still sprawled out on his stomach, his face turned away from the door, it felt like a sign. One that turned her stomach, but she knew was necessary.

She packed her bag as quietly as she could, put on her shoes, and left. Though she hadn't been able to resist turning back once last time when she reached the door before she did.

Ezra was still asleep, still turned away from her, and there was a part of her that prayed—that had actually prayed—he'd turn over so she could see his face one last time. But he hadn't, and she couldn't face going to the other side of the bed. She couldn't risk him waking up and witnessing her cowardice.

She hesitated though. Of course she had. But seconds later she left the cabin and climbed into her car. Now she was on the road, driving away from the lodge in the little town that had changed her life.

It was for the best, she told herself again. She ignored the voice that questioned how many times she'd have to repeat it before she could actually believe it. Instead, she focused on the truth of it. It *was* for the best. Saying goodbye to Ezra would have killed her.

It nearly had the night before.

Their kiss had felt so intimate. It had seared itself into her memory—into her very soul.

Because when they'd kissed last night, she'd poured all the things she couldn't say into it. She poured the *I want to stays* into it; the *I'd miss yous,* too. She'd known what he'd been trying to tell her through the kiss, too. Because of it, the pairing of their lips had moved beyond the physical, the sexual. It had ventured into emotional territory she thought had been torched after her father died.

She stilled, and very slowly tested the word in her head. *Died.* And then the phrase. *My father is dead.* Pain swept through her, stealing her breath. For the next ten minutes she focused on breathing in and out. Focused on keeping her eyes on the road.

When the pain subsided, it felt like a victory. Though

what she won, she didn't know. It hadn't left completely, the pain. She was beginning to think it never would. But this was the first time since her father's death that she'd allowed herself to think of him in that way. As dead. Not passed away, or no longer there. *Dead.* It meant something, she knew. She couldn't deny that that something had to do with Ezra.

Nor could she deny that the fact that she'd slept— really, truly slept—for the first time in years had something to do with him, too. There hadn't been that flutter of anticipation in her chest, tickling her throat, waking her up in panic. There hadn't even been the dreams, the result of the unease that lived in her subconscious.

For the briefest of moments when she woke up, she'd forgotten the pain that she carried with her as though it were a part of her body. She'd been able to breathe easily. And then Ezra had stirred beside her and reality had caught up with her.

Just like now, she thought, the anticipation, the panic, the unease returning. She was going home. She was going to face her sisters, her mother for the first time in years. She was going to have to deal with Sophia's resentment and Zoey's disappointment. She was going to have to deal with her mother and whatever emotions Charlene needed help with.

But there was more to it, too, she realised, as a fresh wave of panic washed through her.

She'd realised she had power and the ability to decide what she wanted for her life the night before. Now it was telling her that she'd made the wrong decision. That leaving Ezra was the wrong decision. That she was choosing a life that would be miserable without him; one where she would have to live with the knowledge that she could have had him, but had been too afraid to risk her heart. To risk her independence.

She slammed her hands against the steering wheel and choked back the sob that threatened. She had reasons for leaving, damn it. The fact that she was even feeling this way meant that she had already become dependent on him. That she had already begun to break in some small way because of it.

Is that really what's happening though?

She frowned at the thought, the question. She had no idea where it had come from, or what it meant. But now that she'd thought it, she couldn't stop thinking about it.

Was this dependence? The desire to be with someone? The change that came from being with that person? The emotions that accompanied it?

If she'd been asked the day before, before Ezra, she would have unequivocally said yes. Needing to be around someone was dependence. Needing someone was dependence. It was the very definition of dependence. But somehow, that definition didn't take into account *wanting* someone. Wanting to be around them. Wanting to change—no, not change, *grow*—because of them.

Just wanting…them.

That was part of it. For her entire life, Angie had believed that needing was a bad thing. Like the need her mother had had for her father's opinion before she would do something. Like the fact that Charlene had wanted his approval before she would say something.

It was not the life Angie had envisioned for herself. She didn't want to look to someone else before feeling what she felt. She didn't want to force the people she cared about to give her permission to do what she wanted. Or to say what she wanted. Or to feel what she wanted. And when they wouldn't or couldn't, she didn't want to force them into doing or saying or feeling something that *they* didn't want to.

That was what dependence had meant to her. And she saw now that the life she carved for herself after her father's death had been running from that, too. Not connecting with anyone. Keeping them at a distance. Controlling her emotions so she couldn't feel the effects of her choices. The emptiness they'd resulted in. Hell, that had been her life before her father's death, too.

She'd seen dependence as a defect. Something that would prevent her from functioning normally. It was something that to Angie, meant brokenness.

But she was beginning to see that she'd defined dependence too broadly. If her mother had displayed it in any way or form, Angie had slapped the 'dependence' sticker onto it.

Wanting to spend time with someone? Dependence. Caring about them? Dependence. Having them influence her or her life? Dependence. Feeling more than she believed she should for them? Dependence. And grieving, which had combined all of those fears into one neat package? *Dependence.*

Breath shuddered through her lips, though she wasn't sure how anything had got past the giant lump in her throat. The lump that told her running had kept her from seeing the truth of this. From seeing that the normal, healthy feelings Charlene had shown in her relationship with Angie's father had somehow conflated with the unhealthy desire Charlene had had to let him do everything for her.

Angie had spent her entire life being afraid of the normal—of the healthy—because of it.

It dried her throat now, sent an anchor slamming into

her heart. She had no idea what to do about it. Had no idea what to think or feel. Did this mean that her father's influence on her life didn't take anything away from her independence? Did it mean she wasn't broken because she'd given in to the grief? Had it affected her relationship with her sisters? Could she finally let go of her fears because of this?

If the answers to those questions were yes, it would change her. It would change her life. She wouldn't have to be scared about what her emotions were anymore. She'd finally be able to face them. She'd be able to face what running from them had done to her relationships.

She would be able to *deal* with them.

Like the guilt that wouldn't simply go away because of her realisations. And how overwhelming it was that she'd hurt her family before figuring them out.

But this was a step forward. A step through. Which meant she could finally stop running.

Because she was still running now. Oh, she'd made up excuses so she wouldn't have to face it. Told herself that being aware that she was running somehow made it better. That her and Ezra's goodbye the night before somehow made it easier. None of that was true. No, she'd run because she'd been scared. Ezra made her feel. And to her, feeling would start the torturous journey to losing herself.

But she was free of that now. She no longer had to be afraid that she cared about Ezra. She didn't have to fear that little burst of warmth she'd felt when he'd held her in the woods as she'd cried for her father. Or the longing that had pulsed in her veins as they'd slow-danced under the moon.

Now that she was free of it, she could see that her feelings for him were significant. She cared enough about him *to* run, after all. Up until that morning, she reserved running for people she'd known her entire life. For people she cared deeply about.

And though she didn't have to be scared, she still was.

Scraping off the layers of her emotional issues had revealed this shiny nugget: she was scared of losing someone again. Of getting hurt. Of having her heart ripped out of her chest again. Hell, she wasn't sure her heart had even returned after being ripped out the first time with her father's death.

So really, it wasn't surprising that she was afraid of putting herself in the position to feel that way again. Except that the fact that she was even considering it meant it was already too late to prevent it.

She waited for the wave of panic, but it was really more of a splash. She knew that was because of Ezra. He'd shown her it was okay to feel again. But not only again; he'd shown her it was okay to feel at all. He'd helped her see that feelings wouldn't turn her into her mother. And wasn't that enough to give him a chance?

Yes.

She almost smiled at the resounding echo in her head, but then she wondered—did it matter?

She was already far enough away from the lodge that Ezra would know she'd left. He'd know that she'd run, despite how he'd denied she was still doing it the night before. She knew that he'd understand. Somehow he always did. But it would have hurt him. And sure, she'd run from something hard; it would have been worth more if she'd stayed. If she'd been courageous. If she chose not to hurt him.

She just hadn't had that courage.

She could have said the same thing regarding her family. The thought sent a hard throb of pain, of shame through her body. It stayed with her until she reached the bottom of the slope of the mountain leading into Somerset West. She frowned at the line of cars keeping her from entering the town that would eventually lead her back home, before lifting her eyes to the electronic board on the side of the road:

Accident Ahead. Both Lanes Closed. Expect Delays.

She wasn't there when he woke up. He felt it the moment he opened his eyes. The bed had felt cold. Empty. Something inside him had, too.

Panic shimmered through his body as he got up. As he searched the cabin that had only a bedroom and bathroom. It made no sense, but he searched. Even after he realised her suitcase was gone, he searched.

Then he sat on the bed, wondering what the hell he was going to do about the fact that she wasn't there.

There was a part of him that urged him to go outside. To check whether she was there. It was the same part of him that was determined to believe she hadn't left. That despite the evidence, she'd just gone out to the café to get them coffee. To order breakfast.

He shook his head, flopped onto his back, and let out the air in his lungs. Forced it out, really, and then sucked it back in, as if somehow, the oxygen would bring sanity to the parts of him that were clearly malfunctioning.

If that were the case, they'd started malfunctioning the day before—the moment Angie had slid into the booth opposite him. Because that was the moment he'd felt the interest. Interest that had turned into attraction, which itself had turned into something more. The something more that had him on his back, hoping she was still out there.

That was at the heart of it all. She'd given him hope.

He'd been simmering in his unhappiness before her. In the fact that no matter what he did, he always disappointed his family. She'd somehow made him realise that he'd been caught in that disappointment. In that unhappiness. That he must have liked it if he wouldn't choose to escape from it.

Now he believed he *could* escape from it. Or rather, that he could focus on more than just the negative of it. He could focus on the love behind it, too. If he did, he wouldn't be hurting himself with decisions he knew in his gut were wrong for him, but he made for the sake of his family.

Well, he thought after a moment. He hadn't quite got that far in his introspection the day before. The night before—or the morning, really, because he'd only fallen asleep when the sky had already started going light.

It probably had something to do with what he'd told Angie: that she could choose the life she wanted for herself. He'd be a hypocrite if he didn't listen to his own advice. To his own gut. Because now that he was learning to let go and to trust it, he could see the decisions he'd made in the past had been the wrong ones. More importantly, he could see that Angie was the right one.

He sat up slowly. Then he stood, opened the curtains, and let the sun warm him. It was a long while before he left his post. Before he went to the bathroom, followed his usual routine. Before he got out of the shower, got dressed.

Then there was no more delaying.

With another breath, he went to the door and walked outside, hoping he'd find either Angie or her car there.

He found neither.

Angie's fingers tapped against the steering wheel as the minutes ticked by.

This was the last thing she needed. Standing still in

the middle of nowhere. Having nothing else to think about besides what she was heading toward. About what she was leaving behind.

About how that last thing had somehow become more consuming than the first; the thing she'd been dreading for years.

The accident ahead of her showed no signs of clearing up. Since it was coded in her DNA to think, it didn't surprise her when a seed was planted in her mind.

The longer she sat there, the more her thoughts nurtured it, watered it, offered it sunlight. Before she knew it, it had grown into a force of nature she couldn't ignore. And she knew she couldn't, because she tried. The more she did, the more it nudged her. The more her heart thumped in her chest.

When those thumps became sharp, rapid beats, she let out a shaky breath. Asked herself what she could possibly achieve by following that inner voice. The one that told her she shouldn't be sitting in traffic. She should be turning back. She should be taking a chance with the man who'd restored her belief in love, in a future. She should be giving them a future.

She resisted for as long as she could. Because there was still a part of her that was afraid. That urged her to run. But the force of nature wouldn't go away. It not only throbbed in her mind, but through her body now, too. And before she knew it, she'd switched on the car and had made a U-turn to go back up the mountain.

She left. Angie had left.

It shouldn't have surprised him. It didn't. Hadn't that been part of why he'd been delaying? Because if he'd gone out as soon as he'd known he'd wanted her in his life, he would have had to face this feeling sooner. The complete hopelessness. The emptiness. Neither of which compared to what he woke up with that morning.

Now he was angry, too, though. Oh, he'd talked a good game about the goodbyes and the fact that they'd said goodbye the night before. He'd comforted himself with it, with thinking that not doing it now, that not saying goodbye now, didn't matter. But he'd lied to himself before. Hell, he was constantly lying to himself.

This was no different.

He *wanted* a goodbye. He wanted to look at her face before she left. So he could memorise her features one last time. So he could run his fingertips over her cheeks, her lips. So he could kiss her again, and etch the taste of her, the feel of her, into his mind. His soul.

So he'd have proof that this magical day at a wedding one Christmas had actually happened.

Regret mingled with anger deep inside him, and then he was walking back to his room. He let the passion of it fuel his movements, throwing the things he'd unpacked into his bag. He refused to let the smell of her that still lingered in the room distract him. He would leave now, too. He would leave the place that reminded him only of her and go home. Where he should have gone from the beginning.

It wasn't so bad now. He could look forward to going back to them without the fears he used to have. He had other things to focus on. Being back home. Enjoying his new job. Being patient with himself as he figured out how to choose a life that would finally bring him fulfilment. *Him.* And not the people in his life he thought he had to pretend for.

Why then had the anger, the regret sizzled down to a spark that buzzed throughout his body? A spark that told him a fulfilling life included Angie?

He zipped his suitcase closed, then rested his hands on it. He didn't know how to answer those questions. Or he did, but he wasn't sure what those answers would bring him. More heartache? More disappointment, this time in himself?

Only if things go wrong.

He straightened. Wondered at that voice that had sounded in his head. In his gut. This was what it felt like, he thought. This was what it was like to have a gut instinct in real time. That instinct that told him he needed to take a chance. That even if things went wrong, he'd always regret it if he didn't try.

He had to try.

Thirty minutes into his trip, Ezra began to think he'd made a mistake.

It started with the line of traffic he saw a few kilometres ahead of him at the top of the mountain leading down to Cape Town. It was compounded by the fact that doubt had infringed on the emotion he'd been using as motivation to follow Angie. It ended when the half-hour news bulletin on the radio informed him an accident had caused the delay, and that there was no foreseeable end to it.

He knew Angie was somewhere in that line of traffic. Somewhere right at the beginning of it, he realised, considering the time she must have left that morning. For the first time, he thought about the logistics of his plan. Logistics that told him that even if there hadn't been an accident, there was almost zero chance he'd have caught up with her.

As clear as it had been when he set out on his plan, he only now realised the extent of its foolishness. He'd made it with his heart, with his gut, and he could now see that those parts of him needed to work in conjunction with his head.

Using his head forced him to acknowledge that he might never see Angie again. He knew nothing about where she was going to except the suburb where she lived, and he couldn't exactly drive through the whole of Kuils River hoping to find her. He didn't even know if that's where he *would* find her. Perhaps her family had moved. Perhaps she'd stay somewhere other than her family home.

He wouldn't be able to find her because he knew nothing practical about her.

It didn't matter that his heart was screaming about what he did know. Like the fact that she was one of the bravest people he'd ever met. That she had a will strong enough to defeat even the toughest of opponents. That she had a heart compassionate enough to help a stranger face his issues.

Defeat struck his body as his head asked him how knowing all that helped. *This* had to be enough. The memories had to be enough.

Yet something deep inside him knew they never would be.

Chapter Twenty

It was insane, Angie thought as she drove. Insane that she was going back for a man she'd met the day before. Insane that that man had somehow burrowed his way deep into her heart. Insane that she was going back even though she wasn't sure what she'd face when she got to him. Or what getting to him would mean.

Despite the insanity of it, she knew she was doing the right thing. If she wasn't, there wouldn't be this fierceness inside her urging her on.

She wasn't sure what had her turning her head right at that very moment, and she knew she would give fate a fleeting thought later. Christmas magic, too, though that was ridiculous.

But on the side of the road she saw Ezra's car.

She slowed down, pulled over. It took her a moment to think about how safe it would be to cross a busy national road to get to him. Not very, she knew immediately. And in the same moment, she knew she'd still do it. Before she could think about it anymore, she crossed the road, taking brisk steps to the driver's seat of his car.

When she got there, all she saw was a mess of dark hair that told her his head was resting on the steering wheel. She rapped her knuckles against the glass, and his head shot up. Disbelief crossed his face. He blinked once, twice, and then got out of the car and pulled her into his arms.

Her breath gushed from her lungs. Partly because it was an unexpected response; partly because she was so relieved she'd found him. She let herself melt into his arms. Told herself to enjoy being there.

But the moment passed before she was ready, and then he took her hand and pulled her to the front of his car.

'What—'

'This isn't the place to have a conversation,' he told her, folding his arms.

'On the side of the road? I agree.' She frowned. 'Though it's not like the front of the car is any safer.'

'It's safer than talking at the side of the car.'

As if to prove his point, a car passed them, sending a force of wind their way that had her hair flying.

Silence beat between them. Two more cars passed before either of them spoke.

'Why are you here?'

'Why are you?' she shot back, strangely annoyed by the detached tone of his voice. Or the stiff way he held himself. If it hadn't been for the hug, she'd wonder if he wanted her there.

'I'm on my way home,' he replied.

'Really? I thought you had another day left at the lodge?'

'I don't.'

The silence stretched again, and she sighed. 'I'm sorry I left this morning, if that's what you're angry about.'

'I'm not angry that you left.'

'No? Because you're doing a pretty good impression of—'

'I'm angry that you didn't say goodbye,' he interrupted, his eyes flashing. 'I know things were…strange, between us. But you didn't say goodbye.'

'We said goodbye.' She shifted her weight to the other leg. 'Last night.'

'That wasn't a goodbye.'

'It was for me.'

'Why are you here then?' he asked. 'Why are you driving in the opposite direction of home when you already said goodbye to me?'

'There's an accident.'

She wasn't sure why she said it. Probably to annoy him. When his gaze went hot, then cooled, she knew she'd succeeded.

'You weren't returning for me at all?' he asked. She didn't reply. 'Or maybe you thought you'd come back to check whether I was still there? Whether I'd notice you were gone?'

'No, no.' How had this gone so pear-shaped? She sighed again, and told herself to tell him the truth and accept whatever came after. 'The accident gave me some time to think. And I thought that…that I didn't want to leave things the way they were—' she lifted a hand '—*are* between us.'

'Why?'

'Because…' A little helplessly, the words spilled from her lips. 'Because I like you, damn it. Somehow you've crept into my mind and other places—' she waved her hand in the direction of her chest '—and I couldn't stop thinking about how much you've helped me.' The steam ran out at the end, and she shut her eyes for a moment before she continued. 'You didn't deserve me running.'

Time ticked by, and he didn't reply. Instead, he stuffed his hands into his pockets as he studied her.

'You stopped. Running, I mean,' he added. 'I still believe that.' Her heart ached. 'Besides, you came back now. You're facing it. Same like what you're doing with your family.'

'I'm trying to,' she said genuinely. 'Some recent re-alisations have shown me that I have a lot to do in that regard.'

She released the breath that had stuck even at the thought of what she'd be going home to. She wasn't looking forward to it. Of course, she hadn't ever looked forward to it, but it was different now. She was different now, and she had to find a way to reconcile the guilt and responsibility she still felt with regard to her family with this different version of herself.

'Ezra, I—'

'No,' he interrupted, 'don't say anything. Let me talk.' But he didn't, not for a long while. And then he sucked in air, let it out on a hiss. 'I was coming after you.'

'What?'

'You were right. I was supposed to check out tomorrow. I left this morning because I was coming after you.' He paused. 'I've made some poor decisions in my life, but…but you're not one of them. You're not Ana, and you're not Liesel.' He shuffled his feet. 'I know this feels quick. But it also feels right. At least to me.' Now he let out a breath. 'I don't want you to do anything that you don't want to. But I'd never forgive myself if I didn't ask for a chance.'

Her lips spread even as her heart filled.

'I did stop running. For family, first, yes, but now… now I've stopped running for you,' she said. 'I'm not scared that I'm going to break anymore. Which doesn't mean I'm not scared by what I'm feeling for you. Because I am. I'm scared of losing the independence I've worked my entire life to get. I'm scared of the work that's obviously going to have to go into this relationship because of that fear.' She took a breath. 'But I'm choosing you, Ezra. And whatever my parents' faults were, they chose one another. They were happy.' She paused. 'I want a chance to be happy, too. I want to have a chance to be happy with you.'

His lips curved into a half smile. 'Yeah?'

'Yeah.'

They stood like that for a few seconds, dorkily smiling at each other, before his smile sobered.

'What about…everything?'

'I don't know,' she admitted. 'I do know that it's going to be a lot. Readjusting the way I've been thinking about it is going to be a long process which might not end up with me staying.' She took his hands. 'But I want to figure this out. With you. If you want, and…' she trailed off, then forced herself to say the words. 'And only if you're really over what happened to you. It wasn't that long ago—'

'I was over Liesel long before things ended between us,' he interrupted. 'You've helped me through what happened to me. I might not be over it, but I'm working on it. On me. I'd like to keep doing that with you.' He brushed the hair from her forehead. 'You healed something inside of me.'

When she sucked in a breath, he smiled.

'I'm not saying I love you, Ange. But I could, someday. And I'd very much like the chance to fall.'

His head lowered until their lips touched, and Angie nearly gasped at the lightness, the tenderness of the kiss.

Like he was trying to convince her that it was okay—
that it would always be okay. She ignored the hoots as
the cars drove passed them, ignored the fact that they
were in the middle of nowhere, kissing, and gave her
own promise in the kiss.

No matter what happened, they could figure it out.
They could fall. Together.

When he drew back, she felt slightly dizzy, and her
lips spread into a smile. 'I don't think I would have ever
believed I would be kissing a man I'd only just met in
the middle of the road a week before Christmas.'

'It's the magic of the day,' he said with a grin.

'What day? It's not technically Christmas.'

He pulled a face. 'Let me have this.'

'It would be way too easy. It would also set a precedent I have no intention on keeping.'

'Touché.' He paused. 'Maybe we should go back to
the cabin and check whether my room is still available
so I can set a precedent I *do* intend on keeping. Talking,' he said with a laugh when she poked him in the
stomach. 'I meant talking.'

'Sure you did.' She tilted her head. 'It's not a bad
idea though. Going back to the café. We could have a
proper breakfast.'

'We could have our first date.'

She smiled. 'I'm in if you are.'

'I am. Come on—' he pressed a kiss to her forehead
'—I know just the booth.'

Epilogue

Christmas, one year later

'Whose decision was it to host our families for Christmas?' Angie asked, not for the first time that month.

Or that week.

Or that day.

Ezra winced. 'Ours,' he replied, unconvincingly. 'Because we're married now, and my ideas are your ideas, and vice versa.'

She stopped chopping vegetables to give him the death glare. 'So this was your idea.'

'Ours,' he insisted again. She aimed the knife at him.

'I swear, I will make your death look like an accident.'

'I knew murder was your intention all along. I'm impressed by the long con.'

She hissed out a breath, then shook her head. 'I genuinely hope you don't die in mysterious circumstances. Considering how much you're clinging to this murder thing, I wouldn't be surprised if you carried a note in your wallet detailing your suspicions that your wife might be poisoning you.'

'Nah. You're much too bloodthirsty for poison.'

She barely looked up at him now, and he realised he pushed his luck as far as it would go. He valued his life.

A new life, he thought, and nearly let a smile slip past his basic human instinct to live. Instead, he grabbed a knife and helped her chop the rest of the vegetables, enjoying the rhythm of it.

Of the task, and of how appropriately it described his new life—his wife, annoyed beside him as they tackled existence together.

He couldn't have been happier.

He would never have said it aloud since he knew he was being a little dopey. And no matter how much he tried to snap out of it, he couldn't. It was the time of year that had changed his entire life. He met his wife a year before, and their life together since had been solid.

Not quite the sexy word he thought should describe dating—though there had been plenty of sexiness in between—but it suited what they'd been through, right from the moment they'd left Caledon one year before. He had been nervous about what he'd be returning to. He'd been worried about what Angie would be returning to, too. But they agreed to meet their families separately that day, and meet again that evening for a debriefing.

His reconciliation with his family had been somewhat predictable. They opened their arms to him, told him he'd been an idiot for doing what he'd done, and then it was over. He had their unconditional support when he introduced Angie a month later. He hadn't even got so much as an eyebrow raise when he told them he wanted to marry her seven months after that. Which of course proved to him he'd been an idiot for doubting them at all.

Or maybe it proved that Angie was someone they approved of because she was finally the right woman for him?

Either way, the experience had been much more positive than Angie's. Her reconciliation had been similarly predictable, so less pleasant. Her sister Sophia was… prickly. It was the best word he could think of to describe her. She had Angie's dry humour, though it came with an edge Angie didn't have. Angie claimed it was a sign of fierce loyalty; Sophia hadn't been thrilled by Angie leaving. Ezra could have sworn it was more that she wasn't thrilled Angie had come back.

Angie's youngest sister was charming. Exuberant and bubbly —and according to Angie, hiding something. And none of this even touched on Angie's mother, who seemed genuinely lovely, if a little…reserved. Which, of course, frustrated Angie beyond belief as she somehow identified it as a failed attempt at independence.

He didn't understand most of it, but somehow they dealt with it. Angie navigated her family as best she could, which had involved putting up boundaries to protect herself. It had taken some convincing from his part, and had led to more than one argument, but they'd figured it out. They were solid, after all. Enough so that eight months after they'd met, he'd wanted to propose.

No, that wasn't entirely accurate. It had taken him eight months because he'd been worried about moving too fast. About pushing her when she was still struggling with what she'd discovered about herself. But he'd known from the day they'd met he wanted to spend his life with her. It had just taken them both some time to come to terms with it.

Mostly her.

It hadn't been a long period of time, those eight months, but it had been enough to tell him all he needed to know about his feelings for Angie. Though it still hadn't made her saying 'no' when he asked any more amusing.

'It was a joke!' she said immediately after.

'It wasn't funny.'

'Maybe not right now, but—' she cut off. 'I'm so sorry. It was in terrible taste. But I thought you'd know—' She gave him an apologetic look. 'Will you ask me again? Please?'

'Are you going to take it seriously this time?'

'I took it seriously the first time.'

'Yeah, ri—'

'Just ask me again.'

And he had.

After they kissed, when she pulled back, she said, 'This still doesn't mean I need to be around you.'

'I know.' His arms tightened around her. 'You just want to be.'

'Yes.' She leaned her forehead against his. 'And I'm not going to stop writing my book.'

'I'm already thinking about the holiday house we'll buy because of its success.'

Her lips curved. 'We'll stay here—because this is where I want to start our family—but we'll need to travel. To get away every now and then since I'm sure I'll need a break from the intensity of my family stuff.'

He leaned back. 'Are you sure? We haven't talked about it for a long time—' and the fact that he hadn't been worried about it told him solid was sexier than it sounded '—but you don't have to do this for me.'

'I'm not. I need to be here. This is…this is home.'

He lowered his head to touch his lips to hers. 'It will be.'

Because they'd had no desire to wait, a short month later they'd got married. First, because they'd had to be creative to secure the venue on such short notice, they'd celebrated early one Tuesday morning at the Durbanville quarry. The short aisle had been covered in white petals. The tree under which they'd had the ceremony hadn't been oak and its leaves hadn't been orange since it was spring, not autumn. It had been draped in white chiffon though.

They'd said their vows, kissed—and had then done it all over again immediately after at a nearby church for the sake of their parents.

For the rest of his life, Ezra would never understand what he'd done to deserve the woman he'd met a year before. He would never know what he'd done to have her sit at his table that day. Or why she'd taken a chance on him.

He was willing to believe it was Christmas magic. Which was why he wanted to make their first Christmas as a married couple special.

'Are you done?' he asked when she sprinkled chopped coriander over the salad.

'With this, yeah. I still have to finish up the cake. It's been in the fridge overnight, so I have to take it out and decorate it. And then,' she said, looking down at herself, 'I should probably have a shower before our families arrive in an hour.'

'Right,' he replied. 'We have time then.'

She squinted at him. 'Did that sound like we have time?'

He didn't answer, only took her hand and led her into their living room. They were renting a place for a year, and it was cosy with its warm, cream walls, beige couches and bright yellow pillows, along with assorted pops of colour on shelves that stood on two of the four walls.

'Before you say anything,' he said, when he lowered

to the couch, bringing her down with him, 'this is going to be quick. I need to give you your Christmas present.'

She frowned. 'I thought we did that last night?'

He snorted. 'You thought I got you a foldable Bluetooth keyboard for Christmas?'

'Um, yeah? It's a damn good gift.'

He knew it had been, though the small smile on her face made him feel a million times better about it. He hoped she'd feel the same way about this.

'Well, I have another one for you.'

He took a breath to calm the sudden nerves, and reached for the present under the Christmas tree. The area was still peppered with gifts for their family; it had been the perfect place to hide it. He handed it to her.

With a questioning look, she began to open it. Her hands stilled halfway, immediately after she'd seen the front of it.

'You—' she stopped on a shaky exhale. Then she looked him dead in the eye. 'I thought you said you didn't have time to read it.'

'This doesn't mean I've read it.'

'No?' she asked, and her voice caught at the end, making the word sound like a sob. She took a loud breath. 'So you're saying you just bind manuscripts into books without reading them?'

He took the book from her and gently undid the rest of the wrapping. He gave it back.

'I was going to say "I did with you," but I don't want to lie.' He didn't smile when he saw the nerves on her face, though he wanted to. 'It's good, Ange. It's raw and sexy and romantic. Though I did think the hero was a bit of a geek at times—'

'Must have been the PhD,' she retorted, though it was more absent than dry, and she blinked rapidly, before looking up. When she looked at him again, there was still a sheen to her eyes. 'I can't believe you did this.'

'Does that mean you like it?'

'Do I like this book you had made from the manuscript I gave you three weeks ago?' She held the book up accusingly; he didn't think she realised how menacing it looked. 'I love it. I'm literally holding a book I wrote in my hands.'

'Your second attempt at a full-length romance novel. A pretty good one at that.' He took her hand. 'I think you've lived up to that promise your dad said you had.'

She didn't even bother blinking back the tears now. 'Low blow, Doctor,' she said, using her free hand to wipe her face. 'I told you that in confidence.'

'And I'm telling you this pretty confidently, too. This is a good book.'

She gave him a look. 'You have to say that.'

'But I wouldn't,' he said, 'if I didn't think so. It needs work, sure—' he laughed when she swatted the book at him '—but it's got good bones.' He paused. 'I had this done because I believe that. I believe in you. This dream is going to come true, baby. I can feel it.'

She pursed her lips together, and didn't say anything for a long time.

'I love you. I never thought I'd say that to a man and not be afraid, but here I am. I love you,' she repeated, 'and I've never felt safer.'

He brought her hand to his lips. 'I'll take it as a compliment.'

'Please do,' she said, with a slight laugh. And then something changed. She sat up straighter, her hand tightening in his, her face sobering, and his heart began to race.

'What?' he asked. 'Are you okay?'

'Fine.' She immediately cleared her throat, which made him doubt her answer. 'So, this dream… It's about to become a little more complicated.'

'What do you mean?'

'You know how I've been a little…moodier than usual today?'

'We're seeing your family,' he replied, as if it explained all.

'Yes.' She took a deep breath. 'But also… Three pregnancy sticks are trying to convince me that I'm pregnant.'

He kept looking at her, as if he hadn't just heard what she'd said. He blinked, as if somehow, that would help him with the information he'd heard, but wasn't processing.

'Excuse me?' he said after a long pause. 'Can you just— Did I just—' He blew out a breath. 'Did you just say that you were pregnant?'

'I said the three sticks I peed on this morning are trying to convince me I'm pregnant.' She got up. Paced. 'I mean, I'm not convinced. How accurate are those things anyway? Besides, we've been careful.' She threw a hand up, though he had no idea why. 'No, I'm not pregnant,' she decided. 'It's probably just the tea I've been drinking. I had three cups this morning alone. It must have had—'

She broke off when he stood, her eyes growing wider when he stopped in front of her.

'What?' she asked.

'All the sticks were positive?'

She blew out a breath. 'All of them. And they were different brands, too, so it's not like one might be faulty.'

She was moaning. If he wasn't still struggling with this new information, he would have smiled.

'So… We're pregnant?'

'*I'm* pregnant,' she corrected him. 'None of this "we" stuff since you're not the one carrying the baby and oh my word I am carrying a baby.' She blinked up at him. 'I'm pregnant.'

'You're having a baby,' he teased, when a giddiness he had no idea could come from him took hold of his tongue.

'*We're* having a baby. I'm pregnant, but we're having a baby.'

Her eyes softened, and giddiness turned into a love so damn fierce he had no idea what to do with it. Good thing he'd married the woman who inspired it.

'We're having a baby, Ez,' she whispered, and gave him a smile so bright he thought he'd seen the sun.

'We're having a baby,' he confirmed, and smiled back.

* * * * *

Author's Note

Although Caledon, South Africa, is a real place, the lodge and café where Angie and Ezra meet is fictional.

Acknowledgements

Thank you to those at Harlequin who have supported me and my writing from the beginning. My Mills & Boon family, for putting in a good word for me, and the team at Carina Press, who've been wonderful about *A Wedding One Christmas* and me. A special thank-you has to go to John Jacobson, my Carina Press editor. Your belief in me has meant more than you can know, and I've already learnt so much from your expertise and intuition.

To my writing friends, who provided moral support with this book. Jenni Fletcher, you're my rock; Olivia Dade, I will always be grateful for your kindness, especially when it came to *A Wedding One Christmas*. To Collette Kelly and Dorothy Ewels, you know how thankful I am to you both for everything. For Dani René and Lucy Parker, who patiently answered all my questions, and Rae Rivers, who was willing to bounce ideas around when I needed it.

To my sister, Lunelle, who listens to all my publishing woes even though she knows little about the industry and still tries to help. And to my husband, who will never know how much his unwavering belief in me has contributed to my dream coming true—and staying true.

I appreciate you all dearly.

*To find out about other books by Therese Beharrie
or to be alerted to new releases and other updates,
sign up for her newsletter
at theresebeharrie.com/newsletter.*

*Can an unlikely romance return the magic of
Christmas to an entire town?
Read on for a sneak peek of* Christmas Catch *by
Mary Shotwell.
Available now from Carina Press.*

Chapter One

Monday, December 7

"I'd like to thank all my guests this evening, especially Dr. Ambrosia. It's always a pleasure to hear how the simple things we do in a day, like keep a gratitude journal, can invoke a positive response in our mental and physical health."

Charlee Ridgeway closed the fluffy gray sweater jacket tight around her chest. Her recording studio was permanently cold, despite Atlanta's stuffiness.

"And remember, there are only a few days left to get in your submissions to the Cheery Christmas Contest. All contest rules are up on my website, cheerycharlee. com. Many of you doubt I can top last year's hurricane-stricken Gulf Coast home rebuild, but just you wait! This is Cheery Charlee. As always, new podcasts are posted on Tuesday nights. Until next Tuesday, stay cheery."

Charlee pulled off the headphones, the metal bracket on the right speaker holding her curls hostage.

Her audio editor, Vanessa Herivaux, walked into the recording room wearing a ribbed tank top and A-line skirt. Her dark silken skin and tall stature made Charlee feel even paler and shorter. "Another great one."

"A little help," Charlee said.

Vanessa untangled Charlee's hair off the headphones. "I don't know why you insist on wearing these huge things."

"Earbuds hurt after a while. Besides." She stood up from the swivel chair. "It drowns out all your tapping on the window."

Vanessa leaned against the recording booth's desk. "If you would stay on target with time, I wouldn't have to tap." Her Haitian Creole accent thickened whenever she grew angry, even after living most of her life in Georgia.

"But that's why I have you." Charlee placed her hand on Vanessa's shoulder. "The whole point of being a production editor is to *edit*."

"Yes, as in add cheerful background and smooth transitions to elevate Cheery Charlee's cheerfulness. Not filter out half the show in our twenty-four hour window before broadcast."

"I love you." Charlee stretched her grin as far as it could go and spread her arms out for a hug.

Vanessa obliged. "You'd better stop before I melt. Or you do."

Charlee let go and unraveled her layers, taking off the sweater jacket and turtleneck and hanging them over her swivel chair.

"Is all that really necessary?" Vanessa said.

"You try sitting in here for hours. It's freezing."

Vanessa shook her head with a smile. "No thanks."

Located in midtown Atlanta near Ansley Park, the studio was a major upgrade from where they had started out. It didn't take much to be better than the sixth floor of a college dormitory lacking central air. Now Cheery Charlee Productions was at home in an old studio between two larger modern buildings. The original brickwork formed the two shared walls, and tinted windows in the front kept sunlight to a minimum. It made for a cool workspace, in stark contrast to the literal sweat they had poured into starting up the podcast.

Charlee placed her hands on her hips. "Lunch?"

"Charlee," Vanessa said. "Your production editor has to edit. Sometimes I think it would be easier to be behind the microphone."

"You hate speaking in public, even when it's behind the mic in a private office."

"And heavily edited, if the editor had a chance to do so."

Charlee scoffed, brushing off the friendly jab. It took some level of guts to have her voice out in the world, even if the mistakes and ramblings were flawlessly omitted, thanks to Vanessa. "I didn't go over too much, did I?"

"You really want me to answer that?"

"Nope. But you have to eat at some point. My treat."

"Okay, now you're talking."

They left the recording room and grabbed their purses. The bright Atlanta midday sun shocked Charlee's eyes. She walked with Vanessa along the sidewalk of Peachtree Avenue, its broad road busy with lunch traffic. Although Atlanta served as Charlee's home base, she spent most of the year traveling the country for on-location broadcasts. The city was loud, hot and crowded, and was only getting worse over time with traffic, all of which made it even more tempting to pack up and head off to somewhere new. When she was in town, she spent most of her time in the same square mile corner of Midtown.

"Usual food court?" Charlee said.

"Sounds good to me."

The food court was fast but also the best way for them to agree on anything. Vanessa was not just Charlee's editor but her best friend too, and they couldn't be more opposite. Their differences weren't just superficial. They disagreed on food, music, clothes, men. But they had shared Barbies as neighbors and never looked back. Nobody knew Charlee like Vanessa.

"So." Vanessa set down her tray of stir-fry. "How does it feel to be so close to one million subscribers? You realize you're going to hit that mark before your twenty-fifth birthday, right?"

Charlee smiled with her mouth full of pasta. She wiped her face and took a drink. "It is crazy. Can you believe it? Over two years of shows. One hundred podcasts."

"One hundred and nine, if you're including the one you just finished," said Vanessa.

"This year's contest should put me over the top."

"Which, by the way, you need to decide on ASAP."

"I know, I know." She took a bite of meatball.

"What's the matter? You love the contest."

"I just haven't been…inspired yet by any of the entries. Nothing is giving me that spark of energy and creativity." It was beyond worrisome now. Not only was the deadline drawing near, but she hadn't hit a block like this before. With so many podcasts under her belt, she was bound to reach a stagnant point. But that wasn't supposed to happen until the ten or fifteen year mark. She hadn't even reached five years. The anxiety gnawed at her, deep in her stomach.

"You put a lot of pressure on yourself," Vanessa said. "It's okay to sit this one out if you want. I can edit a 'best of' podcast to highlight the past year's most inspirational and positive moments. Then you wouldn't have to worry and you could finally spend Christmas with my family."

"Thank you, really."

"You know they love you, all five feet three inches. You're part of the family, Charlee. Or close to it." Her up-to-something smile grew across her face. "My brother is going to be there."

"Vanessa." Charlee shook her head.

"He tries, God bless him. Every time I talk to him he asks about you, and I confirm you're single. Unless you're not telling me something." She pointed her fork at Charlee.

"What? No. You know I tell you everything. You're the only person I do tell things to."

"Okay, okay. Well, if not for a possible romance with my brother, then do it for yourself. When's the last time you spent the holidays with family and friends?"

"The last time I had a family." Charlee set her fork down on her plate. "The year my mom died."

"That was five years ago," Vanessa said. "I don't mean to rush you, but come on, Charlee. You stayed cooped up on campus at Christmas in graduate school, and the last two years you went across the country for the contest. Maybe this year you should actually celebrate it, with your people."

"My people?"

"Yes. Believe it or not, you have people. Like me and my family. I'll invite the Cheery Charlee assistants over too. It'll be a big get-together."

"Our assistants don't even want to leave their homes to work in the office."

"That's because you said they could work virtually."

"True."

"That's not the point. Just because we're not blood doesn't mean we're not your people."

Charlee sighed. Vanessa's efforts were charming but didn't overcome the pressures of sustaining and growing a business. "I can't do that to my listeners. Not now. They're expecting bigger and better. And reaching a million subscribers would be great news for the both of us. I don't want to let you down, and I can't let our audience down."

"*Your* audience. I'm just in it for the food."

Charlee's resolve broke and she laughed. They finished their meals as the noon lunch crowd grew. The food court would be depleted of empty tables and oxygen for talking, with the noise level rising to intolerable. Time to return to work. They walked the busy sidewalks toward the studio. The heat brought Charlee to a near sweat, but the studio quickly chilled her back to her usual popsicle body temperature.

Vanessa clapped her hands. "Now how about we check up on the latest submissions? Several came in while you were recording."

Charlee let Vanessa's eager optimism propel her along, but by twenty seconds in, she knew her answer.

"So please, please, please, Cheery Charlee, pick me—I mean, my boyfriend, Nathan." A twenty-something flipped her hair one last time over her shoulder, her neon yellow tank top strap accentuating her spray tan. "Surprising him with a visit on Christmas morning would make his holiday!"

Judging from the background, Charlee guessed the video had been shot in front of a closet devoted to a designer shoe collection.

Charlee switched her gaze from the computer to Vanessa, who hovered over the desk chair. "Well?"

Charlee closed her eyes for the length of ten blinks before opening them again. "Well... Maybe I should take her gum away. I'm sure her boyfriend, Nick, or whatever his name is, would appreciate not having to listen to her chomp on it for another second."

"Okay, okay," Vanessa said. "So it's not exactly what you're looking for."

"Not exactly? Not even broadly." Charlee slumped and stared at the monitor. It was a good thing they had finished recording tomorrow's podcast material. It looked like deciding on the contest winner was going to take the rest of the day. Or year.

Vanessa rolled her dark eyes and mimicked the hair flip, although her smoothed-back onyx hair barely reached her nape. "Don't worry. There has to be at least a single worthy entry in all of these."

"I looked over the ones you gave me yesterday," Charlee said. "If those were the ones that passed your initial judgment, I'd hate to see the ones that didn't."

Vanessa shook her head, eyes closed. "I wish I could unsee some of those."

"We have to top last year's." Charlee stood and folded her arms, leaning on the desk.

"How are you going to top rebuilding an old lady's destroyed-by-a-hurricane house? Build two houses? I don't know if our budget can handle that."

Charlee had teamed up with Vanessa for her editing skills but also for her business savvy. Her strict adherence to their budget, as well as schedules and talking points for each episode, could occasionally suck some of the joy out of the job. On the other hand, it was impossible to imagine achieving their accomplishments without her. But none of that would matter if Charlee couldn't find inspiration soon.

"I don't know," she said. "We'll cross that bridge when we find the right one."

Don't miss Christmas Catch *by Mary Shotwell, available now wherever Carina Press books are sold.*

www.CarinaPress.com